"The carefully layered drawing-room psychology of Agatha Christie cross-pollinated with the pure squishy terror of Stephen King."
—*Entertainment Weekly*

"What a box of tricks! This full-throttle thriller, dark and driving, rivals Agatha Christie for sheer ingenuity and James Patterson for flat-out speed. Swift, sharp, and relentless."
—A. J. Finn, #1 *New York Times* bestselling author of *The Woman in the Window*

"An intense, brutal, no-holds-barred thriller dripping with adrenaline, a heart-pounding story of courage and sacrifice featuring a heroine unlike any you've ever seen. Don't start unless you're prepared to read straight through, because I guarantee you will not be able to stop turning the pages."
—Karen Dionne, author of the international bestseller *The Marsh King's Daughter*

"An enthralling tale that features a wonderfully relatable and gutsy heroine. Give it to readers looking for a female-led drama in the mode of *The Girl with the Dragon Tattoo* and its sibling works."
—*Booklist*

"Everything I want in a thriller: ingeniously crafted, unapologetically relentless, and shamelessly suspenseful. The twists go off like a series of expertly planted detonations and the tension never lets up. I was blown away. *No Exit* is a damn good time."
—Joe Hill, #1 *New York Times* bestselling author of *The Fireman*

"[A] nail-biting thriller. . . . The action drives to a climactic and emotionally charged ending."
—*Publishers Weekly*

"*No Exit* opens with an ingenious, chilling setup and then delivers a wicked ride of psychological tension. Taylor Adams is a master of suspense. I'm already impatient to see what he does next."   —Michael Koryta, *New York Times* bestselling author of *How It Happened*

"This well-written, fast-paced thriller . . . has enough twists to ensure an enjoyable read for even the most seasoned suspense fans."   —*Library Journal*

"If you love a good twist ending, you'll love this psychological thriller that's snapping up comparisons to suspense masters from Agatha Christie to Stephen King."   —*Parade*

"This gripping thriller with a young, witty female protagonist will keep even the most experienced readers guessing until the end."   —*Shelf Awareness*

"There's a cinematic propulsion to *No Exit* that commands the reader's attention, and Mr. Adams times his shocks with a sure hand."   —*Wall Street Journal*

"One of the year's most unforgettable reads. . . . Adams does for highway rest stops what Stephen King did for shuttered resort hotels, psychotic nurses, and clowns under bridges."   —Bookreporter.com

"This nail-biting thriller will have you guessing at each twist of the surprising and complicated plot as its smart and gutsy protagonist fights to outwit a psychopath, rescue a girl, and make it home alive."   —*Mystery Scene*

NO EXIT

ALSO BY TAYLOR ADAMS

Hairpin Bridge
Our Last Night
Eyeshot

NO

_wm_ WILLIAM MORROW
An Imprint of HarperCollins_Publishers_

EXIT

A NOVEL

TAYLOR ADAMS

NO EXIT. Copyright © 2019 by Taylor Adams. All rights reserved. Printed in the United States of America. No part of this book may be used or reproduced in any manner whatsoever without written permission except in the case of brief quotations embodied in critical articles and reviews. For information, address HarperCollins Publishers, 195 Broadway, New York, NY 10007.

HarperCollins books may be purchased for educational, business, or sales promotional use. For information, please email the Special Markets Department at SPsales@harpercollins.com.

Originally published in the United Kingdom in 2017 by Joffe Books.

A hardcover edition of this book was published in 2019 by William Morrow, an imprint of HarperCollins Publishers.

FIRST WILLIAM MORROW MASS MARKET EDITION PUBLISHED 2019.

FIRST WILLIAM MORROW TV TIE-IN EDITION PUBLISHED 2022.

Designed by William Ruoto

Library of Congress Cataloging-in-Publication Data

Names: Adams, Taylor, author.

Title: No exit : a novel / Taylor Adams.

Description: First edition. | New York, NY : William Morrow, 2019.

Identifiers: LCCN 2018018489 | ISBN 9780062875655 (hardcover) | ISBN 9780062875662 (trade pbk.)

Subjects: | GSAFD: Suspense fiction.

Classification: LCC PS3601.D3973 N6 2019 | DDC 813/.6—dc23 LC record available at https://lccn.loc.gov/2018018489

ISBN 978-0-06-325447-3 (TV tie-in)

22 23 24 25 26 LSC 10 9 8 7 6 5 4 3 2 1

FOR RILEY

NO EXIT

DUSK

"SCREW YOU, BING CROSBY."

Darby Thorne was six miles up Backbone Pass when her windshield wiper broke, and that bass baritone voice was just kicking into the second chorus. It was official: he'd be getting his white Christmas. He could shut up about it now.

She thumbed the radio dial (nothing else but static) and watched her left wiper blade flap like a fractured wrist. She considered pulling over to duct-tape it, but there was no highway shoulder—just walled embankments of dirty ice crowding her right and left. She was afraid to stop anyway. The snowflakes had been big and soppy when she'd blown through Gold Bar forty minutes ago, but they'd grown smaller and grittier as her altitude climbed. They were hypnotic now in her racing headlights, a windshield of stars smearing into light speed.

CHAINS MANDATORY, the last sign she'd seen had warned.

Darby didn't own snow chains. Not yet, at least. This was her sophomore year at CU-Boulder and she'd never planned on venturing any farther off campus than Ralphie's Thrift-way. She remembered walking back from there last month, half-drunk with a gaggle of half friends from her dorm, and when one of them asked her (only half giving a shit) where she planned to go for Christmas break, Darby had answered bluntly that it would require an act of God himself to make her come back home to Utah.

And apparently he'd been listening, because he'd blessed Darby's mother with late-stage pancreatic cancer.

She'd learned this yesterday.

Via text message.

Scrape-scrape. The bent wiper blade slapped the glass again, but the snowflakes were dry enough, and the car's speed fast enough, that the windshield stayed clear. The real problem was the accumulating snow on the road. The yellow lane mark-ers were already hidden by several inches of fresh white, and periodically Darby felt her Honda Civic's chassis rake the sur-face. The sound returned like a wet cough, a little worse every time. On the last one, she'd felt the steering wheel vibrate be-tween her knuckled fingers. Another inch of powder and she'd be stranded up here, nine thousand feet above sea level with a quarter tank of gas, no cell coverage, and only her troubled thoughts for company.

And the brassy voice of Bing Crosby, she supposed. He crooned the final chorus as Darby took a sip of warm Red Bull.

Scrape-scrape.

The entire drive had been like this—a blurry, bloodshot charge through miles of foothills and scrub plains. No time to stop. All she'd eaten today was ibuprofen. She'd left her desk lamp on in her dorm room, but she'd only noticed this as she left the Dryden parking lot—too far to turn back. Stomach acid in her throat. Pirated Schoolyard Heroes and My Chemical Romance tracks looping on her (now dead) iPod Touch. Racing green signboards with faded fast food decals. Boulder had vanished in her rearview mirror around 3:00 P.M., and then the foggy skyline of Denver with its fleet of grounded jets, and finally little Gold Bar behind a screen of falling snow-flakes.

Scrape-scrape.

Bing Crosby's "White Christmas" faded, and the next holi-day song cued up. She'd heard them all twice now.

Her Honda bucked sharply left. Red Bull splashed in her lap. The steering wheel went rigid in her grip and she fought it for a stomach-fluttery second (*turn into the skid, turn into the skid*) before twisting the vehicle back under control, still moving forward and uphill but losing speed. Losing traction.

"No, no, no." She pumped the gas.

The all-weather tires gripped and released in the sludgy snow, heaving the car in violent contractions. Steam sizzled off the hood.

"Come on, Blue—"

Scrape-scrape.

She'd called this car Blue since she got it in high school. Now she feathered the gas pedal, searching for the sensory feedback of traction. Twin spurts of snow kicked up in her rearview mirror, lit vivid red by her taillights. A harsh rat-tling sound—Blue's undercarriage scraping the snow's surface again. The car struggled and fishtailed, half boat now, and—

Scrape—

The left wiper blade snapped off and twirled away.

Her heart sank. "Oh *shit*."

Now the incoming snowflakes stuck to the left hemisphere of her windshield, rapidly gathering on the unguarded glass. She'd lost too much speed. In seconds, her view of State Route Six had narrowed into tunnel vision, and she punched her steering wheel. The horn bleated, heard by no one.

This is how people die, she realized with a shiver. *In blizzards, people get trapped out in rural areas and run out of gas.*

They freeze to death.

She sipped her Red Bull—empty.

She clicked off the radio, leaned into the passenger seat to see the road, and tried to remember—what was the last car she'd seen today? How many miles back? It had been an orange snowplow with CDOT stenciled on the door, hugging the right lane and spouting a plume of ice chips. At least an hour ago. Back when the sun had been out.

Now it was just a gray lantern slipping behind jagged peaks, and the sky was dimming to a bruised purple. Frozen fir trees becoming jagged silhouettes. The lowlands darkening into lakes of shadow. The temperature was four degrees, according to the Shell station signboard she'd passed thirty miles back. Probably colder now.

Then she saw it: a half-buried green sign in a snow berm to her right. It crept up on her, catching the glow of her Honda's dirty headlights in a flash: 365 DAYS SINCE THE LAST FATAL ACCIDENT.

The count was probably a few days off due to the snowstorm, but she still found it eerie. One year exactly. It made tonight some sort of grim anniversary. It felt strangely personal, like one of her gravestone rubbings.

And behind it, another sign.

REST AREA AHEAD.

SEEN ONE? YOU'VE SEEN THEM ALL.

One longhouse structure (visitor center, restrooms, maybe a volunteer-run convenience store or coffee shop) nestled among wind-blasted firs and chapped rock faces. A bare flagpole. A drumlike slice of an ancient tree. A crowd of bronze statues buried to their waists; taxpayer-funded art honoring some local doctor or pioneer. And an offshoot parking lot with a handful of parked cars—other stranded motorists like herself, waiting for the snowplows to arrive.

Darby had passed dozens of rest areas since Boulder. Some bigger, most better, all less isolated. But this one, apparently, was the one fate had chosen for her.

TIRED? asked a blue sign. FREE COFFEE INSIDE.

And a newer one, stamped with the Bush-era Homeland Security eagle: SEE SOMETHING? SAY SOMETHING.

A final sign, at the end of the off-ramp, was T-shaped. It directed trucks and campers to go left and smaller vehicles to go right.

Darby almost ran it over.

Her windshield was now opaque with heavy snow—her right wiper was failing, too—so she'd rolled down her window and palmed a circle in the glass. It was like navigating while looking through a periscope. She didn't even bother finding a parking space—the painted lines and curbs wouldn't be visible until March—but nuzzled Blue in beside a windowless gray van.

She cut the engine. Killed the headlights.

Silence.

Her hands were still shaking. Leftover adrenaline from that first skid. She squeezed them into fists, first the right, then the left (*inhale, count to five, exhale*), and watched her windshield gather snowflakes. In ten seconds, the circle she'd wiped was gone. In thirty, she was sealed under a wall of darkening ice, facing the fact that she wouldn't make it to Provo, Utah, by midnight tonight. That optimistic ETA had hinged on her beating this blizzard over Backbone Pass before 8:00 P.M., and it was almost 6:00 already. Even if she didn't stop to sleep or pee, she wouldn't be able to speak to her mom before the first surgery. That window of time was CLOSED INDEFINITELY, like yet another mountain pass on her news app.

After the surgery, then.

That's when.

Now her Honda was pitch black. Snow packed against the glass on all sides like an arctic cave. She checked her iPhone, squinting in the electric glow—no service, and a depleting battery. The last text message she'd received was still open. She'd first read it back on the highway around Gold Bar, crossing some causeway slick with ice, hauling ass at eighty-five with the little screen trembling in her palm: She's okay right now.

Right now. That was a scary qualifier. And it wasn't even the scariest part.

Darby's older sister, Devon, thought in emoticons. Her texts and Twitter posts were allergic to punctuation, often-breathless spurts of verbiage in search of a coherent thought. But not this one. Devon had chosen to spell out *okay*, and end the sentence with a period, and these little details had lingered in Darby's stomach like an ulcer. Nothing tangible, but a clue that whatever was happening at Utah Valley Hospital was less than *okay* but couldn't be expressed via keypad.

Just four stupid words.

She's okay right now.

And here Darby was, the underachieving secondborn, trapped at a lonely rest stop just below the summit of Backbone Pass, because she'd tried to race Snowmageddon over the Rockies and failed. Miles above sea level, snowed in inside a '94 Honda Civic with busted windshield wipers, a dying phone, and a cryptic text message simmering in her mind.

She's okay right now. Whatever the hell that meant.

As a girl, she'd been fascinated by death. She hadn't lost any grandparents, so it was still an abstract concept, something for her to visit and explore like a tourist. She loved gravestone rubbings—when you tape rice paper against a headstone and rub black crayon or wax to take a detailed imprint. They're beautiful. Her private collection included hundreds of them, some framed. Some unknowns. Some celebrities. She'd jumped a fence at Lookout Mountain, outside Denver, last year to capture Buffalo Bill's. For a long time she'd believed this little quirk of hers, this adolescent fascination with death, would better prepare her for the real thing when it entered her life.

It hadn't.

For a few moments, she sat in her darkened car, reading and rereading Devon's words. It occurred to her that if she stayed inside this cold vault alone with her thoughts, she'd just start to cry, and God knows she'd done enough of that in the last twenty-four hours. She couldn't lose her momentum. She couldn't sink into that muck again. Like Blue bogging down in this heavy snow, miles from human help—it'll bury you if you let it.

Inhale. Count to five. Exhale.

Forward motion.

So she pocketed her iPhone, unbuckled her seat belt, slipped a coat over her Boulder Art Walk hoodie, and hoped that in addition to the promised free coffee, this dingy little rest area would have Wi-Fi.

INSIDE THE VISITOR CENTER, SHE ASKED THE FIRST PERSON she saw, and he pointed to a cheaply laminated sign on the wall: WI-FI FOR OUR GUESTS, COURTESY OF CDOT'S PROUD PARTNER-SHIP WITH ROADCONNECT!

He stood behind her. "It . . . uh, it says it'll bill you."

"I'll pay it."

"It's a bit steep."

"I'll pay it anyway."

"See?" He pointed. "$3.95 every ten minutes—"

"I just need to make a call."

"For how long?"

"I don't know."

"Because if it's going to be more than twenty minutes, you might want to do their RoadConnect monthly pass, which says it's only ten dollars for—"

"Holy shit, dude, it's *fine*."

Darby hadn't meant to snap. She hadn't gotten a good look at this stranger until now, under the sterile fluorescent lights—

late fifties, a yellow Carhartt jacket, one earring, and a silver goatee. Like a sad-eyed pirate. She reminded herself that he was probably stranded here, too, and only trying to help.

Her iPhone couldn't find the wireless network anyway. She scrolled with her thumb, waiting for it to appear.

Nothing.

The guy returned to his seat. "Karma, eh?"

She ignored him.

This place must have been a functioning coffeehouse during daylight hours. But here and now, it reminded her of an after-hours bus station— overlit and bare. The coffee stand (Espresso Peak) was locked behind a roll-down security shutter. Behind it, two industrial coffee machines with analog buttons and blackened drip trays. Stale pastries. A blackboard menu listed a few pricey frou-frou drinks.

The visitor center was one room—a long rectangle following the spine of the roof, with public restrooms in the back. Wooden chairs, a broad table, and benches along one wall. Against the other, a vending machine and racks of tourism brochures. The room felt both cramped and cavernous, with a sharp Lysol odor.

As for the promised free coffee? On Espresso Peak's stone-and-mortar counter was a stack of Styrofoam cups, another of napkins, and two carafes on warming plates guarded by the shutter. One labeled COFEE, one labeled COCO.

Someone on state payroll is zero for two on spelling.

At ankle level, she noticed the mortar was cracked and one of the stones was loose. A kick could dislodge it. This irritated a small, obsessive-compulsive part of Darby's brain. Like the need to pick at a hangnail.

She heard a low buzzing noise, too, like the thrum of locust wings, and wondered if the site was on backup power. That could have reset the Wi-Fi, maybe. She turned back to the goateed stranger. "Have you seen any pay phones here?"

The man glanced up at her—*oh, you're still here?*—and shook his head.

"Do you have a cell signal?" she asked.

"Not since White Bend."

Her heart sank. Although the regional map on the wall didn't mark their location, Darby could deduce that this rest stop was the one called Wanasho (roughly translating to *Little Devil*, courtesy of a long-forgotten local tongue). Twenty miles north was another rest area—the similarly named Wanashono, for *Big Devil*—and then ten miles farther, downhill, was the town of White Bend. And tonight, on the eve of Snowmageddon, or Snowpocalypse, or Snowzilla, or whatever meteorologists were calling it, White Bend might as well be on the moon—

"I got a signal outside," said a second male voice.

Behind her.

Darby turned. He was leaning against the front door with one hand on the knob. She'd walked right past him when she first came inside (*how did I miss him?*). The guy was tall, broad-shouldered, about a year or two older than her. He could be one of the Alpha Sig guys her roommate partied with, with a slick mop of hair, a green North Face jacket, and a shy smile. "Just one bar, though, and just for a few minutes," he added. "My carrier is, uh, T-Mobile."

"Mine too. Where?"

"Out by the statues."

She nodded, thinking. "Do you . . . hey, do either of you know when the snowplows are coming?"

Both guys shook their heads. Darby didn't like standing between them; she had to keep turning her head.

"I think the emergency broadcasts are down," the older one said, pointing to a nineties-era AM/FM radio buzzing on the counter. The source of the staticky insect noise she'd heard. It was caged behind the security grate. "When I got here, it was playing traffic and EAS stuff on a thirty-second loop," he added. "But now it's just dead air. Maybe their transmitter's covered with snow."

She reached through the grate and straightened the antenna, causing the garbled static to change pitch. "Still better than Bing Crosby."

"Who's Bing Crosby?" the younger man asked.

"One of the Beatles," the older one answered.

"Oh."

Somehow, Darby liked the older one already, and regretted snapping at him about the Wi-Fi.

"I don't know much about music," the younger one admitted.

"Clearly."

On the big table, she noticed a deck of dog-eared playing cards. A little Texas Hold 'em apparently, to bond two strangers stranded by a blizzard.

A toilet flushed in the restrooms.

Three strangers, she tallied.

She slipped her phone back into her jeans pocket, realizing both men were still staring at her. One in front, one behind.

"I'm Ed," said the older one.

"Ashley," said the younger one.

Darby didn't give her name. She elbowed out the front door, back into the subzero chill outside, and stuffed her hands into her coat pockets. She let the door swing shut behind her, hearing the older man ask the younger one: "Wait. Your name is Ashley? Like the *girl* name?"

He groaned. "It's not just a girl name—"

The door closed.

The world outside had darkened under shadow. The sun was gone. Falling snowflakes glittered orange in the visitor center's single exterior lamp, which hung over the doorway in a big pan. But Snowmageddon seemed to have thinned out for a few moments; against the descending night she could see the outlines of distant peaks. Craggy shards of rock, half shrouded in trees.

She drew her coat up to her neck and shivered.

The crowd of statues that the younger guy—Ashley—had mentioned was to the south of the rest area, past the flagpole and picnic area. Near the off-ramp she'd taken. From here, she could barely see them. Just half-buried forms in the snow.

"Hey."

She turned.

Ashley again. He let the door click shut and caught up to her, taking high steps in the snow. "There's . . . so, there's a really particular spot I had to stand. That's the only place I could pick up a signal, and it was just one bar. You might only be able to send a text."

"That'll still work."

He zipped up his jacket. "I'll show you."

They followed his old footprints out there and Darby noted

that they were already half filled with several inches of fresh powder. She wondered, but didn't ask, how long he'd been stranded here.

Gaining some distance from the building, she also realized this rest area was nestled on a precipice. Behind the back wall (the restrooms), scoured treetops marked an abrupt cliff. She couldn't even see exactly where the land started to drop, as the blanket of snowpack disguised the verticality. One misstep could be fatal. The flora up here was equally hostile—Douglas firs whipped into grotesque shapes by powerful winds, their branches jagged and stiff.

"Thanks," Darby said.

Ashley didn't hear. They kept lurching through waist-deep snow, arms out for balance. It was deeper here, off the footpath. Her Converse were already soaked through, her toes numb.

"So you go by Ashley?" she asked.

"Yeah."

"Not, like, Ash?"

"Why would I?"

"Just asking."

Again, she glanced back to the visitor center, and spotted a figure standing in the amber glow of the building's single window. Watching them from behind the frosted glass. She couldn't tell if it was the older man, Ed, or the person she hadn't seen.

"Ashley is not just a girl's name," he said as they trudged. "It's a perfectly viable man's name."

"Oh, definitely."

"Like Ashley Wilkes in *Gone with the Wind*."

"I was just thinking that," Darby said. It felt good to bull-shit a little. But still, the wary part of her brain that she could never quite disengage wondered: *You're familiar with that old-ass movie, but you don't know who the Beatles are?*

"Or Ashley Johnson," he said. "The world-famous rugby player."

"You made that one up."

"Did not." He pointed into the distance. "Hey. You can see Melanie's Peak."

"What?"

"Melanie's Peak." He seemed embarrassed. "Sorry, I've been stuck here a long time, reading everything in the information center. See the big mountain over there? Some guy named it after his wife."

"That's sweet."

"Maybe. Unless he was calling her frigid and inhospitable." Darby chuckled.

They'd reached the icicled statues now. There was probably a plaque detailing what it all meant, under the snow somewhere. The sculptures appeared to be children. Running, jumping, playing, cast in bronze and coated with ice.

Ashley pointed at one wielding a baseball bat. "There. By the little leaguer."

"Here?"

"Yeah. That's where I got a signal."

"Thanks."

"Do you . . ." He hesitated, his hands in his pockets. "Need me to, uh, stick around?"

Silence.

"You know. I mean, if—"

"No." Darby gave him a smile, a genuine one. "I'm fine. Thanks."

"I was hoping you'd say that. It's cold as *balls* out here." He flashed that easy grin of his and walked back to the orange lights, waving over his shoulder. "Have fun out here with the nightmare children."

"Will do."

She didn't realize how unsettling the statues were until she was alone with them. The children were missing chunks. It was an art style she'd seen before—the sculptor used raw hunks of bronze, fusing them in odd and counterintuitive welds that left seams and gaps—but in the darkness, her imagination rendered gore. The boy to her left, the one swinging a baseball bat that Ashley had called the little leaguer, had an exposed rib cage. Others waved spindly, mangled arms, missing patches of flesh. Like a crowd of pit-bull-mauling victims, gnawed half to the bone.

What had Ashley called them? *Nightmare children.*

He was twenty feet away, almost a silhouette against the rest area's orange light, when she turned and called to him. "Hey. Wait."

He looked back.

"Darby," she said. "My name is Darby."

He smiled.

Thanks for helping me, she wanted to say. *Thank you for being decent to me, a total stranger.* The words were there, in her mind, but she couldn't make them real. He broke eye contact, the moment evaporating . . .

Thank you, Ashley—

He kept walking.

Then he stopped again, reconsidering, and said one last thing: "You do know Darby is a guy's name, right?"

She laughed.

She watched him leave, and then she leaned against the statue's baseball bat, frozen midswing, and held her iPhone skyward against the falling snowflakes. She squinted, watching the cracked screen's upper left corner.

No service.

She waited, alone in the darkness. In the right corner, the battery had fallen to 22 percent. She'd left her charger plugged into an outlet in her dorm. A hundred miles back.

"Please," she whispered. "Please, God . . ."

Still no signal. Breathing through chattering teeth, she reread her sister's text: She's okay right now.

Okay is the single worst word in the English language. Without context, it's an utter non-thing. *Okay* could mean her mother, Maya, was doing better; it could mean she was doing worse; and it could mean she was . . . well, just *okay*.

People say pancreatic cancer is a swift killer, because death often follows a diagnosis within weeks or even days—but that's not true. It takes years to kill. It's just symptomless in its early stages, invisibly multiplying inside its host, not manifesting jaundice or abdominal pain until it's far too late. This was a chilling notion; that the cancer had been there inside her mother when Darby was in high school. It'd been there when she'd lied about the broken Sears tags in her purse. It'd been there when she drove home at 3:00 A.M. on a Sunday night, woozy from bad ecstasy with a green glow bracelet on her wrist, and her mother broke down in tears on the front porch and called her a *rotten little bitch*. That invisible creature had been perched there on her shoulder all along, eavesdropping, and she'd been dying slowly, and neither of them had known.

They'd last spoken on Thanksgiving. The phone call had been over an hour of crisscrossing arguments, but the last few seconds lingered in Darby's mind.

You're the reason Dad left us, she remembered saying. *And if I could have chosen him instead of you, I would have. In a heartbeat.*

In a fucking heartbeat, Maya.

She wiped away tears with her thumb, already freezing to her skin. She exhaled into the biting air. Her mother was being prepped for surgery, *right now*, at Utah Valley Hospital, and here Darby was, stranded at a run-down rest area miles into the Rockies.

And she knew she didn't have enough gas to idle Blue here for long. The visitor center at least had heat and electricity. Whether she liked it or not, she'd probably have to make small talk with Ed and Ashley, and whoever had flushed that toilet. She imagined them—a huddle of strangers in a snowstorm, like gold miners and homesteaders who must have shared refuge in these same mountains centuries past—sipping watery coffee, sharing campfire stories, and listening to the radio for garbled clues as to when the snowplows would arrive. Maybe she'd make a few Facebook friends and learn how to play poker.

Or maybe she'd go sit in her Honda and freeze to death.

Both options were equally enticing.

She glanced at the closest statue. "This is going to be a long night, kiddos." She checked her iPhone one last time, but by now she'd given up hope on Ashley's magic signal spot. All she was doing out here was wasting battery and courting frostbite.

"One *hell* of a long night."

She headed back to the Wanasho building, feeling another migraine nip at the edges of her thoughts. Snowmageddon had kicked up again, obscuring the mountains with windswept snowflakes. A sharp gust of wind raced up behind her, creaking the fir trees, whipping her coat taut. She unconsciously counted the cars in the parking lot as she walked—three, plus her Honda. A gray van, a red pickup truck, and an unidentified vehicle, all obscured by rolling waves of frost.

On her way, she chose to circle through the parking lot, around this small collection of trapped cars. No reason, really. She would later look back on this mindless decision many times, and wonder how differently her night might've played out if she'd merely retraced Ashley's footprints instead.

She passed the row of vehicles.

First was the red truck. Sandbags in the bed, webbed tire chains. Less snow heaped on it than the others, meaning it hadn't been here long. She guessed thirty minutes.

The second car was completely buried, just an unrecognizable mound of snow. She couldn't even discern the paint color—it could be a Dumpster for all she knew. Something broad and boxy. It'd been here the longest of the four.

Third was Blue, her trusty Honda Civic. The car she'd learned to drive in, the car she'd taken to college, the car she'd lost her virginity in (not all at the same time). The left wiper was still missing, tossed into some snow berm a mile down the highway. She knew she was lucky to have made it to a rest area.

Last was the gray van.

This was where Darby chose to cut between parked cars

and take the footpath to the building's front door, some fifty feet away. She planned to pass between the van and her Honda, leaning on the doors of her own car for balance.

Printed on the side of the van was an orange cartoon fox, like a counterfeit Nick Wilde from *Zootopia*. He wielded a nail gun the way a secret agent holds a pistol, promoting some sort of construction or repair service. The company's name was covered by snow, but the slogan read: WE FINISH WHAT WE START. The van had two rear windows. The right one was blocked by a towel. The left one's towel had fallen away, leaving clear glass that caught a blade of reflected lamplight as Darby passed it, and in it, she glimpsed something pale inside the van. A hand.

A tiny, doll-like hand.

She halted midstep, a breath trapped in her lungs.

This little hand gripped a grate-like material behind the icy glass—white fingers gently unwrapping one by one, in that uncoordinated way of a child still mastering their own nervous system—and then abruptly, it drew back into the darkness. Gone from view. It all happened in three, maybe four seconds, leaving Darby in stunned silence.

No way.

The interior was quiet. Motionless again.

She crept closer, cupping her hands against the window, squinting inside. Her eyelashes fluttering on cold glass. Barely visible in the blackness, near where the tiny hand had vanished, she made out a small crescent, a barely-there reflection of dim sodium-vapor light. It was a circular combination lock. Holding a latticework of metal bars, which the child's hand had been gripping. Like the kid was in a kennel.

Then Darby exhaled—a mistake—and the glass went opaque with her breath. But she'd seen it. There was no un-seeing it.

She stepped away, leaving a handprint on the door, feeling her heartbeat pounding in her neck. An intensifying rhythm.

There's . . .

There's a child locked inside this van.

SHE WENT BACK INSIDE.

Ashley glanced up. "Any luck?"

She didn't answer.

He was seated now, at the wood table, playing cards with Ed. A new woman was here, too—Ed's wife, apparently—sitting beside him. She was a fussy little fortysomething with a black bowl cut and a crinkly yellow parka, busily popping cartoon bubbles on her tablet. She must have been the one in the restroom.

As the door slid shut at Darby's back, she tallied three possible suspects: Chatty Ashley, sad-eyed Ed, and Ed's frumpy wife. So who did the gray van belong to?

Oh my God, there's a kid outside in that van.

Locked in a cage or something.

It hit her again, all at once. She tasted raw oysters in the back of her mouth. Her legs went mushy. She needed to sit down, but was afraid to.

One of these three people did it—

"Make sure the door is shut," Ed said.

Like nothing had happened, the card game resumed. Ashley checked his hand and glanced sideways at Ed. "Four of hearts?"

"Go fish. Two of spades?"

"Nope."

Something else was wrong, Darby realized. The math didn't add up. There were three cars outside besides her own. Three suspects in here. But Ed and his wife had almost certainly traveled together. Right? So there had to be a fourth person at the rest stop. *But where?*

She glanced from Ashley, to Ed, to Ed's wife, scanning the room front to back, her heart seizing with slippery terror. *Where else could—*

Then she felt a warm breath touch the back of her neck. Someone was standing behind her.

"Jack of clubs."

"Go fish."

Darby stood still, hairs prickling on her skin. A chill racing down her spine. She wanted to turn around, but she couldn't. Her body wouldn't move.

He's right behind me.

He was breathing down the back of her neck. A mouthy waft, lifting her auburn hair, tickling her bare skin. Gently whistling past her ear. Somehow she already knew this fourth traveler was a man—women just didn't *breathe* like that. He was standing less than eighteen inches behind her. Close enough to touch her back, or reach around her throat and put his fingers to her windpipe.

She wished she could turn around and face this fourth person, whoever he was, but the moment felt strange, floaty. Like trying to throw a punch in a nightmare.

Turn around, she urged herself. *Turn around now.*

In front of her, the card game continued: "Queen of hearts?"

"Ah! Here you go."

"Nine of diamonds?"

"Nope."

Behind her, the breathing halted for a few seconds—long enough that she briefly hoped she'd been imagining it, all of it—and then it sucked in a heavier gulp. Mouth-breathing. Standing there in rigid silence, Darby realized she'd done it again. She'd entered the room without checking the corner on her left.

Jesus, Darby, just turn around.

Face him.

Finally, she did.

She turned slowly, casually, with one palm up, like she was just obliging Ed's request to ensure the door was closed properly. She turned—turned until she was face-to-face with the man.

Man was a stretch. He was tall but slouching, rail thin, nineteen at most. A weasel-like profile to his acne-encrusted face, all overbite above a shapeless chin shrouded with peach-fuzz whiskers. A Deadpool beanie and a baby-blue ski jacket. His narrow shoulders were speckled with snowflakes, like he'd just been outside, too. But outside doing what? He was staring at her, so she met his gaze—tiny black pupils, rodent-like in their flat stupidity—and returned a shy smile.

The moment smeared.

Rodent Face's breath reeked of milk chocolate mixed with the earthy sourness of Skoal. His right arm lifted without warning—Darby flinched—but he was reaching to press the door shut. It engaged with a deadbolt click.

"Thanks," Ed said, turning back to Ashley. "Ace of hearts?"

"Nope."

Darby broke eye contact and left the man by the door. Her heart banged against her ribs. Her footsteps sounded magnified. She squeezed both hands into fists to hide their shaking and took a seat at the table with the others. She pulled up a chair between Ashley and the older couple, and the wooden legs honked on the tiles.

Ashley gritted his teeth at the harsh sound. "Uh, nine of hearts."

"Shit."

Ed's wife smacked his elbow. "Language."

Darby knew Rodent Face was still watching her with those dim little eyes, studying her. And she realized she was sitting rigidly—too rigidly—so she sprawled in her chair a bit and pretended to play with her iPhone. Hunching her knees up to the table. She was play-acting now, just an overcaffeinated art major with a Honda full of gravestone rubbings and an exhausted phone battery, stranded here at the edge of civilization like everyone else. Just a harmless CU-Boulder sophomore.

He lingered by the door. Still watching her.

Now Darby began to worry. Could he know? Maybe he'd been looking out the west-facing window and seen her peering inside his van. Or maybe her demeanor gave it all away the second she'd wobbled back inside the lobby with her nerves frayed and her heart in her throat. She was usually a good liar, but not tonight. Not now.

She tried to find an ordinary explanation for what she'd witnessed—like, one of these four people's not-yet-mentioned kid was just napping in the back of their van. That was plausible, right? It had to happen all the time. That's what rest stops are for. Resting.

But that didn't explain the circular padlock she'd glimpsed. Or the wire bars the hand had been gripping. Or, come to think of it, the deliberate placement of the towels on the rear windows—to conceal what was happening inside. Right?

Am I overreacting?

Maybe. Maybe not. Her thoughts were scattering, her caffeine high deserting her. She needed some damn coffee.

And speaking of *overreacting*, she'd already tried calling 911 outside. Still no signal. She'd tried several more times near the Nightmare Children, in the magic spot Ashley had described to her. Nothing. She'd even tried sending a text message to 911—she recalled reading once that text files take up a fraction of the bandwidth required for a phone call, and are the best way to summon help from cellular dead zones. But that hadn't worked, either: Child abduction gray van license plate VBH9045 state route 6 Wanasho rest stop send police.

This text message, tagged UNABLE TO SEND, was still open. She closed it, in case Rodent Face looked over her shoulder.

She'd also tried opening the van's rear door (which could've been a fatal error if the vehicle had possessed a car alarm), but it was locked. Of course—why would it *not* be locked? She'd lingered out there, peering into the darkness with cupped hands, tapping the glass with her knuckles, trying to coax the tiny form into moving again. No luck. The van's interior was pitch black, and the rear doors were heaped with blankets and junk. She'd only glimpsed that little hand for a few seconds. But it'd been enough. She hadn't imagined it.

Right?

Right.

"Ace of spades."

"Goddammit."

"Language, Eddie—"

"For *Christ's sake*, Sandi, we're snowed in inside a taxpayer-funded shithouse in Colorado and it's almost Christmas Eve. I'll put a twenty in my swear jar when I get home, okay?"

The lady with the black bowl cut—Sandi, apparently— glanced across the wide table to Darby and mouthed: *Sorry about him.* She was missing a front tooth. In her lap, her rhinestone purse was embroidered with Psalm 100:5, FOR THE LORD IS GOOD AND HIS LOVE ENDURES FOREVER.

Darby smiled back politely. Her delicate sensibilities could handle a little cussing. Plus, Ashley still thought Bing Crosby was one of the Beatles, and that made Ed a decent guy in her book.

But . . . she was aware that she was developing another blind spot here, just like when she'd entered the building without checking her corners. Her gut said that Rodent Face was the driver of the gray van. But that was an assumption. She knew the kidnapper/child abuser could be anyone here. Any of the four strangers trapped at this roadside shelter could be—no, *was*—a suspect.

Ashley? He was cleaning up at Go Fish right now. He was witty and friendly, the kind of sanguine charmer she'd dated once but never twice, but there was something about him she didn't trust. She couldn't put her finger on exactly why. Was it a mannerism? A choice of words? He just felt *false* to her, his social engagements carefully managed, the way a store clerk puts on a cheery face for customers but talks shit about them in the break room.

As for Ed and Sandi? They were nice, but something was off about them, too. They didn't seem like they were married. They didn't even seem like they particularly liked each other.

And Rodent Face? He was a walking AMBER Alert already.

Everyone here was guilty until proven innocent. Darby would need to match each individual to a vehicle outside, and then she could be certain. She couldn't just openly ask, either—or the true kidnapper/abusive parent would know she was onto them. She'd need to ply this information gently. She considered asking Ashley, Ed, and Sandi what time they'd arrived and deducing from the amount of snow piled on the cars outside. But that, too, could attract too much attention.

Then again, what if she waited too long?

The kidnapper wouldn't linger here. The instant the blizzard cleared, or the CDOT snowplows arrived, he (or *she*, or *they*) would get the hell out of Colorado. Leaving Darby with only a suspect description and a license plate number.

Her phone chirped in her pocket, startling her. Twenty percent battery.

Ashley glanced up at her over a handful of grubby cards. "Signal?"

"What?"

"Any luck catching a cell signal? By the statues?"

She shook her head, understanding this was an opportunity. She knew her phone wouldn't last the night, so now would be an appropriate time to ask, in character: "Anyone here have an iPhone charger, by chance?"

Ashley shook his head. "Sorry."

"I don't," said Sandi, nudging Ed's elbow, and her tone morphed from sweet to venomous. "What about you, Eddie? Do you still have your phone charger, or did you pawn that, too?"

"You don't pawn things in the twenty-first century," Ed said. "It's called Craigslist. And it's not my fault Apple makes overpriced—"

"Language—"

"Trash. I was going to say overpriced *trash*, Sandi." He slapped his cards to the table and looked at Ashley, forcing a grin. "I broke an iPhone in my pocket once, just by sitting down. A seven-hundred-dollar gadget, destroyed by the simple act of *sitting down*. The flimsy little thing bent like a leaf against my—"

"Language—"

"—hip. My hip. See, despite what Sandi here thinks, I'm actually capable of completing an entire sentence without resorting to—"

Ashley interrupted: "Four of clubs?"

"*Fuck*."

Sandi sighed and popped another bubble on her tablet. "Careful, young man. Eddie-boy flips tables when he loses."

"It was a chessboard," Ed said. "And it was *once*."

Ashley grinned, taking his new four of clubs.

"You know, Eddie, you're never going to get another job

if you don't get that cussing under control." Sandi pecked at her screen with a thumbnail, and a cartoon failure sound chimed—*whomp-whomp.*

Ed forced a smile. He started to say something, but reconsidered.

The room cooled.

Darby crossed her arms and let the words sink in—bottom line, no white Apple charging cord for miles. She guessed her phone had a few hours of battery life left on power-save mode, if she kept it idle. Rodent Face hadn't answered her question, of course, or even spoken at all. He was still standing by the front door, blocking the exit with his hands in his pockets, his fuzzy chin down, his red-and-black Deadpool beanie cloaking the upper half of his face.

He's watching me. Just like I'm watching him.

She had to act natural. Her best friend had once told her that she suffered from RBF ("resting bitch face"), and yes, it was true that Darby rarely smiled. Not because she was bitchy, or even unhappy. Smiling made her self-conscious. When the muscles in her face tensed, the long, curved scar over her eyebrow became visible, as clear as a white sickle. She'd had it since she was ten. She hated it.

Crackle-snap.

A ragged sound, like tearing fabric, and Darby jolted in her seat. It was the radio behind the security shutter hissing to life. Everyone looked up.

"Is that—"

"Yep." Ed stood. "The emergency freq. It's back."

Another slurp of grungy static, reaching a garbled peak. Like a phone dropped underwater.

She didn't realize Rodent Face had crept closer until he was standing directly over her left shoulder, still mouth-breathing, joining the group in frozen attention as the ancient Sony AM/FM leaked electronic slush from the counter. Under the feedback noise, she recognized . . . yes, there it was . . . the faintest murmur—

"A voice," she said. "Someone's talking."

"I can't hear anything—"

"Hang on." Ed reached through the security grate and twirled the volume dial, lifting tinny fragments out of the muck. It sounded like an automated voice, stilted with inhuman pauses: "—has issued a w-nter st-rm w-rn-ng -ffecting Backb-ne Pass with bl-zzard conditions and extr-me prec-pitation. State Route Six is closed to all tr-ffic between exits f-rty-nine and sixty-eight unt-l f-rther notice—"

Ashley blinked. "Which exit number are we at?"

Ed raised a finger, clattering the shutters. "Shh."

"—Em-rgency and road maint-n-nce crews exp-ct signif-icant delays of eight to t-n hours due to m-ltiple collisions and heavy sn-wfall. All mot-rists are adv-sed to st-y off the roads and r-main indoors until c-nditions impr-ve."

A long, crackly pause. Then a faint beep.

Everyone waited.

"The n-tional weath-r service has issued a w-nter storm w-rning affecting Backb-ne Pass . . ." The broadcast repeated, and everyone in the room deflated at once. Ed lowered the volume and huffed.

Silence.

Sandi spoke first. "Eight to ten *hours*?"

Darby's legs nearly folded under her. She'd been half standing, arched forward to listen, and now she slumped back into her chair like a rag doll. The rest of the room processed this information in hushed voices, swirling around her:

"Is that right?"

"Eight to ten freakin' hours."

"All night, basically."

"Better get comfy."

Sandi pouted and closed her tablet's leather case. "Figures. I'm already on the last level of *Super Bubble Pop*."

All night. Darby rocked in the cheap chair, her knuckles clasped around her knees. A strange sensation of alarm washed over her, a sluggish sort of horror, like what her mother might've felt when she found that first lump under her armpit. No panic, no fight, no flight, just that shivery little moment when daily life goes rancid.

It'll be all night until the snowplows get here—

Rodent Face cleared his throat, a juicy gurgle, and everyone glanced at him. He was still standing behind Darby's chair, still breathing down her neck. He addressed the entire room, his words slow and clotted: "I'm Lars."

Silence.

"My . . ." He inhaled through his mouth. "My name is . . . Lars."

No one responded.

Darby tensed, realizing this was likely the first time Ashley, Ed, and Sandi had heard him speak as well. The awkwardness was tangible.

"Uh . . ." Ashley flashed his easy smile. "Thanks, Lars."

"You know . . ." Lars swallowed, both hands in his jacket pockets. "Since we'll be . . . ah . . . here a while. Better make introductions. So, ah, hello, my name is Lars."

. . . And I'm probably the one with a kid locked in my van.

Darby's mind raced, her thoughts fluttering out of control, her nerves writhing and sparking like live wires.

And we're trapped here with you.

In this tiny rest stop.

All night.

"Nice to meet you," said Ed. "What're your thoughts on Apple products?"

———

TWENTY MINUTES OF STRATEGIC SMALL TALK LATER, DARBY had all the parked vehicles matched to their drivers.

The buried one belonged to Ashley. He'd been the first one here, having arrived sometime after 3:00 P.M. this afternoon to find a deserted rest area with a murmuring radio and stale coffee. He'd been in no hurry to cross the pass, and figured he'd play it safe. He was a college student, like herself—Salt Lake City Institute of Tech or something. Now that the ice was broken, he was an absolute chatterbox with a Cheshire grin full of white teeth. Darby now knew he was planning a Vegas trip with his uncle to see some illusionist show. She knew he hated mushrooms but loved cilantro. Good lord, could he talk: "And *Ashley* is a perfectly good male name."

"Uh-huh," said Ed.

The two older folks were more guarded, but Darby learned the red F-150 was actually Sandi's—not Ed's, as she'd originally guessed. She was also surprised to learn they weren't married, although they sure bickered enough to be. They were *cousins*, actually, and Sandi was driving them both to Denver to visit family for Christmas. A bit of an eleventh-hour trip, by the sound of it. Ed had been in some sort of recent trouble, since he didn't have a car or (apparently) a steady job. Prison time? Maybe. He seemed to be something of a beached male; a fiftysomething man-child with an earring and a biker goatee, and Sandi seemed to love babying him, if only so she had an excuse to hate him.

So Darby had eliminated three people, and two vehicles.

This left Lars.

He hadn't spoken at all since he'd told them his name, so Darby couldn't get a firm idea of exactly when he'd arrived here, but judging by the snowpack she estimated maybe thirty minutes before Ed and Sandi. She watched Lars fill a Styrofoam cup with COCO and return to his sentry spot at the door, taking a childish slurp. She hadn't seen him sit down once.

As she sipped her own drug of choice, COFEE, Darby tried to plan her next moves. But there were too many unknowns. She couldn't involve Ed, Ashley, or Sandi—not yet—because then she'd lose control of the situation. Involving other people had to be a last resort. You can't put the pin back in the grenade. Right here, right now, she had the element of surprise, and the worst thing she could possibly do was waste it.

Still, her mind conjured worst-case scenarios. She imagined telling Ashley (the youngest and most physically able) that she suspected they were sharing oxygen with a child molester, and Ashley understandably blanching. Lars would notice this, yank a gun from his baby-blue jacket, and kill them both. Ed and Sandi would be witnesses, so they'd die, too. Four bullet-riddled bodies in a glossy pool of blood. All because Darby opened her mouth.

And the flipside—what if there wasn't a child in Lars's van? *What if I imagined it?*

What if she'd seen a plastic doll hand? A dog paw? A kid's empty glove? It wouldn't explain the bars or the combination lock, but still, it could've all been her tortured imagination, a trick of light and shadow, and it had lasted only a few seconds anyway. Her mind swirled a little.

She'd been certain thirty minutes ago, but suddenly her conviction disappeared. She could imagine a dozen scenarios more probable than this one. What were the odds of stumbling across a kidnapping in progress? While trapped overnight in a snowy rest stop? It was all too fantastical to be a part of Darby's life.

She tried to mentally reconstruct the scene. Step by step. The van's rear window had been frosted with ice. The interior had been dark. And Darby herself? She was a wreck—anxious, sleep-deprived, her blood surging with Red Bull, glimpsing starbursts behind her own dry eyelids. What if this was just her vivid imagination at work, and Lars was just an innocent traveler like the others? Attacking him could be a felony.

If I'm wrong about this . . .

She finished her last gulp of coffee and for some reason, her mind darted to her older sister. Twenty-three-year-old Devon, who had her first tattoo etched on her right shoulder blade. A few Chinese characters, bold and elegantly drawn. They translated to: "Strength in Chinese."

The lesson there? Double-check everything.

She needed to go back outside to the van. She needed to see this child. Really *see* this child.

And she couldn't rush to action. She had plenty of time; she had eight to ten hours of it, in fact. If this really was a kidnapping, Lars would run the van's heat periodically tonight to keep the child from freezing. Darby had enough time to think. And she needed to be certain before making her move.

Right?

Right.

She rubbed the goose bumps on her arms and scanned the room. At the table, they'd finished Go Fish—Ashley was now trying to convince Ed to play a new card game called War. Sandi had plucked a yellowed paperback from her purse and raised it like a defensive wall. And Lars, the star of tonight's nightmare, was still guarding the front door, sipping his Styrofoam cup of coco. She'd been counting; this was his third refill. He'd be hitting the restroom soon.

That's when, she decided. That was when she'd slip outside. Last time she'd stumbled into the scene, off guard and frightened. This time, she'd be ready.

Ashley riffled the cards, having given up on Ed, and nodded at Sandi's paperback. "What're you reading?"

She grunted. "A murder mystery."

"I like murder mysteries." He hesitated. "Well, actually, to be honest, I don't read much. I guess I just like the *idea* of murder mysteries."

Sandi forced a polite smile, turning a page. *Why'd you ask, then?*

It was barely two hours into Darby's stay at the Wanasho

rest area, and she was already getting annoyed at Ashley. He was a talker, all right. And he was still going like a windup toy, his hooks latched into Sandi: "How far . . . uh, how many chapters in are you?"

"Not many."

"Has the victim been murdered yet?"

"Yep."

"I like gore. Was it gory?"

Ed stirred uncomfortably and his chair croaked. He watched Sandi, who was turning another page and hadn't even answered Ashley's last question when he pelted her with another: "Can you guess who the murderer is?"

"Not yet," she said dryly. "That's the point."

"It's always the nice guy," Ashley said. "Again, I don't really read, but I've seen a lot of movies, and that's even better. Whoever seems like the nicest character, at first, will always turn out to be the asshole in the end."

Sandi ignored him.

Please stop talking, Darby thought. *Just stop.*

"That truck," he continued, glancing out the window. "That's yours, right?"

"Mm-hmm."

"Reminds me of a joke. What does *Ford* stand for?"

"I don't know."

"*Found on road, dead.*"

Sandi grunted and kept reading.

Finally, Ashley took the hint. "Sorry. I'll let you read."

Lars watched this interaction from the door. He licked his lips, and Darby was struck by how small his teeth were. Just two little rows of stunted kernels, like baby teeth, half-formed, still encased in pink gums. He gulped the last of his COCO and threw his empty Styrofoam cup at the garbage can, missing by three full feet.

No one commented on this.

Not even Ashley.

Darby watched the white cup twirl on the tile and considered—assuming her suspicions were confirmed—maybe she'd be able to break into Lars's van and quietly move the child into her Honda. Hide him or her in the back seat, perhaps, under the heap of rice paper she used for her gravestone rubbings. Or better yet, the trunk—if there was enough oxygen and heat. When the snowplows arrived early tomorrow morning, everyone could go their separate ways, and Lars might drive away without even realizing his prey had escaped—

No. That was wishful thinking. Lars would be back to run the engine. He would notice his captive had disappeared.

She took in a rattling breath. She counted to five before letting it out, just as her mother once taught her.

Right now, the advantage is mine.

I can't waste it.

She wished it could be someone else in this situation. Someone smarter, braver, steadier, more capable. Someone from her college's ROTC program, one of those sweaty girls in urban digital camouflage lugging heavy rucksacks up and down campus. Someone who knew jujitsu. Hell, *anyone* else.

But it was just her.

Just 110-pound, five-foot-two Darby Thorne, the weird girl who hid from parties inside a dorm room wallpapered with black crayon rubbings stolen from strangers' graves, like some kind of spiritual vampire.

As the snowstorm intensified outside, she swiped her iPhone and quickly typed another text. Just a draft message. Just a backup, in the event of the unthinkable, but it brought tears to her eyes all the same.

Mom, if you find this message on my phone, something happened to me. I'm trapped overnight at a rest stop as I write this, and one of the people here might be dangerous. I hope I'm just being paranoid. But if I'm not . . . just know that I'm sorry for everything. All the things I said and did to you. I'm sorry about our phone call on Thanksgiving. You don't deserve any of that. Mom, I love you so much. And I'm so sorry.

Love, Darby.

FIFTEEN MINUTES LATER, LARS WENT TO THE RESTROOM.

He passed by Darby's chair, and she noticed something strange. He'd peeled his black ski gloves off, exposing the pale skin on the back of his left hand. It was peppered with tiny, raised bumps. Like mosquito bites. Or maybe scar tissue, though she couldn't imagine what grisly tool could do that to a human hand, short of a cheese grater—

Then he shuffled past and vanished into the men's restroom. The door swished shut, taking forever before finally clicking.

Now.

Darby scooted her chair out and stood up on quivering knees. Ed and Ashley glanced up at her. This was her chance, her thirty-second window to sneak outside and confirm the unthinkable. Her phone in her hand, she moved to the front door, her lungs swelling with held breath—but on the way she surprised herself. She did something utterly illogical.

She approached the second carafe, labeled COCO, and quickly refilled her eight-ounce Styrofoam cup. She didn't even like hot chocolate.

But kids do. Right?

She heard a urinal flush. Lars was coming back.

Hurrying now, she sipped the warm drink while she crossed back to the front doorway, then tugged the door open, aware that Ashley was still watching her. "Yo, Darbs, where are you going?"

Darbs. She hadn't been called that since fifth grade.

"Trying again to get a cell signal. My mom's got pancreatic cancer and she's in a hospital in Provo." Without giving Ashley time to respond, she stepped outside into the howling storm, flinching against a wall of bone-chilling air, and recalled an offhand little saying she'd heard once from her mother. *The easiest lies to tell are the true ones.*

NIGHT

8:14 P.M.

DARBY WALKED TO THE NIGHTMARE CHILDREN FIRST.

This was part of her plan—it would be suspicious to bee-line straight for the cars, and she had to assume Lars would look out the window after he exited the restroom and found her not there. Plus, she was leaving tracks in the snow. She recognized her own from over an hour ago, and Ashley's, and possibly Lars's (her size-eight shoes were so much smaller than theirs). All filling with snowflakes.

Tonight, every decision would leave footprints.

As for decisions, the hot chocolate had been a dumb one. About as dumb as Devon's "Strength in Chinese" tattoo. She didn't know why she'd taken the time to pour a drink while a possible child predator took a leak one room over. She'd just done it. She'd burned her tongue when she sipped it on her way outside, like a real badass.

She circled the chewed-up statues, and then looped back around the visitor center. The building teetered by the cliff's edge—just a narrow precipice behind a cement foundation wall, made narrower by stacked picnic tables. On the building's back wall, she spotted two more windows. One for each restroom. They were small and triangular, about eight feet off the ground, nestled under the icicled overhang of the roof. She was certain Lars was finished in there already—she'd heard the urinal flush minutes ago—but she moved quietly, just in case.

She walked uphill, still play-acting the role of Girl Without Cell Service. Of course, her iPhone detected nothing. She tried resending her 911 text message every few paces, but it never took. Her battery was now at 17 percent.

From up here, she could survey the entire rest area, laid out like a diorama. Wanasho—*Little Devil*, in the local tongue. The stout little building. The flagpole. The cedar trunk. The Nightmare Children. The huddle of snowbound cars. Particularly, she watched the visitor center's front door, waiting for Lars to step outside under the orange glow of the sodium-vapor lamp. Waiting to see if he'd follow her trail.

The door didn't open.

No sign of Rodent Face.

Melanie's Peak towered to the left, a sloping shadow. The intensifying snowfall had obscured most of it, but it was still the tallest mountain within view. It would be a useful landmark for navigation.

From this vantage point, she could also see State Route Six, bathed in circles of overhead light. It looked like a giant ski ramp, glittering with fresh powder. Utterly impassible for everything here except (maybe) Sandi's truck. Blue wouldn't make it five feet up—or *down*—that.

She waited there with snowflakes in her hair, listening to

the distant gusts of high-altitude wind. Between them, a bleak silence. And in it, Darby's own tortured thoughts ran wild, looping endlessly.

You're the reason Dad left us. And if I could have chosen him instead of you, I would have. In a heartbeat.

In a fucking heartbeat, Maya.

Before hanging up, her mother had answered: *If he really wanted you, Darby, he would have taken you.*

She sipped her cocoa again. Lukewarm.

Now that she was certain Lars wasn't following her, she could finally approach his van. She crossed the exit ramp and came at it from the north, her eyes never leaving Wanasho's front façade. From the interior window, you could see the van's right side but not the left, and she had to assume Lars would be keeping an eye out. Walking in the deep snow was exhausting; she clambered and panted, spilling her drink. The air was abrasive on her throat. Her nose burned. She felt the moisture freeze on her eyelashes, turning them crunchy.

Strangely, though, her body itself wasn't cold. Her blood was hot with adrenaline. She felt radioactive. She didn't even have gloves, but she felt like she could spend all night out here.

Crossing the section of the parking lot designated for RVs and semi trucks, she was close enough now to the building that she could discern seated figures through the smudged glass. She saw Ashley's shoulder. The top of Ed's balding head. No sign of Lars, though, which suddenly worried her. What if he'd followed her outside after all? What if he'd just exited the building when she was *behind it*, and he was tracking her footprints right now, creeping after her in the darkness?

She couldn't decide what was scarier—seeing Rodent Face,

or not seeing him. Her hot chocolate would soon freeze in its cup.

She kept moving toward that mysterious van, and the stupid cartoon fox floated closer with every lurching step. That slogan: WE FINISH WHAT WE START. The powder on the parking lot was shallower; only ankle-deep under a skin of ice. It had been plowed within the last twenty-four hours, which was reassuring. Approaching from the left, she used the van's long side as cover.

She approached the van's rear doors. A Chevrolet Astro. She assumed AWD stood for all-wheel drive. An older model, judging by the hard wear. Dirty scrapes on the bumper. Charcoal-gray paint, peeling off in crunchy blisters. To the right, she recognized the faint outline of her own footprints from earlier, passing between the van and her Honda, and pausing right here. This was where it happened. This was where her night took a hard turn.

And now, this was her moment of truth.

She set her Styrofoam cup in the snow and leaned up to the Astro's rectangular back windows, half-obscured with knives of creeping frost. She cupped her hands to the glass again and peered inside. It was even darker than she'd remembered. No shapes. No movement. Just murky blackness, like she was looking into a stranger's closet.

She tapped the glass with two fingertips. "Hey."

No answer.

"Hey. Is someone in there?" It was strange to be talking to a van.

Nothing.

Only Darby Thorne, standing out here like a car prowler,

feeling more and more awkward with every passing second. She considered using the LED flashlight on her iPhone, but that would consume battery and worse, be as bright as a supernova. If Lars happened to be facing the window, he'd definitely see it.

She rapped on the metal door twice with her knuckle, just above the California license plate, and waited for a response. No activity inside. Nothing at all.

I imagined it.

She stepped back from the door, sucking in a cold breath. "Listen up," she hissed, her voice hoarse. "If there's someone trapped in there, make a noise right now. Or I'm leaving. This is your last chance."

Still no answer. Darby counted to twenty.

I imagined that little hand. That's what happened.

Now, in the luxury of hindsight, she knew exactly why she'd taken the time to fill a cup of hot chocolate back in the visitor center. It was her own form of denial. She'd done something similar after Devon had texted last night with a message that imploded her world: Call me mom has cancer.

The first thing she'd done?

She'd set her phone down, slipped on a jacket, and then walked from Dryden Hall to the student union building and ordered a cheeseburger. She'd watched it come to her, greasy and squashed, paid $5.63 with a crumpled ten, found a seat in the deserted cafeteria, and taken two half-hearted bites before bolting to the restroom and vomiting. She'd called Devon right there in the stall, her elbows on bleached porcelain, her cheeks burning with tears.

There's refuge in normalcy—if you can hold on to it.

Outside Lars's van, she kept counting.

By now she'd reached fifty, and still seen no sign of this imaginary child. It made sense, right? The same way perfectly rational people swear to see red lights in the sky, or phantoms in mirrors, or Bigfoot in national parks—Darby Thorne had just imagined a child's hand inside a stranger's car, and nearly taken serious and violent action based on that half-glimpsed mirage. Too much caffeine, not enough sleep.

This wasn't a movie. This was just real life.

And this was all just a misunderstanding, a false alarm, and Darby suddenly couldn't wait to return to that stuffy little visitor center. Now the company didn't seem so bad at all. She'd try to play cards with Ashley, maybe chat with Ed and Sandi. Perhaps doze off on the bench until CDOT updated the emergency frequency with more weather details.

Because Lars wasn't a kidnapper after all. He was a creep with a stutter and a bumpy skin condition on his hands, sure, but the world was brimming with creeps. Most were harmless. Since the owner of this Astro likely was, too, she regained some courage and pressed her phone to the van's back window and engaged her LED flashlight, triggering a wash of blinding blue-white. Just to put the last of her suspicions to rest, to finally confirm there was nothing—

Behind the glass, she saw a little girl's face staring back at her.

Darby dropped her phone.

The LED light landed sideways at her feet, facing the Wanasho visitor center like a beacon, throwing jagged shadows in the snow. She dove for it, covering it with her cupped hands and fumbling for the button.

Stillness in the van again. The girl had retreated back into the darkness.

And again, Darby had only glimpsed her. But in the harsh flash the afterimage was scorched into her retinas, like she'd stared into the sun. Details lingered. The oval shape of her face. Maybe eight or nine years old, with matted, dark hair. Wide eyes, flinching at the brightness. Dark tape clamped cruelly around her mouth, shiny with dripped snot. She was behind something metallic and gridded, like a black wire cage. As Darby had initially suspected. A dog crate.

Oh my God. Her mouth is duct-taped shut and she's stuffed inside a dog crate.

For the first time since she'd stepped outside, Darby shivered. All of the heat seemed to leave her body in a single, bracing instant. It was all confirmed. It was all true. It was all exactly as she'd suspected. It was all really happening, right now, in vivid color, and a little girl's life was really on the line, and tonight's title match would be between a sleep deprived art student and a human predator.

She stood again.

Stupidly, she retried the Astro's rear door. Still locked. She knew this already. She went for the driver's door next. She wasn't thinking; she was acting on instinct. Just reflexes, raw nerves. She was going to break into Rodent Face's van. She was going to get this little girl *the hell out of there*, and hide her in her Honda. The trunk, maybe. She'd be safe in there, right?

Breaking glass would be loud, and would leave evidence. Instead, Darby peered through the driver window. The Astro's interior was cluttered with receipts on the dashboard and yellow burger wrappers on the seats. The cup holders bulged with Lars's empty Big Gulps. She swept away fresh powder and searched for the door's lock pin behind the icy glass—yes, there it was. Thank God for old cars—

Darby, think this through.

She crouched and ripped the white shoelace from her right shoe. Gritting her teeth, she tied a slipknot down the middle. Drew it tight, like a miniature lasso. She'd only done this once before.

Darby, stop.

No way. She palmed more snow off the top of the door, dropping scabs of ice, and pressed her shoelace into the upper corner. With her fingertips, she gripped the metal and pulled, just enough to relieve the pressure between the door and its frame. Just a millimeter or two. After thirty seconds of fidgeting, the lace slipped right through and dangled behind the glass.

Stop.

She couldn't. She fed the shoelace in careful inches, lowering the loop to the lock. And something miraculous happened— the lasso dropped onto the pin and encircled it on her first try. This was the hardest part, the part that had taken forty-five frustrating minutes last time, but amazingly, Darby had it here on her very first attempt. This was a promising omen, like God was on her side. She sure hoped he was. Tonight, she'd need all the help she could get.

Her better judgment was still protesting: *Darby, don't be impulsive. After you break her out, then what? You can't take her inside. You can't hide her in Blue's trunk all night. First, take a step back—*

Nope. All she could think about was that girl. That terrified little face, still flash-burned onto her mind.

Think this through—

She repositioned left, sliding along the door's perimeter, and tugged the shoelace horizontal. The slipknot tightened around the lock, like a noose squeezing a neck. Then she repositioned it vertically, adjusted her grip, and tugged a little harder (too hard, and she'd lose her grip on the pin and have to start over), and a little harder, and harder still, and the shoelace quivered with sweaty tension, and the pin creaked, and now she was committed and couldn't stop . . .

Darby, you're going to die tonight.

Click.

The door unlocked.

Her heartbeat accelerating, Darby grabbed the door handle and wrenched it open, and to her horror, the Astro's dome light kicked on. A glaring brightness.

LARSON GARVER SAW A LIGHT OUTSIDE.

He was slouching by the brochure rack, studying the Colorado Air pamphlet and trying to tell if their Robinson copter was an R66 or an R44, when he noticed it. Glimmering at the edge of his peripheral vision. A soundless little flash from the parked cars, reflected backward on the window. From *his van.*

He felt a knot of panic tighten in his gut.

The rest of the room was oblivious. Ashley and Ed's card game continued, their voices a gentle back-and-forth:

"Nine of diamonds?"

"Agh. You got me."

Lars held his breath. His angle on the unknown light outside wasn't good enough; it could be just a reflection on the glass.

So he stuffed the Colorado Air brochure into his pocket—where it would join Springs Scenic (a Cessna 172) and Rocky Vistas (a DHC-3 Otter)—and hurried to the paneled window, craning his neck for a clearer view—

DARBY FOUND THE DOME LIGHT BUTTON AND PUNCHED IT OFF.

Darkness again.

Holy shit. She gasped, her heart thudding, her eardrums ringing, full of blood. That had been stupid. Reckless. Dangerous. She'd acted without thinking and allowed herself to be ambushed by a door-activated light bulb.

Still, no one had seen it. *No harm, no foul, right?*

. . . Right?

The van smelled like stale sweat. It reminded her of a gym locker room. The leather seat cover was clammy under her fingers. A model airplane on the dashboard. The floor was a sea of crumpled yellow Jack in the Box and Taco Bell bags, slimy and transparent with congealed grease. She groped for the center console and opened it—more bulging trash. She'd been hoping for a handgun or something. She wanted to try the glove box, but she knew there'd be another light bulb in there, ready to go off like a tripwire. She couldn't risk that again.

Inside the door panel, she found the interior locks.

Click-click.

The Astro's rear doors were now unlocked. The cab was separated from the cargo bay by a metal screen, like in a Catholic confessional. Too dark to see the girl from here. So, carefully, she scooted back outside, retrieved her shoelace slipknot, thumbed the lock pin, and gently shut the driver's door with her palms. She could see the building's window over the van's hood. She dreaded seeing Lars silhouetted behind the glass—investigating the dome light—but the window was still empty. Just the top of Ed's head, and part of Ashley's shoulder, as Go Fish continued.

So far, so good.

Darby crept back along the van's left side, retracing her steps past the stupid cartoon fox, clambering through heaped snow. She stuffed her shoelace into her jeans pocket; no time to relace her shoe right now. She circled the back of the Astro, grabbed the left door handle, and tugged it open.

The girl was inside a dog cage. One of those black wire-grate ones that can be collapsed for flat storage. This one was sized for a collie, reinforced with a padlock and dozens of knotted zip-ties. She was hunched on her knees because there wasn't enough room to stand. Her tiny fingers gripped the wire bars. Duct tape was looped around her mouth in clumsy twists.

Darby smelled a damp sourness. Urine.

For a long moment, she couldn't speak. What could you possibly say? There were no words for this situation. As if swallowing a mouthful of peanut butter, she finally managed to move her lips and say: "Hi."

The girl stared at her with wide eyes.

"Are . . . are you okay?"

She shook her head.

Well, no shit.

"I'm . . ." Darby shivered under a gust of chilling wind, realizing she hadn't planned this far ahead. "Okay, I'm going to take the duct tape off your face, so you can talk to me. Is that all right?"

The girl nodded.

"It might hurt."

The girl nodded harder.

Darby knew it *would* hurt; it was gummed up in her hair. Lars had wrapped it lazily around her head, and it was the black electrical kind. She reached through the gaps in the dog kennel and found the tape's seams with her fingernails. Carefully, she peeled off the first loop, and then the second, and as the little girl worked the rest, Darby asked: "What's your name?"

"Jay."

"Do you know the man who drives this van?"

"No."

"Did he take you?"

"Yeah."

"From your house?" Darby rephrased: "Wait, okay, Jay, where do you live?"

"1145 Fairbridge Way."

"Where is that?"

"By Costco."

"No. What's the name of the *city* you live in?"

"San Diego."

This made Darby shudder. She'd never driven to the West Coast before. Lars must have been on the highways for days, with this girl penned up in the back. That explained the fast food trash. She glimpsed more of the van's interior as her pupils adjusted to the darkness—blankets and rugs heaped to cover the cage. Plywood shelving on the walls, all empty. Coca-Cola bottles, the glass kind, jangling on the metal floor. Loose sawdust. Nails. A red gas can with a black spout. Children's clothing bundled up in white Kmart bags, although Darby doubted Lars had changed Jay once since he'd abducted her from her hometown. All the way in *Southern California*.

"Right by the Costco," Jay clarified.

Darby noticed a circular logo on the girl's shirt, and recognized it—the ball-shaped device from the Pokémon games. A Poké Ball, she remembered, from the iPhone app that had briefly taken CU-Boulder by storm. "What's your last name?"

"Nissen."

"Is . . ." Darby rattled the circular padlock securing the kennel door. "Is Jay short for something?"

"Jaybird."

"No. A longer name. Like . . . Jessica?"

"Just Jay," the girl said.

Jay Nissen. Age nine. Reported missing in San Diego.

The realization crept up on Darby—this would be on the news. She'd just broken into a man's car (already technically a crime) and decisions were being made, right now, that would later be recited to a courtroom. Attorneys would nitpick the minute-to-minute details. If she survived, she would have to answer for every single choice she'd made, good and bad. And thus far, all she'd really accomplished was asking the kidnapped girl with her mouth duct-taped shut if she was *okay*.

Darby had always been awful at speaking to children. Even back to her babysitting days, she'd lacked that maternal instinct. Kids were just messy, belligerent little creatures that stressed her out. She'd often wondered how her own mother could've handled her, especially since she'd been unplanned.

Her sister Devon had been deliberate, of course. The darling firstborn. But then three years later, along came baby Darby in the wake of a shattering marital split. Divorce paperwork, late rent, and a side of morning sickness. *I thought you were the stomach flu*, her mother told her once with a crooked grin. Darby never quite knew how to feel about this.

I thought you were the flu.

I tried to kill you with Theraflu.

Now this little abducted girl raised her other hand to grip the kennel, and Darby realized it was bandaged. Jay's palm was wrapped and sealed with more loops of sloppy electrical tape. Too dark to make out details.

Darby touched it—and Jay flinched away sharply.

"Did he . . . did he hurt you?"

"Yeah."

Her gut stirred with rage. She couldn't believe it—how much worse this night seemed to get with each passing second—but she steadied her voice and asked through chattering teeth: "What did he do to your hand, Jay?"

"It's called a yellow card."

"A *yellow card*?"

The girl nodded.

Darby's mind fluttered—like in soccer?

Jay lowered her injured hand and leaned back, creaking the kennel, and Darby felt something crusty coating the wire bars. It flaked off under her fingernails, smelling coppery. Scales of dried blood.

A yellow card.

That's the kind of psycho I'm up against—

Fifty feet away, the building's front door opened, and then banged shut.

Jay froze.

Approaching footsteps, coming fast. Ice crunching under treaded boots. Darby hesitated there where she stood, leaning into the back of the child abductor's Chevrolet Astro. Half in, half out. Afraid to move, afraid to stay. Paralyzed by building terror, she looked into the little girl's wide eyes as the footsteps stomped closer in the darkness.

And another sound, fast approaching.

Mouth-breathing.

8:39 P.M.

RUN OR HIDE?

As Lars approached his van, Darby chose *hide*. She scooted all the way into the vehicle, tucking her knees inside and gently closing the rear door behind her—but it shut on a towel.

His footsteps crunched closer.

"*Shit—*"

She tugged the towel inside and eased the door shut. It clicked home. She was now sealed inside the predator's van, wedged between the rear door and Jay's dog kennel. She sank as low to the floor as she could, contorting to fit the cramped space, and covered herself with heaped blankets and scratchy rugs. Coca-Cola bottles jangled underneath her. The musty odor of dog blankets. Her forehead pressed to the cold metal door, her right elbow squished crookedly behind her back. She fought to control her breathing, to keep her panicked gulps of air silent: *Inhale. Count to five. Exhale.*

Inhale. Count to five. Exhale.

Inhale. Count to—

Now she heard Rodent Face's footsteps circle the vehicle's right side, past the nail gun–wielding cartoon fox, past the WE FINISH WHAT WE START motto, passing between his van and her own Honda. She tasted a seasick mix of fright and vindication—if she'd chosen *run* instead of *hide*, he would have certainly spotted her. He kept coming, wheezing softly between his too-small teeth, and she saw his silhouette pass by the rear window over her head. He paused there, glancing inside, twelve inches away from her, his breath fogging on the glass.

Darby held hers.

If he opens that door, I'm dead—

But he didn't. He kept walking, completing a full circle around the van, then came up to the driver door. Unlocked it. Darby heard the door screech open on bad hinges, and the vehicle sank on its suspension as a third human body lurched inside. The jingle of car keys on his lanyard.

With one eye uncovered, careful not to disturb the glass bottles underneath her, Darby glanced over at Jay inside her dog kennel and raised one trembling index finger to her lips: *Shhh.*

Jay nodded.

In the driver's seat, Lars sniffled, leaned forward, and clicked a key into the ignition—but he didn't turn it. Darby heard a long, thoughtful pull of breath. Then silence. Too much silence.

Something is wrong.

She waited, her eardrums ringing with building pressure. Gut muscles clenched. A breath held in swollen lungs. Rodent Face was a dark form at the wheel, separated by a caged divider and silhouetted against the opaque snow on the windshield. With her one uncovered eye, Darby could see that his head was turned sideways. He was looking up, and to his right. At the Astro's dome light.

The dome light she'd switched off.

Oh no.

She could imagine the thoughts inching through his brain. He was wondering why the light bulb hadn't clicked on automatically when he opened the door, as it usually did. Now, what did that suggest? That someone else had entered his van. That, upon closer examination of the mixed footprints and displaced snow outside, someone was *still inside* his van, buried in the back under a musty Navajo rug, sweating and trembling with nerve-shredding panic—

Lars twisted the key.

The engine turned over smoothly and Darby exhaled with relief. He hunched forward in his seat and angled the air vents. Clicked the heater dial to full blast. Set his Deadpool beanie on the dashboard beside his model airplane, crinkling a fast food wrapper.

Darby heard movement beside her. It was Jay, quietly rewrapping the electrical tape around her mouth. *Smart girl*, she thought.

The next twenty minutes felt like hours, as the van slowly filled with heat and moisture. Lars idled the engine and scanned radio stations. He found only different flavors of garbled static, the repeating robovoice of that CDOT transmission, and once again, Bing Crosby's goddamn "White Christmas."

I can't escape that song, Darby thought. *It'll probably play at my funeral.* She'd always imagined that they would have invented flying cars by then. Now, slumped in a kidnapper's humid van, breathing through her nose, she wasn't so sure.

Naturally, Lars listened to the entire song, which meant Darby had to as well. Listening to the lyrics made her appreciate it a bit more. She'd always just assumed it was about snow, but there was a homesickness and longing to it. As Bing Crosby crooned, she imagined some poor farm boy just out of high school, hunkered in frozen foreign dirt, fighting someone else's war, dreaming of loved ones back home. She could relate to that.

Lars probably wasn't thinking quite as deeply about it. He munched a candy bar, chewing loudly. He picked his nose and studied his findings in the glow of the dash. Farted twice. The second one made him giggle, and then he suddenly turned around and grinned at the back of the van with a mouthful of small, pointy teeth, and Darby's chest tightened, her heart a clenched fist.

"Warmed it up for you," he said.

He was looking at Jay's kennel in the darkness, but he had no idea he was also looking directly at Darby. Just a layer of fabric covering her, and one exposed eye. All it would take was a little more light.

He's looking right at me.

Rodent Face's grin vanished. He kept staring.

Oh God, he can see me, Darby thought, her sides cramping, feeling spiders crawling on her skin. *His eyes are adjusting to the dark, and now he knows I'm in here, and oh my God, he's going to kill me—*

He farted a third time.

Or that, I guess.

This was a long one, a blaring honk, and then he exploded into hard laughter. He *screamed* his laugh, punching the passenger seat. He was immensely pleased with himself, barely choking out words to his captive: "You're . . . ah, you're welcome for the cheek-rumbler. Nice and warm, huh, Jaybird?"

Darby heard Jay's electrical tape crease as her head tilted slightly. She imagined the girl making a *See what I've been dealing with?* eye roll.

Then Lars's belly laughs morphed into coughs. They were wet, bubbly, like he was nursing a sinus infection. That explained the mouth-breathing.

Darby's feet were pressed up against the five-gallon gas can she'd seen before, and beside it, she now noticed a second white jug. A Clorox logo barely visible in the dashboard light. Bleach, probably.

Five gallons of gasoline.
And bleach.

Materials to clean up a crime scene, maybe?

After the radio cycled through a few more holiday songs ("Grandma Got Run Over by a Reindeer," which he sang along to, and "Silent Night," which he didn't), Lars cut the Astro's engine and stuffed the keys into his jacket pocket. By now the van was an eighty-degree sweatbox; the windows steamed with condensation. Beads of dewy lamplight sparkled on the glass. Trapped under that smothering blanket, the perspiration and melted snow had turned Darby's skin clammy. Her coat's sleeves stuck to her wrists, and underneath it, her Art Walk hoodie was soaked with dread-sweat.

Lars scooted outside, slipped his Deadpool beanie back over his scalp, and glanced back at the dome light. He was still mildly perplexed by that detail. But then he turned around, ripped ass one final, emphatic time into the cab, fanned it with the door, sealed Jay (and Darby) inside with it, and left.

Darby listened to his footsteps fade. Then, distantly, she heard the visitor center's front door open and shut with a dim clap.

Silence.

Jay peeled the electrical tape off her mouth. "He farts a lot."

"I noticed."

"I think it's the burgers."

Darby threw the bristly blanket off her shoulders, wiping damp tangles of hair from her face. She kicked open the Astro's rear door and climbed back outside. It felt like escaping a sauna. Her Converse were soaked, her socks grossly squishy inside them, and her right shoe was still missing a shoelace.

"He puts ranch sauce on everything," Jay continued. "He asks the drive-through for a cup of it to dip his fries in, but that's a lie. He just pours it on—"

"Right." Darby wasn't listening. The subzero chill was invigorating, like shedding fifty pounds of sweaters. She felt agile and alive again. She knew what she had to do—she just didn't know how the hell she was going to do it. She stepped back, raised her iPhone, and snapped two quick photos.

Jay didn't blink, her bloodstained fingers on the kennel bars. "Be careful."

"I will."

"Promise you'll be careful—"

"I promise."

The girl extended her unhurt hand to Darby. At first she thought it was a handshake, or a pinkie-swear, or some other half remembered artifact from her own childhood, but then Jay dropped something into Darby's palm. Something small, metallic, as cold as an ice cube.

It was a bullet.

"I found it on the floor," Jay whispered.

It was lighter than Darby would have guessed, like a blunt little torpedo. She rolled it left to right on her skin. Her palm was shaking; she almost dropped it. This wasn't a surprise, exactly, just a grim confirmation of her worst-case scenario.

Of course Lars has a gun.

Of course.

She should have guessed. This was America, where cops and robbers carry guns. Where, as the NRA tells us, the only thing that stops a bad guy with a gun is a *good guy with a gun.* Hokey, but true as hell. She'd never even handled a firearm before, let alone shot one, but she'd sell her soul to have one right now.

She realized Jay was still looking at her.

Usually, she hated talking to kids. Whenever she was trapped with her cousins or her friends' younger siblings, she'd treat them like smaller, dumber adults. But now it came easy. She didn't need to mince words. She meant every bit of what she said, and rewording it would only dilute its simple power:

"Jay, I promise I will get you out of here. I *will* save you."

10:18 P.M.

DARBY HADN'T SEEN HER FATHER IN ELEVEN YEARS, BUT AS a high school graduation gift two years ago, he'd mailed her a multi-tool. The funny part? The drugstore Hallmark card congratulated her for graduating *college*.

Oops, huh?

But as gifts go, it wasn't bad. It was one of those red Swiss Army variants that unfolded in a fan—corkscrew, metal saw, nail file. And of course, a two-inch serrated blade. She'd only used it once, to help open the blister package encasing her roommate's new earbuds, and then she'd forgotten about it for the rest of her college career. She kept it in Blue's glove box.

It was in her back pocket now. Like a prison shiv.

She was seated on the stone coffee counter, her back against the security shutter, her knees tucked up to her chest. From here she could watch the entire room—Ed and Ashley finishing their millionth game of Go Fish, Sandi reading her paperback, and Lars guarding the door in his usual spot.

From the back seat of her Honda outside, under her sheets of rice paper for gravestone rubbings, she'd also grabbed a blue pen and one of her college-ruled notepads. It was in her lap now.

Page one was doodles. Abstract shapes, cross-hatched shadows.

Page two—more doodles.

Page three? Carefully shielded from view, Darby had sketched possibly her finest-ever rendering of a human face. It was nearly flawless. She'd studied Lars, every slouching inch of him. His blond whiskers, his slack overbite, his mushy chin and slanted forehead. The pronounced V shape of his hairline. She'd even captured the dim glaze of his eyes. The police would find it useful; maybe they'd even release it to the media to aid the coming manhunt. She also had the van's make, model, and license plate. Plus a blurry photo of the missing San Diego girl. It would look great on CNN, blown up on forty-inch LCD screens across the country.

But was it enough?

Driving was impossible now, but tomorrow morning when the snowplows arrived and opened up Backbone Pass to traffic, Lars would take Jay and leave. Even if Darby could manage a 911 call immediately afterward, the police would still be acting off a last known location. Maybe he'd get caught, but *maybe he wouldn't*. He'd have ample time to slip through the patchy net, to vanish back into the world, and that would be a death sentence for nine-year-old Jay Nissen. Jaybird Nissen. Whatever her name was.

According to the regional map on the wall, State Route Six intersected two other highways near the pass. Plus a major interstate running like a vein to the north. Whether Lars drove east or west, he'd have plenty of escape routes. On closer inspection, she also learned that the Wanasho (Little Devil) rest stop was twenty miles downhill. This one, the one they were all stranded at, was actually Wanashono. She'd misread the map earlier. They were twenty miles *farther* from civilization.

Wanashono translated to *Big Devil*.

Of course it did.

Darby still had the bullet in her pocket, too. She'd inspected it under fluorescent lights in the women's restroom. The bullet's blunt nose was split with four cross-cuts, which appeared deliberate, for some unknown reason. The bottom of it, the brass rim, had stamped lettering: 45 AUTO FEDERAL. She'd heard of guns called *forty-fives* before, in cop movies. But it was chilling to think that there could be a real one right here, in the room with her, tucked under Lars's jacket. Just a few feet away.

Darby had known this in her gut for an hour now, but her mind was finally coming around to it, too. A suspect description and a blurry, half-assed photo wouldn't be good enough. It would be enough for the media to brand her a hero if things worked out nicely, but it wasn't enough to guarantee Jay's rescue.

And afterward, if the cops never found Lars, what would she tell the poor girl's parents? *Sorry your kid is dead, but I called the police and wrote down the license plate and ran everything through the proper channels. I even drew a picture.*

No, she needed to take action.

Here. Tonight. In this snowbound little rest area. Before the plows arrived at dawn, she needed to stop Lars herself.

Somehow.

That was as far as her plan went.

She sipped her coffee. This was her third cup, bitter and jet black. She'd always loved her stimulants—espresso shots, Red Bull, Full Throttle, Rockstar. NoDoz pills. Her roommate's Adderall. Anything for that addictive little buzz. Pure rocket fuel for her paintings and oil pastels. Depressants—alcohol, weed—they were the enemy. Darby preferred to live her life wide-eyed, tormented, running, because nothing can catch you if you never stop. And thank God for it, for caffeine's acidic little kick. Because tonight, of all nights, she would need to stay pin sharp.

Above the regional map, she noticed an old analog clock. *Garfield* themed. In its center, Garfield courted the pink female character—Arlene—with a handful of crudely drawn flowers. The clock's hour hand indicated it was almost midnight, but she realized it was an hour ahead. Someone had missed winter daylight savings.

It wasn't even eleven yet.

Come to think of it, she wasn't sure which was more nerve-racking—running out of time, or having too much of it. As she completed her sketch (shadowing the lumpy slope of his forehead, which reminded her of a human fetus) she noticed Lars was finally warming up to the others. At least, there was a little more of a group dynamic now. Ashley was showing Lars and Ed a card trick, something he called a Mexican turnover. From what Darby overheard, you flip over a card using another one in your hand—but really, you're switching them. In plain view. Lars was fascinated by the maneuver, and Ashley seemed delighted to have an audience.

"So that's why you keep winning," Ed said.

"Don't worry." Ashley flashed a huckster's grin, hands up. "I beat you fair and square. But yes, if I may be permitted to toot my own horn, I did take silver in a stage magic competition once."

Ed snorted. "Yeah?"

"Yeah."

"That's a thing?"

"*Of course* it's a thing."

"Second grade?"

"Third, actually." Ashley shuffled cards. "Thank you very much."

"Did you wear a little tux?"

"You have to."

"How's the current job market for silver-medal magicians?"

"Staggeringly poor." Ashley shelved the cards with a rattle-snake chatter. "So I went to school for accounting instead. And let me tell you, that's where the *real* magic is."

Ed laughed.

Lars had been listening to their conversation, his hairy lips pursed, and now he seized this pause to involve himself in it: "So, then, were the . . . ah, were the magic tricks real?"

The blizzard intensified outside. The window creaked under the pressure of gusting wind. Ashley glanced to Ed for a smirking moment (*Is magic real? Really?*), and Darby watched him decide whether to play it straight or to indulge in a little sarcasm at the expense of the armed child abductor.

Don't do it, Ashley.

He turned back to Lars. "Yep."

"Really?"

Ashley's grin widened. "Absolutely."

She felt a shivery pool of dread growing in her stomach. Like witnessing the moments before a car accident. The scream of locked tires, the unyielding kinetic power of momentum: *Stop it, Ashley. You have no idea who you're talking to—*

"So it's real?" Lars whispered.

Stop-stop-stop—

"Oh, it's all real," Ashley said, milking it now. "I can bend time and space, pull surprises out of my sleeves, make people misremember. I can cheat death. I can dodge bullets. I'm a *magic man*, Lars, my brother, and I can—"

"Do you know how to cut a girl in half?" Lars asked abruptly.

The room went quiet. The window creaked under another howl of wind.

Darby glanced back down and pretended to doodle again with her blue pen, but she realized with a sour tremor—he was staring across the room at her. Lars, the chinless child abductor with a Deadpool beanie and a child's fascination with magic tricks, was looking *directly at her.*

Ashley hesitated. His bullshit machine was out of gas. "I . . . uh, well . . ."

"Do you know how to cut a girl in half?" Lars asked again, eagerly. Same tone, same inflection. His eyes were still pinned on Darby as he spoke. "You know. You put her in a big wooden box, like a coffin, and then you . . . ah, you cut it with a saw?"

Ed stared at the floor. Sandi lowered her paperback.

Again: "Can you cut a girl in half?"

Darby's fingers tightened around her pen. Her knees hunched closer to her chest. Rodent Face was standing about ten feet from her. She wondered—if he went for the .45 under his jacket, could she yank the Swiss Army knife from her pocket, extend the blade, and cross the room quickly enough to stab him in the throat with it?

She rested her right hand on the countertop. Near her hip.

Lars asked again, louder: "*Can you cut a girl in—*"

"I can," Ashley answered. "But you only win gold if she survives."

Silence.

It wasn't particularly funny, but Ed forced a chuckle.

Sandi laughed too. So did Ashley. Lars cocked his head—like he had to squeeze the joke through the clockwork of his brain—and finally gave in and laughed along with them, and the room thundered with belly laughs, ringing in the pressurized air, until Darby's migraine threatened to return and she wanted to clamp her eyes shut.

"See, I got silver," Ashley added. "Not gold—"

Under another crescendo of strained laughter, and still grinning widely, Lars whipped his coat aside and reached for something on his hip. Darby grabbed the knife in her pocket—but he was just adjusting his belt.

Jesus. That was close.

He'd moved quickly, though. If he were really going for his gun, she realized, he could have killed everyone in the room.

"Gold medal," he chuckled, tugging his belt around his scrawny ass, pointing a thumb at Ashley. "I, ah, like his jokes. He's funny."

"Oh, give me time," Ashley said. "You'll find me quite grating."

As the false laughter faded, Darby processed something else. A small detail, but something deeply unsettling about the way the abductor had laughed. He'd seemed too alert. Normal people blink and let their guards down. But not Lars. His face laughed but his eyes *watched*. He scanned everyone's faces, pupils searching the room, coldly assessing while he showed his mouthful of pointy teeth.

That's the grinning, stupid face of evil, Darby realized.

That's the face of a man who stole a little girl from her home in California.

The lights flickered. A seizure of icy darkness. Everyone glanced up at the fluorescent overheads, but as they came back on and the room filled again with light, Darby was still studying Lars's whiskery face.

That's what I'm up against.

THERE'S A TIME, DEEP INTO THE NIGHT, WHEN THE FORCES of evil are said to be at their strongest. *The witching hour*, Darby's mom used to call it, with a silly little voodoo twang to her voice.

It's 3:00 A.M.

Supposedly this was the devil's mockery of the Holy Trinity. Growing up, Darby had respected this superstition but never really believed it—how can one time of day be more evil than any other? But still, throughout her childhood, whenever she woke up from a nightmare, her breaths hitching and her skin glazed with sweat, she'd glanced to her clock radio or phone. And eerily, the time had always been close to 3:00 A.M. Every time she could remember.

The time she dreamed that her throat closed up in seventh grade Social Studies class and she vomited a three-inch maggot, pale and bloated, writhing on her desk?

3:21 A.M.

The time a man stalked her on her way to 7-Eleven, whistling at her, and then cornered her in the restroom, produced a tiny handgun, and shot her in the back of the head?

3:33 A.M.

The time that tall ghost—a gray-haired woman with a floral skirt and double-jointed knees, both bending backward like a dog's hind legs—came lurching through Darby's bedroom window, half floating and half striding, weightless and ethereal, like a creature underwater?

3:00 A.M. exactly.

Coincidence, right?

Witching hours, her mother used to say, lighting one of her jasmine candles. *When the demons are at their most powerful.*

Then she'd snap her Zippo lighter shut for emphasis—*click*.

Here and now at the Wanashono rest area, it was only 11:00 P.M., but Darby still imagined a darkness gathering in the room with her, with all of them. Something sentient pooling in shadows, giddily awaiting violence.

She hadn't yet decided how she'd attack Lars.

She'd already memorized the floor plan of the visitor center. It was simple, but honeycombed with significant details. The rectangular main lobby with two gendered restrooms, crusty drinking fountains, and a locked supply closet labeled EMPLOYEES ONLY. The stone-and-mortar coffee counter encircling the closed coffee shop, sealed off with padlocked security shutters. One highly visible front door with a squeaky hinge. One broad window overlooking the parking lot, half blocked by a shelf of windswept snow. And a small triangular window in each restroom, nestled into the ceiling, eight feet off the tile floor. Like a jailhouse window, minus the bars. She'd remembered this, because it seemed like a detail others would forget.

Outside felt like another planet entirely. The moonlight snuffed by clouds. The temperature had dropped to negative two, according to the mercury thermometer dangling outside. Heaped snow crowded up to the window, still accumulating. The wind came in shrill spurts, slashing flurries of dry snowflakes that tapped the glass like pebbles.

"I could sure go for some global warming right now," said Ed.

Sandi turned a page. "Global warming is a hoax."

"I'm just saying, thank God we're indoors."

"That's true," Ashley murmured, tilting his head in Lars's direction, "until someone gets locked in a wooden box and sawed in half."

Rodent Face was back to hovering by the door, picking at the brochure rack. Darby couldn't tell if he'd heard Ashley's joke. She wished he would stop tempting fate. This situation couldn't possibly sustain itself for eight more hours. Sooner or later, Ashley would wander onto a verbal landmine.

Weapons, then.

That was what tonight would come down to. And as far as Darby could tell, this public rest area was as harmless as a preschool. Outside the security shutters, the coffee bar had only plastic forks and spoons. Paper plates and brown napkins.

There was the janitorial closet, but it was locked. No tire irons, or flare guns, or steak knives. Her best offensive option, unfortunately, was the two-inch serrated blade on her Swiss Army multi-tool. She patted her jeans pocket, reassured that it was still there.

Could she stab Lars with it? More important, would it even stop him? She didn't know. It was barely a weapon, unlikely to pierce a rib cage. She'd need to catch Rodent Face off guard, and she'd need to plunge it directly into the soft flesh of his throat, or his eyes. No time for hesitation. It was possible, she knew, but not exactly plan A.

The cracked mortar under the counter, she remembered. *The loose stone.*

That could be useful.

She stood from the bench and approached the coffee counter, pretending to fill another Styrofoam cup. When no one was looking, she raised her right foot, rested it on the wobbly stone, and leaned forward. She applied a little pressure, then more, then more—fussing with the COFEE carafe's lever to conceal the noise—until the stone popped free and clacked to the tile floor. Lars, Ed, and Ashley didn't notice. Sandi glanced up briefly, and then resumed reading.

When the woman's attention was back on her paperback, Darby scooped the stone up. It was a little smaller than a hockey puck, smooth and egg-shaped. Just large enough to bash out a few teeth, or to throw hard. She pocketed the cold rock and returned to her seat on the bench, taking mental inventory.

A two-inch knife.

A medium-size rock.

And a single .45-caliber bullet.

I'm going to need help, she realized.

She could try to take down Lars herself, of course. Surprise him, injure him, twist the gun from his jacket and detain him with it until the snowplows arrived at dawn. Hogtie him with his own electrical tape, maybe. And if things went to hell, she supposed she'd be mentally prepared to kill him. But attempting it right now, solo, would be irresponsible. She needed to share her discovery with someone else here, in case Lars managed to overpower her and quietly hide her body without the others realizing. She couldn't save Jay if she got herself killed first.

The difference between a hero and a victim?

Timing.

At the table, Ashley fanned out the cards in a smooth rainbow, all facedown except a single, upturned ace of hearts. "And *here's* your card."

Lars gasped, like a caveman discovering fire.

Ed shrugged. "Not bad."

From the bench, Darby assessed her potential allies. Ed was pushing sixty and carried a belly. His cousin Sandi might as well be made of balsa wood and hairspray. Ashley, though—as gratingly chatty as he was—was broad, muscular, and quick on his feet. The way he moved to pick up dropped cards, the way he confidently shimmied around chairs—he had the swooping, ducking grace of a basketball player. Or a stage magician.

A *silver-medal* stage magician.

"Do another one," said Lars.

"That's the only authentic trick I remember," Ashley said.

"Everything else was kiddie stuff. Fake sleeves, trapdoors in cups, that sort of thing."

"You missed your calling," Ed said.

"Yeah?" He smiled, and for a split second, Darby glimpsed pain in his eyes. "Well, accounting is pretty badass, too."

Lars moped by the door, disappointed that the show was over.

Darby decided that her next step had to be Ashley. He was strong enough to fight, at least. She'd catch him alone, in the restroom maybe, and tell him about the girl. She'd make sure he understood the gravity of the situation; that right now, a child's life was at stake outside. Then she'd have backup, when she chose her moment to attack and detain Lars—

"Oh!" Ashley clapped his hands together, startling everyone. "I know how we can pass the time. We can play circle time."

Ed blinked. "What?"

"Circle time."

"*Circle time?*"

"Yes."

"What the hell is circle time?"

"My aunt is a preschool teacher. She uses this to break the ice with small groups. Basically, you're all seated in a circle, kind of like we are right now, and you all agree on a topic, like *my favorite pet*, or whatever. And then you take turns, clockwise, sharing your answer." Ashley hesitated, glancing from face to face. "And that's . . . that's why it's called circle time."

Silence.

Finally, Ed spoke. "Shoot me in the face, please."

Everyone was distracted again, so Darby paced back to the

Espresso Peak counter and grabbed a brown napkin. Returning to the bench, she slipped the napkin inside her notebook, clicked her pen, and scrawled a message.

"Guys, we're all snowed in here together, and we've got another seven hours to go." Ashley tried valiantly. "Come on. We're going to get cabin fever if we don't open up and talk a little more."

Ed grunted. "We're talking right now."

"So, circle time, then—"

"I'm not playing circle time."

"I'll go first."

"So help me God, Ashley, if you make me play circle time, the snowplows will arrive tomorrow morning and find a rest stop full of bloody corpses."

Darby clicked her pen. *Let's hope not.*

"I like circle time," Lars chimed in.

Ed sighed. "Yeah, of course *he* does."

"All right. A good icebreaker question is phobias, or biggest fears," Ashley said. "So . . . I'll start off this round, and I'll tell you all my biggest fear. Sound good?"

"Nope," said Ed.

Lars had set down his brochure. He was listening.

"You're all going to think my phobia is weird," Ashley said. "It's not a normal fear, you know, like needles or spiders . . ."

Darby folded the napkin twice with her message inside it. She knew she was about to do something that couldn't be undone. This was tonight's point of no return. From now on, one wrong glance, or misplaced word, and the Wanashono rest area could explode into violence.

"So, I grew up in the Blue Mountains," Ashley told the

room. "When I was a kid, I used to walk the railroad tracks and explore these old, boarded-up coal mines. The hills are just Swiss cheese out there. And this particular mine wasn't on any map, but locally, it was called Chink's Drop."

Sandi frowned. "Okay."

"You know," Ashley said, "as in, the derogatory term for Chinese people—"

"Yeah, I figured."

"I'm guessing a miner must have fallen and died, and—"

"I get it—"

"And he must have been Chinese—"

"I *get it*, Ashley."

"Sorry." He hesitated. "So, uh, I'm seven and dumb as hell. I crawled under the barricade and went alone, without telling anyone, and brought just a flashlight and some rope. Like a pint-sized Indiana Jones. And, I mean, it wasn't scary at first. I followed the narrowing tunnel deeper, and deeper, past these ancient ore carts, over these mangled eighteenth-century train rails, through one blocked door after another. Sound carries funny down there, all warbling and ringing. And I'm sliding around this old wooden door, and I rested my hand on the corroded hinge for maybe a second. And . . . something awful happens."

Darby noticed Lars's attention had drifted back down into his Colorado Air brochure, so she seized her moment. She slid off the bench, and her wet Converse hit the floor with squishy thuds.

Ashley made an abrupt *slice* motion. "The door swings shut. The hinge snaps closed, like these two rusty metal jaws, obliterating my thumb, fracturing three metacarpals. Boom. It didn't hurt at all at first. Just shock. And this door was three hundred pounds of solid oak, completely unmovable. And there I was, alone in the pitch black, a half mile below the surface."

Darby walked toward him.

"Two days without food or water. I slept a few times. Scary dreams. Fatigue, dehydration. I didn't have a knife, but I seriously considered losing my thumb. I remember staring at it with my dying flashlight, wondering how hard I'd have to twist my body weight against the hinge to . . . you know."

Ed leaned forward. "You've still got both thumbs."

Darby passed around Ashley's chair and discreetly dropped her folded napkin in his lap. Like kids passing a note in high school.

He noticed—but smoothly finished his story, giving Ed an ironic thumbs-up: "Correctamundo. Turns out all I had to do was wait. Some teenagers from a different town happened to break into Chink's Drop and they walked right into me. Saved by pure, dumb, lottery-ticket luck."

"And . . ." Sandi looked at him. "Your phobia is . . . what, being trapped?"

"No. Door hinges."

"Door hinges?"

"I *hate* door hinges," Ashley said, making an exaggerated shiver. "They freak me out, you know?"

"Huh."

Darby stopped by the window, watching snowflakes pelt the glass, and waited for Ashley to read her note. In her periphery, she saw him lift the napkin and unfold it under the table's edge to furtively read it on his knee, out of Ed and

Sandi's view. In scratchy blue pen, Darby had written: MEET ME IN THE RESTROOM I HAVE SOMETHING YOU NEED TO SEE.

He paused.

Then he produced a black pen from his pocket, thought for a moment, and scribbled a response. Then he stood up and casually approached the window, too, fluidly slipping the napkin back into Darby's hand as he passed. He did this as naturally as a pickpocket.

She unfolded it and read his handwriting.

I HAVE A GIRLFRIEND.

She sighed. "Jesus Christ."

He looked at her.

She mouthed: *Not what I meant.*

He mouthed: *What?*

Not. What. I. Meant.

Now they were both standing conspicuously by the window with their backs to the room. Lars was probably watching them, wondering what they were mouthing to each other. Ed and Sandi, too—

Ashley touched her shoulder, mouthing again: *What?*

Darby felt it, that familiar paralysis locking up her bones. Like climbing onstage and forgetting your lines. If she spoke, they'd overhear. If she didn't, she risked making a scene. The entire world teetered on a knife edge. She chanced a look over her right shoulder, toward Rodent Face, and as she'd feared, he was watching them. She noticed something else, too, and her blood turned to ice water.

Lars had placed something white on the brochure rack. A Styrofoam cup, flattened from being inside his pocket.

Her cup.

The eight ounces of misspelled COCO that she'd stupidly filled up and carried outside earlier. She'd set it in the snow by the Astro's rear door, right before she broke in and spoke to Jay. Then she'd forgotten about the cup, leaving it out there in the dark for him to find. Near her clustered footprints.

He knows, she realized. And something even worse occurred to her—that now, the quiet danger cut both ways.

He's planning to attack me.

The same way I'm planning to attack him.

"Trapped in a coal mine," Sandi echoed to Ed. "Scary stuff."

"Eh." Ed shrugged. "I would've just cut off my thumb."

"I don't think it's that easy."

"Just saying. When you're facing a lunch date with the Reaper, what's a few little bones and tendons?"

Lars kept quietly watching them, and what frightened Darby most was the deep, dumb calm in his eyes. A criminal with any sense of self-preservation would have his gun out by now. But Lars was chillingly uninterested, untroubled, his vapid little eyes regarding her like she was nothing more urgent, or dangerous, than a spill on the floor that needed to be mopped up in the next hour or so. That was all.

Another black thought slipped into her mind, and somehow, she was certain it was prophecy, turning up like one of her mother's musty Tarot cards: *That man is going to murder me tonight.*

This is how I die.

She looked back to Ashley and whispered: "Follow me. Right now."

11:07 P.M.

IN THE MEN'S RESTROOM, SHE TOLD ASHLEY EVERYTHING.

The van. The dog kennel. The little girl named Jay from San Diego. The electrical tape, the padlock, the unknown menace of a yellow card. Even the farts. And no matter how quietly she whispered, her words seemed to echo inside the restroom, ringing off tile and porcelain. She was certain the others could hear.

Ashley exhaled, visibly shaken. His eye sockets shadowed harshly under the fluorescent lights, like dark bruises, and for the first time all night, he looked as tired as Darby felt. And, another first—he was speechless.

She watched him, trying to get a read. "So."

"So?" he replied.

"So. We have to do something."

"Obviously, but what?"

"We stop him."

"*Stop* him? That's vague." Ashley glanced back, watching

the restroom door, edging closer to her. "Do you mean kill him?"

She wasn't sure.

"Jesus, you're talking about killing him—"

"If it comes to that."

"Oh my God." He rubbed his eyes. "*Right now?* With what?"

Darby opened her two-inch Swiss Army blade.

Ashley choked on a laugh. "He's going to have a gun, you know."

"I know."

"So what's your plan, then?"

"We stop him."

"That's not a plan."

"That's why I told you. And guess what, Ashley? You're involved now. It's 11:10 P.M. on a Thursday night, and there's a child abductor in the next room, and a little girl locked in his shitty van outside, and that's the hand we've been dealt. And I'm asking you now—will you help me?"

That seemed to get to him. "You're . . . you're sure?"

"Positive."

"That Lars kidnapped her?"

"Yeah." She reconsidered. "If that's even his real name."

Ashley ran a hand through his hair and took a step back, leaning against a stall door. PAUL TAKES IT IN THE ASS had been scratched on it. Ashley gulped hard breaths, staring down at his shoes, like he was trying not to faint.

She touched his arm. "You okay?"

"Just asthma."

"Don't you have an inhaler?"

"No." He smiled sheepishly. "I, uh, don't have medical."

Darby realized she might have misjudged this tall, dark stranger. Maybe Ashley—ex-magician, chatterbox, Salt Lake Institute of Tech student—wasn't quite as capable as she'd thought. But then she remembered his impressive sleight of hand when he'd returned her note. She hadn't even felt it. The napkin had just materialized between her fingers, like . . . well, *magic.*

That was something. Right?

He'd caught his breath now, and looked up at her pointedly. "I need proof."

"What?"

"Proof. Can you prove any of this?"

Darby thumbed the photo gallery on her iPhone. Behind her, the restroom door banged open.

It was Lars.

Rodent Face stomped in, wet boots squealing on tile. Just like that, the kidnapper was inside the room with them, breathing the same air. Darby's mind screamed—*we're cornered in here, we're both exposed, there's no time to hide in a stall*—and the slouching figure of Lars whirled to face them, that stubbly, chinless face wheezing through a mouthful of baby teeth—

Then Ashley grabbed her face, his palms to her cheeks—

"Wait—"

—And he mashed her mouth to his.

What?

Then Darby understood. And after another heart-fluttering second, she played along, pressing her body against his, clasping her fingers behind his neck. Ashley's hands groped her back, her hips. His warm breath was inside her mouth.

For a few long seconds, Lars watched them. Then she heard

his squeaky footsteps again, moving to the sinks. A faucet twisted. A rush of water. The soap dispenser pumped once, twice. He was washing his hands.

Darby and Ashley kept going, eyes clamped shut. For Darby it hadn't been this excruciatingly awkward since her ninth-grade Sadie Hawkins dance, just pawing movement and mis-placed squeezes and half-held breaths. He was either a godawful kisser or he wasn't trying; his tongue was like a dead slug in her mouth. After a painful eternity—*don't stop, don't stop, he's still watching us*—she heard the sink twist off, then a paper towel tore and crumpled. Another long silence, and then finally, Lars left the restroom.

The door clicked shut.

Darby and Ashley separated. "Your breath is rancid," he said.

"Sorry, I drank six Red Bulls today."

"No shit—"

"Here." She thrust her phone out to him—a murky photo of Jay caged behind those black kennel bars. Only the girl's bloody fingernails were in focus. "You wanted proof? That's what's at stake. She's out there, in his van, fifty feet from this building, right here, right now."

Ashley barely looked at the photo—he'd already gotten his proof. He nodded nervously, gulping in another breath. "He . . . he didn't come in here to wash his hands. He was checking on us."

"And you're involved now."

"Okay."

"Okay?"

"Okay." He sighed. "Let's . . . do it, I guess."

Darby nodded intently. But her mind had darted back to her mom's pancreatic cancer.

All of that—the miserable twenty-four hours leading up to this—felt like another life entirely; one she'd blissfully stepped away from. Remembering it now hit her like buckshot in the gut. She still hadn't gotten a cell signal. She still hadn't deciphered the meaning behind Devon's stupid, cryptic text, now several hours old: *She's okay right now—*

"Darby?"

Ashley was looking at her.

"Okay, yeah." She composed herself, wiping his saliva from her lip, blinking in the harsh light. "We need to surprise this asshole. And since he suspects we know, he won't turn his back to us."

"Even if he does, that butter knife of yours won't be enough."

"So we'll hit him over the head."

"With what?"

"What do you have?"

Ashley considered. "I . . . I have a jack in my car, I think—"

Too obvious, she knew. Not concealable. But she had a better idea. She reached into her jeans pocket and produced the decorative stone she'd plucked from the coffee counter. "This will work better."

"A rock?"

"Take off your shoe."

He hesitated, then leaned against the stall door and slipped off his left shoe.

"Now your sock," she said. "Please."

"Why mine?"

"Girl socks are too short."

He handed her a white ankle-length sock, warm as a handshake and slightly yellowed. He winced. "My washer's broken."

Darby pulled the sock taut, slipped the rock inside it, and sealed it up with a tight square knot. She swung it once, smacking it into her palm. The arc gave the small stone fierce leverage; even a quick flick of the wrist could fracture an eye socket. Or at least, that was the idea.

Ashley looked at it, then her. "What's that?"

"It's called a rock-in-a-sock."

"I . . . see why, I guess."

She'd seen it on a TV survival show. "Rock-in-a-sock," she repeated.

"The Cat in the Hat's weapon of choice."

She smiled, letting the scar over her eyebrow become briefly visible. "Okay." She hefted the weapon. "Here's my idea. Lars likes to stand by that front door and monitor the exit, right?"

"Right."

"One of us—Person B—will walk past him. Through the front door. Outside, toward his van. He's onto us now, so he'll follow Person B outside. He'll have to. And to do this, he'll go through the door, turning his back to Person A."

She smacked the rock-in-a-sock against her palm. It hurt.

"Person A—who is stronger than Person B—will come up behind Lars and whack him in the back of the skull. One good swing is all it should take to knock him out cold. But if it doesn't, Person B, who has the knife, will turn around and we'll both tag-team him—"

"You mean double-team?"

"Yeah. Tag-team."

"Those don't mean the same thing."

"You know what I mean, then." She was being intentionally vague about this part. In theory, one swing of the rock-in-a-sock would do the job. If it came to a scuffle, it would still be two versus one, and *both* two were now armed. Lars might be a violent sociopath, but how prepared could he be for a surprise attack from two directions?

More important: how fast could he draw his .45 and fire it?

Ashley was starting to get it now. "So Person A is me, huh?"

"It'll be two versus one, using the doorway as a bottleneck—"

"Am I Person A?"

Darby placed the rock-in-a-sock in Ashley's hand and closed his fingers around it, one by one. "You're stronger than me, aren't you?"

"I was . . . I was kind of hoping you were Ronda Rousey or something."

"I'm not."

"Then I guess I'm stronger."

"Two versus one," she repeated, like a mantra.

"What if we kill him?"

"We'll bash him to the floor and empty his pockets. Grab his gun. Grab the keys on that lanyard. If he keeps fighting, so do we. I was inside the van with him. I know what we're up against and I'll *cut his throat myself if I have to*—"

She paused, surprised by what she'd said.

Surprised she'd meant it, too.

"You didn't answer my question," Ashley said, drawing closer. "And just so you understand, Darbs, this is an assault charge if you're wrong."

She did—and she knew she wasn't. She'd spent thirty minutes lying prone in Lars's sweaty van under an Indian blanket, listening to that flat-eyed creature eat and fart and giggle with a nine-year-old girl held captive inside a dog kennel. She knew that whatever happened, she'd be seeing that leering grin in her nightmares: *Warmed it up for you, Jaybird.* But as for Ashley— well, she understood why he had doubts. This had all crashed down on him like a rockslide. All in about ten minutes.

In her other pocket, she still had the .45 round. Pressed tight against her thigh. That was her real fear—Lars's gun. He'd certainly use it if they didn't bring him down swiftly. Even if he only managed to squeeze off a blind shot or two, there were bystanders—Ed and Sandi—to consider. Darby had never actually been in a fight before, so she wasn't sure exactly what to expect, but she knew the movies were wrong.

"If you can," she added, "try to keep one eye closed."

"Why?"

"We're going to fight him outside, maybe in the dark. So try to keep one of your eyes closed now, while you're indoors, in the light, and then you'll have an eye with a little night vision. Make sense?"

He nodded, half-hearted.

"And . . . you said you have asthma?"

"Mild shortness of breath. I've had it since I was a kid."

"Well, when I was little," Darby said, "I used to have panic attacks. Really bad ones that made me hyperventilate and faint. I'd be in the fetal position on the floor, choking on my own lungs, and my mom would always hold me and say: *Inhale. Count to five. Exhale.* And it always worked."

"Inhale. Count to five. Exhale?"

"Yep."

"So, in other words, *breathe*? That's brilliant."

"Ashley, I'm trying to help."

"Sorry." He eyed the door. "I'm just . . . I'm just having trouble with this."

"You saw him, too."

"I saw a run-of-the-mill weirdo." He sighed. "And now we're about to beat the shit out of him."

"I'm sorry," she said, touching his wrist. "I'm so sorry to drag you into this. But I was dragged into it, too. And I can't save her alone."

"I know. I'll help."

"If we don't do something right now, Lars could snap and attack us first. Every second we wait here is a second we *give* him, to decide how to deal with us. If it makes it easier for you, stop thinking about this hypothetical little girl's life, who you've never actually met. Think about yours —"

"I said I'll do it," he said, and the ice-tray lights flickered behind him.

"Thank you."

"Don't thank me yet."

"I mean it, Ashley. *Thank you*—"

"I'll help," he said with a nervous grin, "if you give me your phone number."

Darby grinned, too, all teeth: "If you help bludgeon the shit out of a complete stranger with a rock for me, I might just marry you."

LARS WATCHED AS THEY RETURNED.

He was back at his sentry post, a few paces to the right of the front door in the lobby's natural little blind spot. He was trying vainly to refold a map of Mount Hood, but he tilted his head to follow Darby and Ashley as they crossed the room. Darby kept her head down. Her gray Converse squeaked, her socks still squelching with melted snow.

No eye contact.

Exiting the restroom at the same time had been a huge mistake, Darby realized. Even though both gendered doors were around a corner, only one door had been heard opening, and the timing was suspicious. Both Ed and Sandi had probably noticed, and they'd draw their own conclusions. Behind her, Ashley noisily bumped a chair. Smooth.

Her own heart was booming so loud she was shocked the others couldn't hear it. Her cheeks burned tomato red. She knew she was visibly rattled, but conveniently, it might just fit the bizarre scene. If she'd just met a stranger for a quickie in a public restroom, she'd feel pretty damn anxious about this ten-pace walk of shame.

She carried her Swiss Army knife concealed against her wrist. The metal ice-cold against her skin. She had to be ready—if Ashley's first swing didn't take Rodent Face down, she'd stab him in the throat. The face. Those dim little eyes.

I'll cut his throat if I have to.

She thought about Jay in the Chevrolet Astro outside, crouching inside a dog kennel damp with her own urine, her hand bloodied and bandaged, with five gallons of gasoline and a jug of Clorox bleach sitting nearby. She wondered what would happen to this poor little kid if they failed.

She was still angry at herself for exiting the restroom at the same time as Ashley. That had been stupid.

Ed definitely noticed. He glanced up at them, slurped his coffee, and nodded at the radio. "You missed it."

Ashley prickled. "Missed what?"

"The emergency loop updated again. It's bad. Eastbound is blocked by a jackknifed semi at the bottom of the slope. Multiple fatalities."

"How far from us?"

"Mile marker ninety-nine. So, seven, eight miles?"

Too far to walk.

Darby sighed, glancing back at the big Colorado map on the wall. That would place the wreck somewhere by Icicle Creek, halfway between the blue dots signifying the Wanasho and Wanashono rest areas. It was a little surreal how perfectly trapped they were—a blizzard sweeping in from the west, and a crashed eighteen-wheeler eight miles downhill to the east, cutting off the exit behind them. Like an ambush, every bit as staged as the one they were about to attempt. She wondered if dawn was still the ETA for the road crews' arrival, or if their timeline had slid back into tomorrow afternoon. If so, it would be a hell of a long time to hold a criminal at gunpoint.

Ashley reached through the security grate and adjusted the Sony's antenna. He squinted into the coffee stand, into the dark spaces under the counters. "And . . . do you think they have a real radio back there?"

"What?"

"A two-way radio? Or a landline phone? They'd have to."

Easy there, Ashley.

"Yeah?" Ed grunted. "If they do, it's state property, locked up—"

Ashley pointed. "Held by a dollar-store padlock. One good whack with something heavy, and those shutters come right up."

"I'm not in a felony mood just yet."

"Maybe you'll reconsider," Ashley said, "in the next few minutes."

Darby knew he would. She stood by the window, trying to appear calm, and looked outside into the dark trees. The snowflakes kept coming, some rising, some falling, catching flecks of sodium lamplight like cinders from a campfire. A few paces behind her, she heard Ashley exhale through chattering teeth. He had the rock-in-a-sock stuffed up his right sleeve, ready to drop into his palm and swing.

They'd agreed on a covert signal. When Ashley was ready, he'd cough once. This would be Darby's cue to walk to the front door, pass Lars on her way outside, and set the ambush in motion. Like triggering a bear trap.

Only problem? Ashley wasn't ready.

He hovered there, teeth gritted, sucking in shallow gulps of air. She hoped his shortness of breath wouldn't be a liability. Typical for her luck—*I enlist the aid of the youngest, tallest, strongest-looking guy in the immediate area, and he turns out to have asthma.* Just great. And she couldn't even imagine what was going on in poor Ashley's mind. An hour ago, he'd been demonstrating a Mexican turnover to this guy, and now he'd been asked to slink up behind him and bash his skull in.

It should be me, she realized.

I'm a coward for being Person B.

Maybe. But Ashley was, without a doubt, physically stronger than her. So her being the bait and Ashley being the trap made plenty of logical sense. It just didn't *feel* right.

"Hey." Lars cleared his throat. "Ah . . . excuse me?"

Darby turned to face him, centipedes coiling in her stomach, her Swiss Army knife tucked up her sleeve.

So did Ashley.

"Does . . ." The child abductor was still by the door, squinting into another tourism brochure: "Does anyone know what this word means?"

Sandi lowered her paperback. "Pronounce it."

"Res-plend-ent."

"Resplendent. It means beautiful."

"Beautiful." Lars nodded once, mechanically. "Okay. Thank you, Sandi." His gaze returned to his brochure—but on the way down, it met Darby's from across the room, and for a half second, she was trapped in the heady stupidity of his eyes.

He mouthed: *Beautiful.*

She looked away.

It'd been more than sixty seconds. Ashley was still standing beside her, his feet rooted to the floor, and now she was beginning to worry. She couldn't just tug him back into the restroom for another pep talk—the first one had already drawn too much of the room's attention. She was stuck waiting on his signal.

Come on, Ashley.

She wished he'd just inhale some dust and accidentally cough, so she'd have an excuse to approach the door and kick off the attack. Under her sleeve she pricked her thumb on the Swiss Army blade. It was satisfyingly sharp.

Please cough.

She watched him waver there, like a kid on a high diving board. He'd been so cool, so smooth and confident before, and now he looked like he'd just witnessed a murder. Darby felt a nervous tightness climb her throat. She'd chosen the wrong ally, and now the situation was unraveling.

Cough. Or you're going to give us away—

Ed noticed. "Ashley, you're quiet all of a sudden."

"I'm . . . I'm fine."

"Hey, look, man, I'm sorry about circle time."

"It's all right."

"I was just giving you shit—"

"I'm *fine*. Really." Ashley adjusted his sleeve as he spoke, keeping the rock-in-a-sock from dropping into view.

Ed smiled, tapping the table's edge with two fingers. A quiet little heartbeat, and for a moment the room was silent, and Darby could feel that sound in her bones. "Your big fear is . . . you said it was *door hinges*. Right?"

Ashley nodded.

Sandi set her paperback down. "Mine's snakes."

"Snakes, huh?"

"Mm-hmm."

Ed sipped his coffee, still tapping. "Mine is . . . well, I didn't really know how to put it into words. But I think I can now."

Another growl of wind, and the lights flickered overhead. The room threatened to fall into darkness.

Lars watched like a shadow.

Ashley licked his lips. "Let's . . . uh, let's hear it, then."

"Okay." Ed took an uncomfortable breath. "So . . . here's

some hard-earned wisdom for you kids. You want to know the secret to ruining your life? It's never one big black-and-white decision. It's dozens of little ones, that you make every single day. It's excuses, mostly, in my case. Excuses are poison. When I was a veterinarian, I had all sorts of good ones, like: *This is me time. I earned this.* Or: *No one can judge me for this drink; I just operated on a golden retriever who ran into a barbed wire fence, with her eyeball hanging out on a little string.* See? Horrific. That's how you trick yourself. And then one day I was at Jan's—I mean, my ex-wife's sister's place—a few years back for my goddaughter's big wedding reception. Wine, home-brews. I brought champagne. But I also brought a bottle of Rich and Rare for myself, and I stashed it in their bathroom, inside their toilet tank."

"Why?"

"Because I didn't want anyone to see how much I was drinking."

Silence.

Darby realized his drumbeat on the table had stopped.

Ashley nodded sympathetically. "My mom struggled with that, too."

"But . . ." Ed prodded Sandi's shoulder. "Well, thank God for my cousin Sandi, here, because she called me up at two o'clock yesterday and told me she was going to drive my ass up to Denver for family Christmas. No excuses."

Sandi sniffled. "We missed you, Eddie."

"So, yeah." He straightened. "To answer the circle-time question, my biggest fear is this Christmas in Aurora. I'm afraid my ex-wife and sons will be there at Jack's tomorrow night. And I'm even more afraid they *won't*."

For a long moment, no one spoke.

Ashley swallowed. Some color was back in his cheeks. "Uh, thanks, Ed."

"No problem."

"That couldn't have been easy to say."

"It wasn't."

"Been sober awhile?"

"No," Ed said. "I drank this morning."

Silence.

"That, uh . . ." Ashley hesitated. "That sucks."

"Tell me about it."

Another volatile silence, and the lights flickered again, as five people, with three concealed weapons, shared oxygen in this little room.

"Excuses are poison," Ed repeated. "Doing the right thing is hard. Talking yourself out of it is easy. Does that make sense?"

"Yeah," Ashley said. "More than you know." Then he glanced purposefully over at Darby, and raised a fist to his mouth.

He coughed once.

The trap engaged. She walked, feeling the tiny hairs prickle on her skin. She looked Lars in the eye as she moved toward that front door—he glanced up from his pamphlet and watched her pass, twisting his scrawny neck to follow her—and then Darby tugged the door open. A rush of subzero air. Slashing wind. Gritty snowflakes peppering her eyes.

She stepped outside, her shoulders tense, the knife tight in her knuckles.

Follow me, Rodent Face.

Let's end this.

11:55 P.M.

LARS DIDN'T FOLLOW HER.

The door closed. She took a few shaky steps outside, her Converse sinking into the fresh snow, her heart banging against her ribs. She'd been certain Lars would follow her. He should have been *right behind her*, shadowing her, his slouching frame filling the doorway, his back to the room so Ashley could strike—

He wasn't.

Darby shivered and watched the door. No need for concealment now; she held the Swiss Army knife like an icepick as she stood in the orange light, waiting for the door to creak open. But it didn't.

What had gone wrong?

The eye contact. The eye contact with Lars had been too much, she realized. She'd overplayed her hand. And now the armed criminal was still inside the building, with Ashley and the others, and the trap had failed.

Okay.

Okay, fine.

She had a choice now.

Go back inside? Or keep walking to his van?

Another howl of wind whipped her face with snow. For a moment she couldn't see. She blinked furiously, mashing her eyes with her thumbs. When her vision returned, the world had darkened. She realized the sodium-vapor lamp that hung over the visitor center's front door had fizzled out. Another grim omen to add to the list.

Seconds count, she reminded herself.

Make a choice.

So she did—she decided to keep walking to Lars's van. She'd open the door, check on Jay again, and flick the dome light on. Maybe even the high beams. This would give Lars another reason to come outside. And Ashley would have his chance to attack—if he was still ready. If the ambush could still be salvaged.

Something else occurred to her as she walked—what if there was a gun in the van? Her first search had been brief and frantic. Lars was certainly carrying one, of course, but what if there was another?

Yes, a gun would be a game changer. Her stomach growled.

Shambling through knee-deep snow, her right shoe coming untied, she crossed the fifty feet to Lars's van. Snow had regathered on the windshield, hardened to sheets of ice where it melted. She'd made sure to leave the Astro's rear door unlocked, and she was glad she had.

She circled to the back of the van now. She passed the faded decal of the cartoon fox—the blistered letters of WE FINISH WHAT WE START—and wondered if Lars had bought the vehicle from a business that went chapter 11. Or maybe he'd murdered someone for it. Or maybe Rodent Face was himself a freelance handyman. Maybe that was how he got inside your house and scoped out your kids' bedrooms, opening drawers and sniffing pillows.

Darby glanced over her shoulder, back at the Wanashono visitor center. The front door was still shut. The lamp was still dead. No silhouettes standing near the window, which was surprising. She'd expected to see Lars watching her, or at least Ashley. She couldn't even see Ed and Sandi; they were seated too far back. Save for the dim amber glow behind the half-buried glass, you'd never guess the tiny structure was populated at all.

What's happening in there?

Hopefully nothing. Yet.

She considered jumping into her Honda and punching the horn—that would sure draw some attention. Lars would certainly come outside to investigate that. But so might Ed and Sandi. The situation could unravel. The element of surprise could be lost. Shots could be fired. Bullets could ricochet.

She tugged the Astro's rear door. Still unlocked. It scraped open, dropping a shelf of snow, revealing soupy darkness inside as her pupils adjusted.

She whispered: "Hey."

Silence.

"Jay. It's okay. It's me."

Another tense moment, long enough for Darby to worry—

and then finally the girl stirred, her fingers gripping the kennel bars for balance. The frame made a twanging noise, like taut cables. Darby reached into her jeans pocket for her phone, to turn on the LED flashlight, but it wasn't there. She patted her other pocket. Also empty. She'd left her phone in her purse. On the edge of that porcelain sink, inside the men's restroom.

Stupid, stupid, stupid.

Inside the van, she smelled the same odors—dog blankets, urine, stale sweat—and identified a foul new one.

"I threw up," the girl whispered. A tremor in her voice.

"It's . . . it's all right."

"Sorry. My stomach hurts."

Mine too, Darby thought. She leaned back and peered around the Astro's icy taillight—yes, the building's door was still shut. "I'm sorry, Jay. We're both having a crappy night. But we'll get through it. Okay?"

"I didn't mean to throw up."

"It's fine."

"I never throw up. Ever."

"Believe me, Jay, that'll change in college."

"College makes you throw up?"

"Something like that."

"I *hate* throwing up. If that's what college is like, I'm not going—"

"All right, Jay, listen." Darby touched the kennel, and the little girl's trembling fingers squeezed hers through the bars. "I'm going to help you. And to help you, I need you to first help me. Okay?"

"Okay."

"I need you to try and remember. The farting man . . . can you describe the gun he's carrying?"

"It's little. Black. He keeps it in his pocket."

"Of course." She leaned out and checked the building's front door again—still closed—and asked: "Did you see him keep any knives in here? Bats? Machetes?"

"I don't know."

"Any other guns?"

"One other."

Darby's heart double-tapped. *"Where?"*

"No, it's not a regular gun—"

Her mind raced with possibilities—and she barely choked out: "Why? Is it bigger?"

"It shoots nails."

"Like a . . ." Darby hesitated. "Like a nail gun?"

Jay nodded.

"And you're . . . you're sure?"

She nodded harder.

A nail gun.

Just like the cartoon fox on the van. Darby remembered the bandage on Jay's hand, the bloody little smudge on her palm, and it all fit together. Punishment for an escape attempt, maybe? Or maybe this, this thing he called a *yellow card*, was just an appetizer for whatever horrific main course Lars had in mind for her once he drove her to his remote cabin in the Rockies.

Her hands were shaking again. Not with terror—rage.

A freaking nail gun.

That's the kind of psycho we're up against.

"And the nail gun is here?" she asked. "It's in the van with us?"

"I think so."

Darby doubted a power tool would be an even match against Lars's .45, but it was a hell of an upgrade from a two-inch Swiss Army knife. She'd never operated a nail gun before, or even seen one outside of an Ace Hardware store—but she hoped it would be simple to learn. How far could it fire a nail? Was it heavy? Loud? Would a nail to the skull kill the victim, or just maim? Point and click, right?

She touched Jay's right hand through the bars, and found the nine-year-old's fingers were slick with fresh, cold blood. The scab on her palm must have broken.

Point and click.

Darby vowed she'd kill Lars tonight. Maybe when she and Ashley finally cornered this sicko and pummeled him into a whimpering, broken heap—well, maybe she'd keep stabbing. Maybe she'd cut his throat. Maybe she'd enjoy it.

Maybe.

She leaned back and checked on the building again—still no activity. Now she was getting worried about Ashley, Ed, and Sandi. Was Lars really just standing idly by in there, allowing Darby to poke around the parking lot outside? After finding her Styrofoam cup in the snow? After stalking her and Ashley into the restroom? After she made knowing eye contact with him on her way out the door?

Jesus—what the hell was going on?

Bloody scenarios cycled through her mind like camera flashes. She braced, half expecting the thump of a gunshot. But there was nothing. Only icy silence. Only the distant moan of the wind. Only Jay and herself, standing on shaky legs in that desolate parking lot.

The nail gun, she decided.

Lars's nail gun was her new objective. She'd find it, figure out how to operate it, and then she'd run back inside the visitor center, kick open the door, and whatever was going on inside, she'd fire a nail right into Lars's whiskery little face. *Ka-thunk.* Asshole dead. Innocent child saved. Nightmare over.

That would work.

She looked back at Jay, her teeth chattering. "All right. Where do you think Lars keeps his nail gun? Back here, or in the front?"

"The other one keeps it in an orange box."

"Keeps it where?"

"It used to be back here, but I think they moved it—"

But Darby wasn't listening. Jay's little voice bled away, and in a flash of scalding panic, the prior sentence snagged in her brain and echoed: *The other one keeps it in an orange box.*

The other one.

The other one.

The other one—

Slipping, staggering back outside, she hit her kneecaps on hardened snow, steadied herself against the brake light, and peered around it—

The building's door was now open.

Lars stood in the doorway. Beside him, Ashley.

The other one.

They watched her, fifty feet away, framed by interior light. They appeared to be speaking to each other in guarded whispers so Ed and Sandi wouldn't hear from inside. Their faces were black shadows, unreadable. But Lars had his scrawny arm chicken-winged up inside his jacket, likely resting on the grip of his pistol. And Ashley had the rock-in-a-sock out, in his right hand.

He was swinging it.

Smacking it against his palm.

MIDNIGHT

12:01 A.M.

DECEMBER 24

TWO VERSUS ONE.

She'd been right about that part.

Ashley was in on the kidnapping. He'd lied to her—about driving the other car, about not knowing Lars, about everything. He'd played along with her in the restroom. He'd put his tongue in her mouth. He'd been so authentic, so convincingly human and frightened. She'd believed it all. She'd told him everything. Her entire plan, all of her options, her thought processes, her fears.

She gave him *everything*. Including a new weapon.

She whirled to face Jay. "You didn't tell me there were two of them."

"I thought you knew."

"How could I know?"

"Sorry—"

"Why didn't you fucking *mention* it?"

"I'm sorry." Jay's voice broke.

Darby realized she was yelling at a nine-year-old girl who'd recently taken a steel nail through the palm. What did it matter? It was Darby's fault. Her mistake. Her horrible, fatal miscalculation, and now it was two versus one, and she and Jay were both as good as dead. Or worse.

One of the silhouettes started walking toward them.

Her heart seized up. "Okay. Where's their nail gun?"

"I don't know."

"Front or back?"

"*I don't know,*" the girl said, sniffling.

She needed to find it fast. Under the front seats, maybe? This orange box had to be large; there were only so many places it could fit.

She raced to the driver's-side door, her feet sinking, like she was running in quicksand. She chanced a look over her shoulder—the advancing figure was halfway to them. Twenty feet back, taking high steps on the footpath. She recognized the beanie, the slouching walk. It was Lars. His right hand swung past a slice of light, and she saw a blocky shape.

His .45-caliber pistol.

"Jay," Darby hissed. "Close your eyes—"

"What's going to happen?"

"Just close your eyes." She reached the Astro's driver door, hitting it with both palms, her mind screaming: *Find their nail gun. Kill this asshole. And then take his gun, and kill that lying snake Ashley—*

She tugged the door handle. Locked.

Her stomach plunged.

Because . . . because Lars had relocked it. Of course he had; he was in there last. It was locked, locked, *locked*.

"You, ah . . . you asked my brother to kill me," Lars's gurgling voice called out, drawing closer. "Is . . . is that right?"

They're brothers.

Shit, shit, shit.

Crunchy footsteps, like breaking eggshells, coming toward her. "He says you . . . you asked him to bash my brains in." His voice was so frighteningly *close*. Hoarse, rattling in the crisp air, hot with exhaled fog.

The Astro's driver door was a no-go. Darby scrambled to the rear of the van, catching herself on the ajar door for balance, and looked back inside the dark vehicle. At Jay's eyes, brimming with panicked tears, full of reflected light. At her rash-red cheeks. Her tiny fingernails.

She pleaded: "Run—"

Lars's footsteps crunched closer.

Darby pressed her Swiss Army knife into the little girl's outstretched fingers, almost dropping it. "Use this," she said, touching the serrations on the blade. "Scraping motions, okay? To saw at the kennel bars—"

"He's coming."

"Do it, Jay. Promise?"

"I promise."

"Keep cutting. You'll get out."

"What're you going to do?"

Darby stepped back out and slammed the rear door, dropping a shelf of snow. She hadn't answered Jay's question, because she had no answer.

I have no goddamn idea.

"WHY . . . AH, WHY ARE YOU RUNNING?" LARS CALLED.

Darby scrambled through the snow. It was waist-deep off the path, and moving through it was like hauling herself out of a wading pool over and over with every lurching step. Hard, gasping breaths. Her throat stung. Her calves burned.

"*Hey*. I just wanna talk—"

From the clarity of his voice, he was less than ten feet behind her. Chasing her. His mouth-breathing had morphed into a steady pant. Low, guttural, wolflike. Her right shoe—still untied—tugged off in the snow. She grabbed it and continued, half-shod, as his labored breathing grew louder behind her. He was gaining, she knew. A few paces closer and he'd grab her ankle—

"I'm . . . ah, I'm gonna catch you anyway—"

A metallic rattle. The gun, moving in his hand.

But she knew the pistol was just for intimidation. If Lars really wanted to shoot her, he would've done it already. That would alert Ed and Sandi, so Ashley had probably ordered his brother to run her down, to kill her discreetly, via suffocation or a snapped neck—

His brother.

His *fucking* brother.

Darby passed the bare flagpole and looked back. Lars was a pursuing shadow. He'd lost his Deadpool beanie. She saw weedy blond hair, milky in the dim light, a receding hairline. The furious fog of his breathing. He'd stopped shouting at her; he was too winded now. The deep snow was too exhausting. It was a slow-motion nightmare.

He's going to catch me, Darby knew.

She was already tiring. Muscles throbbing. Joints mushy.

He's going to run me down out here, and wrap his hands around my neck, and choke me until I die—

He was right behind her now. She could smell his salty sweat. She'd lost her lead and given up both of her weapons— the rock-in-a-sock to Ashley, the pocketknife to Jay—and now all she had left was a bullet in her pocket and a size-eight shoe in her hand. She considered throwing it at Lars, but that'd just be a nuisance. He'd swat it away without breaking stride.

There was nowhere to run anyway. Ashley was guarding the building's front door. She didn't have her keys, so locking herself inside Blue wasn't an option. Running wasn't, either—there were only miles of jagged Colorado taiga in all directions, frigid and unsympathetic. Just crunchy alpine trees, sparse ground cover, and fatal plunges concealed by snow. How long would she last before succumbing to the creeping death of hypothermia?

I can't keep running.

She considered stopping, standing her shaky ground, and fighting Lars. Bad odds.

"Turn around," Lars huffed behind her. "Let's . . . ah, let's talk—"

She needed to decide. If she stopped now, she'd have a few seconds to catch her breath before the fight. But if she kept running and he tackled her, she'd be winded, and her odds would be even worse—

Or . . .

The layout of the Wanashono visitor center flashed through her mind again. Walls, corners, blind spots. Although the front door was still blocked by Ashley, there was another way into the building. The little triangular windows in the restrooms. She'd seen one in the men's room, no larger than a doggy door. She could see it from here, leaking a whisper of orange light through hanging icicles, above the stacked picnic tables.

Her purse was inside that restroom. With her keys and her phone.

Okay.

I'll climb those tables, break that window, and get inside.

She changed direction.

Lars noticed. "Where . . . where are you going?"

She didn't have a plan for when she got inside. She just went for it. Because, as Sandi had said, inside was a hell of a lot better than out. Ed and Sandi were in there, and Ashley and Lars wouldn't dare murder her in view of two witnesses.

Would they?

No time to think on it.

The picnic tables were stored in a heap below that window, crusted with snow, so she climbed them, like giant stairs. One, two, three tables up, wobbling under her weight. But she made it, and she hit the triangular window with outstretched hands. Frosted glass, glowing with interior light, bumpy with ice. Too thick to shatter with an elbow. But it was a casement window, opening outward on a rust-eaten hinge, and it seemed to sit crookedly, so she groped for the edges, gripping with numb fingertips—

Lars laughed. "What're you doing up there?"

A twelve-inch icicle dropped from the roof and banged off the table beside her. She winced, gritting her teeth, still pulling, clawing her fingernails into the window's rubber seam—

"Hey, girlie—"

Pull . . . pull . . .

Another icicle dropped and exploded, showering her with ice flecks. Like glass shards on her cheeks.

"Girlie, I'm *comin' for ya*—"

Two more icicles dropped to her right and left, exploding like twin gunshots in her eardrums, and the picnic table wobbled underneath her as Rodent Face climbed up toward her, clambering on elbows and knees like a racing, scuttling animal, but her sole focus was that hinged window. On that warm glow behind the glass, so teasingly close. On her clamped fingertips, wrenching the thing open—

Pull . . .

Pullpullpull—

The mechanism broke. The window came free.

She let it fall, and it shattered off an icy picnic table. Lars raised a hand to shield his face from the shards—*Oh Jesus Christ, he's right behind me*—and Darby was out of time. She lunged inside, face-first, performing a desperate swan dive through the tiny opening—

Icy fingers clasped around her ankle. "Gotcha—"

She kicked free.

12:04 A.M.

SHE TWISTED, DROPPED SIX FEET, AND HIT A URINAL.

Spine-first, slamming into the porcelain lip with the small of her back. She rolled off it, sprawling, and her skull banged against floor tile. Flashbulbs went off behind her eyes.

The urinal flushed.

She scrambled upright, whirling to face the empty window. Just a triangle of darkness. Snowflakes swirled inside. The opening was probably too small for Lars to follow her through, but she couldn't count on that. Plus, Ashley was still around.

She backed away from the window, down the long rectangle of a restroom, past the stalls, past PAUL TAKES IT IN THE ASS, past the other stained urinals, until she bumped into the sink with her bruised back. Another flare of pain. She'd left her purse here. She scooped it up, feeling inside for the reassuring jingle of her Honda keys. And her iPhone.

Seven percent battery.

She held her breath and listened. She could hear Lars's footsteps outside the window, and his wheezing mouth-breaths under the whine of the wind. He was stymied now—unwilling to climb through and risk getting his bony ass stuck, unwilling to leave the little window unguarded and circle around the front. It was eerie. He'd given up speaking to her. Just grunting, huffing animal sounds now.

Keep moving, Darby.

She heard voices from the visitor center lobby. Muffled by the door. Ed and Sandi had probably heard her fall. And she recognized the robotic tones of the radio—another CDOT update. What was the timetable before help arrived, now? Dawn, right? Six hours? Seven?

Don't think about that. Keep moving.

Ashley was nearby but unaccounted for, and this terrified her. Worse, she was unarmed now. She hoped Jay could saw through the kennel bars with her serrated knife, or this was all wasted. She just had to buy the little girl enough time to do so (assuming she could survive the next few minutes in close quarters with two killers) and then drive them both to safety (assuming Blue could limp through Snowmageddon). All in all, three colossal assumptions. *Unlikely* didn't even do it justice.

No, Blue was snowed in. The snow was too deep now—

But what about Sandi's truck?

Tire chains, good lift—yeah, that thing stood a chance.

She closed a fist around her keys, letting the sharp points protrude between her knuckles. She could do some damage to an attacker's face, or gouge an eye if she got lucky. Her Dryden Hall dorm key was particularly sharp, like a little filet knife.

She heard shuffling outside. She froze, listening. Something heavy moved and scraped, followed by a thud of displaced snow. A picnic table shifting. She knew Lars was attempting, a second time, to climb the wobbly stack of tables and follow her inside. Any second now, that chinless little face would appear in the window, grinning with demented cheer—

Time to go.

Darby slipped her right shoe on. Double-knotted the shoelace. Then she slung her purse over her shoulders—car keys still clenched in her knuckles —and pushed out into the Wanashono visitor center lobby.

Ed was fussing with the radio's antenna through the security shutter. He performed a confused double-take in her direction, and she knew why. She'd exited the building twenty minutes ago—and now she'd returned through the restrooms. Beyond him, Sandi napped on the bench, her legs hunched, her paperback covering her face.

"Find a cell signal?" Ed asked.

Darby didn't answer. She looked ahead, past Espresso Peak, at the front door. That was where Ashley stood, his broad shoulders blocking her exit. He was staring at her. The flinching, nervous asthmatic she'd spoken to an hour ago was gone, just a discarded act. This new Ashley was still and solid, with deep, observant eyes. He looked her up and down—she had snow on her knees, her cheeks were flushed red, her skin sticky with sweat, her Honda keys clasped in her fist—and then he glanced at the center table, as if ordering her to take a seat.

She stared back at him, gritting her teeth and trying to appear fearless. Defiant. Like a courageous hero encircled by evil forces.

Instead, she almost cried.

She was certain now—she'd die tonight.

"Hey." Ed leaned between them, straining to remember her name. "Are . . . are you okay, Dara?"

For Christ's sake, it's Darby.

She swallowed, her voice mouse-like. "I'm fine."

She wasn't. She felt sobs trapped in her chest, shuddery spasms struggling to escape. Her spine ached where she'd landed on the urinal. She wanted to jump forward, grab Ed by the shoulders, to scream at this nice old veterinarian and his sleeping cousin: *Run. For the love of God, run right now.* But where?

Ashley nodded again at the table, harder.

At her chair.

She noticed a brown object neatly placed on the center of her seat, and recognized her brown napkin. The same napkin they'd used before, back when she'd thought he was an ally.

She approached the chair and picked up the napkin. Still watching her, Ashley curled his lip. It was the beginning of a smug grin, unnoticed by Ed and Sandi.

She unfolded the napkin with numb, clumsy fingers.

IF YOU TELL THEM, I KILL THEM BOTH.

12:09 A.M.

ASHLEY MOVED TO THE TABLE AND TOOK A SEAT DIRECTLY across from her. He'd crossed the room silently, and he sat now with both palms flat on the tabletop. His hands were large and callused.

Darby refolded the napkin and set it in her lap.

The radio crackled.

"I'm sick of Go Fish," Ashley said crisply. "How about something else?"

She said nothing.

"How about . . ." He thought. "Oh! How about War?"

She glanced over at Ed and Sandi—

Ashley snapped his fingers. "*Hey.* I'm right here, Darbo. Don't worry about the rules. War is real simple. Simpler than Go Fish, even. You just cut the deck in two, see, and take turns drawing, one after the other, and we see who has the higher card. Higher card takes both, and adds them to their deck. You know, because every war is fought one battle at a time."

He grinned, pleased with himself, and fluidly shuffled the cards in front of her. Then he curled them backward with a harsh chatter.

"Winner has a full deck at the end." He looked her in the eyes. "And the loser? Well, she's left with nothing."

Behind her, Ed pumped the COFFEE carafe to fill his cup, and it made that drowning scream again. Like lungs bubbling with water. Something about it made her shoulder blades quiver.

"Bad news, friends." Ed rattled the security shutter. "Coffee's out."

Ashley's eyes goggled with faux-horror. "*What?* No more caffeine?"

"Afraid so."

"Well, I guess we're all going to start murdering each other now." Ashley shuffled the cards a final time. It occurred to Darby, in a slow drip, that these grubby playing cards were probably not a fixture of the Wanashono rest area. The brochure stand was bolted down and the radio and coffee were caged behind a security grate. Ashley had brought these cards himself. Because he was a playful sort of evil, fascinated by games and tricks. Sleight of hand, surprises, and misdirection.

I'm a magic man, Lars, my brother.

The clues had all been there. She just hadn't seen them.

"You should get some rest," Ashley told her. "You look tired."

Her throat felt like dry paper. "I'm fine."

"Yeah?"

"Yeah."

"No rest for the wicked." He grinned. "Right?"

"Something like that."

"How much sleep did you get last night?"

"Enough."

"Enough, huh? What's that?"

"I . . ." Her voice broke. "An hour, two—"

"Oh, no, that's not enough." Ashley leaned forward, creaking his chair, and divvied the cards between them. She marveled; his fingers were so chillingly *fast*.

"Humans are built for six to nine hours of sleep per night," he told her. "I get a solid eight every night. That ain't a recommendation, honey, that's biology. See, less than that erodes your brain function. That's everything—your reflexes, your emotional stability, your memory. Even your intelligence."

"Then we'll be evenly matched," Darby said.

Ed chuckled, returning to his seat. "Kick his ass. Please."

But she didn't pick up her cards. Neither did Ashley. They quietly regarded each other across the table as the wind growled outside. A gust blew through the broken window in the men's restroom, rattling the door on its hinges. The temperature in the room was dropping, but so far no one had noticed.

"Fortunately for you," Ashley said, "the card game War is entirely luck. You know, unlike the real thing."

Darby studied his eyes. They were vast, emerald green, flecked with amber. She searched them for something recognizable, something human to relate to—fear, caution, self-awareness—but found nothing.

Eyeballs are on stalks, she'd learned randomly, back at an art gallery in October. She forgot the name of the artist, but he'd been there mingling with the crowd, sipping a Dos Equis, gleefully explaining that he'd incorporated authentic autopsy photos into his work. To Darby, the shape of the human optic nerves had looked disturbingly insectoid, like antennae on a garden slug. Something about it made her skin crawl. Now, she imagined Ashley's big eyes hanging in their sockets, firing electrical signals along those drooping stalks into the coils of his brain. He was a monster, an alien bundle of nerves and flesh. Utterly inhuman.

And he was still watching her.

"Unlike the real thing," he repeated.

The playing cards sat between them in two ignored heaps. Questions fluttered in her mind like trapped birds, things she desperately wanted to ask aloud but couldn't. Not while Ed and Sandi were within earshot.

Why are you doing this?

Why abduct a child?

What are you going to do with her?

And those green dragon eyes kept staring back at her, full of secrets. Jewel-like, scanning her body, assessing her dimensions, running contingencies and *what ifs*. They were frighteningly intelligent, in all the same ways Lars's had been frighteningly dumb. But it was an icy intelligence.

Other questions sparked in her mind: *How fast are you? How strong are you? If I slashed your face with Blue's keys, could I blind you? Right now, if I ran for the building's front door, could I make it?*

A door opened. A cold draft slipped into the room.

Ed glanced over. "Hi, Lars."

Ashley smirked.

Over a snarl of deflected wind, Rodent Face took position by the door, his right hand tucked in his jacket pocket, wrapped around the grip of that black .45. She'd seen it now, glimpsed it twice when he'd chased her. She knew little about firearms, but she recognized this one as magazine-fed, which meant it held more shots than a revolver's five or six. She could just barely identify its outline under his blue coat, a bulge at his right hip—but only because she knew to look for it.

Ed wouldn't notice it.

And Sandi was asleep.

Darby was surrounded again. Ashley at the table, and Lars posted at the door. She'd been surrounded this entire time—they'd been tacitly coordinating their locations all night—although she sure hoped her swan dive through the restroom window had been a surprise. It'd certainly saved her life, at least for a few more—

"Dara," Ed said, startling her. "You never answered the question, did you?"

"What?"

"You know. The circle-time question. Your biggest fear." He twirled his empty Styrofoam cup on the table. "I gave mine. Ashley gave his door-hinge story. Sandi hates snakes. So what about you?"

All eyes darted to her.

She swallowed. She still had Ashley's IF YOU TELL THEM, I KILL THEM BOTH napkin clutched tightly in her lap.

"Yeah." Ashley suppressed a grin. "Tell us. What scares you, Darbs?"

Words clogged up in her throat. "I . . . I don't know."

"Guns?" he prompted.

"No."

"Nail guns?"

"No."

"Getting murdered?"

"No."

"I don't know. Getting murdered is pretty scary—"

"Failure," she said, interrupting Ashley and looking those green eyes dead-on. "My biggest fear is making the wrong choice, failing, and letting someone get kidnapped or killed."

Silence.

On the bench, Sandi stirred in her sleep.

"That's . . ." Ed shrugged. "Okay, that was a weird one, but thanks."

"She's—" Ashley started to say something but stopped himself. Ed didn't notice, but Darby did, and it thrilled her. What did he almost blurt out?

She's—

She, as in Jay Nissen. The little San Diego girl in the van outside, whose life hung in the balance right now.

It was just a small error, only a fraction of a sentence, but it told Darby she'd caught her enemy off guard. Maybe Ashley and Lars had underestimated her—this 110-pound art major from Boulder who'd stumbled into their kidnapping plot. Surely, they couldn't have predicted that restroom window escape. She was proud of that.

She hoped she was getting under their skin.

They don't want to kill me here, in front of witnesses.

Because then they'd have to kill Ed and Sandi, too, and that seemed to be a last resort. One homicide was probably easier to manage than three. They'd wanted to kill or incapacitate her outside—discreetly—but she'd outsmarted them: hurtled face-first through a tiny-ass window, bruised her spine on a urinal, and earned herself another ten minutes of life.

Those ten minutes were almost up.

Inhale, she reminded herself. *Count to five. Exhale.* She had to keep her breaths full and steady. She couldn't lose it. Not now.

Inhale. Count to five. Exhale.

Ashley glanced over her shoulder, to his brother, and gave a slight but commanding nod. Without question, he was the alpha. If Darby killed one of them tonight, it would need to be him.

She wondered how much of what he'd said was true. The buried car outside wasn't really his. Was he really studying accounting in Salt Lake City? Had he really almost died in a coal mine in Oregon with his thumb crushed inside a rusty hinge? Ashley seemed intoxicated by the act of lying, misdirecting, wearing different hats, presenting different versions of himself. He was a kid performing a magic show.

It was past midnight now. Darby had to make it for another six hours until the CDOT snowplows arrived at dawn and opened up the highway for an escape. That was a lot of ten-minute increments. But she'd try.

She didn't know what Ashley's little nod to his brother had meant—so far, Lars had remained glued to the front door—but she didn't like it. The two brothers had just made another silent chess move against her, and she was now, again, on the defensive.

But as long as Ed and Sandi are here, they won't kill me.

She glanced up at the clock on the wall, and for a bleak moment, she thought about how far away dawn was. How dark and cold the night was. How outnumbered and outmatched she was. They could kill everyone in this room. Maybe they planned to. Maybe the threat on the napkin was just a little game.

Ashley grinned, like he'd read her mind.

This stalemate won't last.

"All right, everyone," he said cheerily. "War with Darbs seems to be a bust. Who's up for a new round of circle time?"

Ed shrugged. "Sure."

"Let's do . . . first job? No. Let's do favorite movies." Ashley glanced around the stuffy room, a beaming game-show host. "Okay if I answer first again?"

"Knock yourself out."

"All right. Actually—well, I don't have a single favorite movie, but rather, a favorite *genre* of movies. Is that acceptable for everyone?"

Ed gave a *who cares* hand wave.

"Monster movies," Ashley said, his eyes darting back across the table to Darby. "Not, like, small monsters like werewolves. I'm talking about the huge, towering ones, twenty stories tall, like Godzilla and Rodan. *Kaiju* movies, they're called in Japan. You know the kind, where something big is terrorizing a city, hurling model cars around?"

Ed nodded, not really listening. He was tilting his coffee cup, trying to capture the last few precious drops.

It didn't matter, because Ashley was only looking at Darby as he spoke, his words clean and composed, revealing his Crest-white teeth: "See, golly, I just *love kaiju* movies. And . . . the thing I find fascinating about them is this: The human heroes—Bryan Cranston and that bland Sergeant Vanilla guy, in the 2014 *Godzilla* reboot, for example—they're just placeholders. They're ciphers for the audience. Do these puny humans have any effect on the actual plot?"

He let his rhetorical question float for longer than necessary.

"*Nope*," he finally answered. "Zero. Their role in the story is entirely reactive. Godzilla, Mothra, the MUTOs—the true stars of the show—they're going to fight and settle their business, and the humans can't possibly hope to stop the carnage. Does this make sense to you?"

Darby didn't answer.

"No matter what you try, the monsters are going to do what they want." Ashley leaned forward, creaking his chair, and she whiffed his moist breath as his voice lowered into a husky croak: "See, the monsters are gonna fight, and flatten skyscrapers and smash bridges, and all you can do is get the hell out of their way, or *you're gonna get crushed*."

Silence.

She couldn't look away. As if staring down a rabid animal.

His breath was overpowering. Like boiled egg yolks and bitter coffee, curdling with meat-like odors. Sixty minutes ago, his tongue had been a warm slug in her mouth. But now his boyish smile returned, like he'd slipped a rubber Halloween mask back on, and in another moment, he was back to being the jovial chatterbox she'd first met. "So, what about you, Darbs? What's your favorite type of movie? Horror? Ghosts? Torture porn?"

"Rom-coms," she answered.

Lars giggled by the front door, a raspy noise that reminded her of a chain saw on idle. Ashley traded glances with his brother, and his lips curled a little as the swirling snow intensified outside. "This is . . . this is going to be a fun night."

Maybe so, Darby thought, looking him in the eye. *But I promise, I won't make it easy.*

"But," Ashley said, rubbing his eyes in stage-managed sleepiness, "I admit, I would kill for a cup of coffee right now."

"Actually . . ." Ed considered. "Hey, you know, we have some in the truck. It's the cheapo instant camping type, where you just pour in the grounds and add hot water. It tastes like river silt, but it's coffee. Anyone interested?"

"Cowboy coffee?" Ashley beamed, like a prospector discovering gold. He'd either planned this or gotten lucky. "That would be wonderful."

"Sandi hates it."

"Well, luckily she's asleep."

"Yeah? Takers? All right." Ed slipped on a pair of black winter gloves, moving to the door. "I'll be back in a sec—"

"No worries." Ashley's grin inflated. "Take your time, amigo."

Darby tried to think of something to say—*wait, stop, please don't leave the room*—but her mind was as thick as peanut butter. The moment passed, and in another stomach-fluttering instant, Ed was gone. The visitor center's front door swung closed, not quite engaging.

Lars pushed it—*click.*

The two brothers glanced at each other, then at Darby. In a microsecond, the room's air pressure changed. The three of them were now essentially alone. For however long it took Ed to walk out to Sandi's truck, open his luggage, grab his camping coffee, and walk back. Sixty seconds, maybe?

Now . . . the only thing keeping Darby alive was Sandi.

And she wasn't even awake. She snored like a purring cat on the blue bench, her arms crossed over her potbelly, her paperback precariously balanced on her face. The lightest breeze could disturb it. For the first time all night, Darby could read the title: *Luck of the Devil*. For the next sixty seconds or so, Darby's life depended on how light a sleeper this middle-aged woman was.

"Rom-coms," Ashley muttered under his breath. "That's cute."

"Better than *Godzilla*."

"All right, Darbs, I'm sick of talking around it." Ashley kept his voice low, controlled, watching Sandi from the corner of his eye. "So here's what's going to happen. I'm going to make you an offer."

She listened, but in the back of her mind she was counting seconds, like steady clockwork: *Sixty seconds for Ed to walk to his cousin's truck and back.*

Fifty seconds, now?

"This offer is going to stand once, Darbs, and then it'll be gone forever. No second chances. So think hard, please, before you make a decision—"

"What're you doing with that little girl?"

He licked his lips. "We're not talking about Jay right now."

"Are you going to kill her?"

"That's not important."

"It's pretty *goddamn* important to me—"

"Darby." He was getting aggravated now, baring his perfect teeth, his voice a strained whisper: "This isn't about her. Don't you understand? This is about you, and me, and my brother, and everyone else caught in the cross fire at this rest stop. This is about the decision you're going to make, right now."

Forty seconds.

She thought about Lars, guarding the door behind her, and

her stomach tightened with queasy horror. His mooning grin, the shiny scar tissue peppering his hands, his flat little eyes. She didn't think she could say it aloud—but then she did: "Is he . . . is Lars going to rape her?"

"What?" Ashley rolled his eyes. "Ew. Gross. Darbs, you're not listening—"

"Answer me," she said, glancing over at Sandi. "Or I swear to God, I'll start screaming bloody murder right now—"

"Do it." He leaned back. "See what happens."

She still had her keys in her knuckles, on her lap. The sharpest one—her Dryden Hall dorm key—was gripped between her thumb and index finger. But she couldn't trust herself to clear the table fast enough. Ashley would see her attack coming; he'd raise a hand to protect his face. It wouldn't work. She wasn't strong enough or quick enough.

"I dare you," he whispered. "Scream."

She almost called his bluff.

Then Ashley glanced over Darby's shoulder. He nodded again, and she realized with a shiver of panic—Lars was now standing directly behind her. She hadn't heard him approach, but now she heard the crinkle of his ski jacket flexing, just inches away. Like the moment they'd first met. She flinched, half expecting those scarred hands to clamp around her throat and squeeze—but Lars knelt instead, snatching her purse from the floor beside her ankle.

"Yoink." He carried it to the door.

Ashley glanced back to her, sucking on his lower lip. "Darbs, so we're clear, I'm giving you a chance to undo all of this. A big red reset button. It's easy, too, because all you have to do is nothing. Just keep your mouth shut."

Twenty seconds.

"See, Darbs, we'll all agree that this little accident never happened. We—my brother and I—we'll pretend you never broke into our van. You'll pretend you never saw Jaybird. We'll all just . . . just erase the last few hours from our brains, and when the snowplows rumble up here at the ass-crack of dawn, we'll all just hop into our cars and go our separate ways. A peaceful resolution for everyone."

Pop-pop. Lars opened the buttons on her wallet. Credit cards click-clacked to the floor. He sniffed, checking out her Utah driver's license, and unfolded a crumpled twenty, which he pocketed.

Ten seconds.

"I'll be honest." Ashley leaned forward. "I'm really, *really* hoping you'll just look the other way. Get some rest. You're tired. You look like boiled crap. You won't stand a chance against Lars and me. So just . . . let the monsters do their thing, okay?"

Five seconds.

"Please, Darbs. It'll be easier on all of us." He glanced at Sandi as he said this, as if his threat weren't already clear enough.

Darby felt her cheeks burn. "I can't."

"We won't hurt Jay, you know." He cocked his head. "Is that it? Is that what you're afraid of? Because if so, I can promise you—"

"You're lying."

"No one will get hurt tonight, if you cooperate."

"I know you're lying."

"She'll be fine," Ashley said, waving his hand. "Hey, by

the way. I saw a bunch of papers in the back seat of your car. Black papers. What's all that?"

"Why do you care?"

His eyes hardened. "You peeked into Garver family business. So I peeked into yours. Answer the question."

"It's . . . just papers."

"For what?"

"Gravestone rubbings."

"What're those?"

"I take . . . I use crayons to, uh . . . to take an imprint of headstones."

"Why?"

"Because I collect them."

"Why?"

"I just do." She hated being studied by him.

"You're kind of a damaged girl," Ashley said. "I like it."

She said nothing.

"And you have a scar above your eyebrow." He leaned over the table, inspecting her in the fluorescent light. "That must have been . . . what, thirty stitches? It's only really noticeable when you furrow your brow. Or smile."

She stared at the floor.

"Is that why you don't smile much, Darbs?"

She wanted to cry. She wished it were over.

"Smile," he whispered. "You'll live longer."

It's been more than a minute.

Where the hell was Ed? Possibilities cycled through her mind. Maybe he couldn't find the camping coffee. Maybe he was sneaking in a drink. Or maybe . . . maybe he'd detected some subtle clue, pieced together the kidnapping plot, and he was attempting to find a cell signal to contact the police right now? Or what if Jay had cut through the kennel bars and run to him? He'd be a second witness. That would give Ashley and Lars no choice but to start shooting.

Every second felt volatile. She glanced up at the *Garfield* clock, and Ashley noticed. "That's an hour fast, you know."

"I know."

"It's only one o'clock."

"I know."

He licked his lips, studying the clock. The image on it of a love struck Garfield offering roses to Arlene. "Hey, what's that cat's name? The pink one?"

"Arlene."

"*Arlene.* That's a pretty girl's name. Like yours."

"Yours too," she said.

He smirked, enjoying the back-and-forth, his attention returning to her eyebrow. "How'd you get the scar, anyway?"

"A fight," she lied. "In junior high."

She'd crashed her bicycle into a garage door. If it could be called a fight, the garage door had won. Twenty-eight stitches and an overnight at the hospital. The other fifth graders had called her *Frankengirl.*

She couldn't tell if Ashley believed her. He licked his lips. "I should warn you, Darbs, if you're . . . you know, planning on fighting us tonight. Are you?"

"Am I what?"

"Planning to fight us?"

"I'm thinking about it."

"Well, if you *are*, you should know. I've always been kind of special."

"I bet you are."

"See, I'm not just lucky—I'm protected, I think. From consequences. It's like a magic I have. In the end, things always go my way." He leaned in closer, like he was imparting a delicate secret. "You might call it luck, but I sincerely believe it's something else. My toast always lands jelly-side up, you could say."

She had to ask. "You don't really have asthma, do you?"

"Nope."

"Do you even go to Salt Lake Institute of Tech?"

His grin widened. "Made-up school."

"What about your phobia of doors?"

"Door *hinges*. That one's true, actually."

"Really?"

"Yeah. They give me the creeps." He held his hand over his heart. "Swear to God. Can't touch 'em, try not to look at 'em. Ever since I almost lost my thumb down in Chink's Drop, they've just bothered the hell out of me."

"Regular door hinges?"

"Yeah."

"I was certain you'd made that up, too. It didn't seem real."

"Why not?"

"Because," Darby said calmly, "I didn't think you'd be such a pussy."

A board creaked.

Ashley looked back at her coldly, like she'd defied his initial assessment, and the lights flickered overhead. Then he sighed, swallowed once, and when he finally spoke again, his voice was tightly controlled: "You're gambling with a child's life. Don't forget that. Tonight could have a happy ending, but you're jeopardizing it."

"I don't believe you."

"It's not a sex thing," Ashley said, frowning with exaggerated disgust. "It's money. If you just have to know."

Sandi stirred again on the bench. *Luck of the Devil* slid a few centimeters down her face. Darby wondered if she was really asleep. What if she was only pretending? What if she'd heard the whole conversation?

"I mean, tell you what." Ashley suppressed a laugh, loosening up again. His demeanor came in chilling phase changes; light to dark and back again. "You should *see* this house, Darbs. Looks like Mr. Burns's mansion. Daddy owns a tech start-up, something to do with a video player. You know, computer shit, which is over my blue-collar head. I'm more of a practical nuts-and-bolts guy Which is why we're borrowing Jaybird here, taking her out to the Rockies for a few weeks, letting Mommy and Daddy get real worried and whip out their checkbooks, and once we're fairly compensated for our work, we'll cash out and leave her at a bus station in some shitsplat town in Kansas. She won't be harmed. It'll be like a vacation. Hell, maybe we'll even teach her how to snowboard while we're—"

"You're lying again."

His folksy grin vanished. "I already told you, Darbs. Try to keep up. We won't hurt her—"

"You *already* hurt her," she snarled, half hoping Sandi really was awake under her paperback, really was listening. "You shot a goddamn nail through her hand. And I swear to God, Ashley, if I get the chance, I'll do worse to you."

Silence.

Lars slipped her wallet back into her purse, and then he returned it to the floor at her feet. She didn't look at him.

"So . . ." Ashley paused. "You saw Jay's hand?"

"Yes."

He considered this for a few moments, sucking his lower lip again with a lizard slurp. "Okay. Good." He hardened, another eerie phase change. "Good, good. *Great*, even. Let's call this a teachable moment, okay? If it's in my best interests to keep Jaybird alive—shaken, but alive—and yesterday morning I got sick of her whining and put a cordless nailer to her palm and pulled the trigger . . . well, Darbo, just imagine what I'll do to someone who I *don't* have to keep alive. Imagine what I'll do to this rest stop. What I'll do to Ed and Sandi. What I'll make you watch. And it'll all be your fault, because you felt too morally superior to play ball here. So I'm asking you again, Darby. And I'm warning you, too—think long and hard about what you say next, because if it's the wrong thing, I *promise* you, you won't be the only one who dies tonight."

She stared back at him, afraid to blink.

"Also," he added, "your nose is bleeding."

She touched her nose—

He lunged forward, grabbed a fistful of her hair, and slammed her face into the tabletop. Fireworks behind her eyes. Dizzying pain. The cartilage in her nose made a wet *crunch* and she recoiled backward, nearly falling off her chair, clasping both hands to her face.

Across the room, Sandi jolted awake. Her paperback clapped to the floor. "What . . . what happened?"

"Nothing, nothing," Ashley said, looking at Darby. "We're fine."

Darby nodded, pinching her nose. Hot blood dribbled down her wrists, vivid red. Her eyes stung, fighting back tears.

Don't cry.

"Oh, honey, your nose—"

"Yeah. I'm fine." Darby tasted coppery blood in her teeth. Big drops tapped the tabletop. Her fingers stuck together.

"What happened?"

"High altitude," Ashley said crisply. "Low air pressure. It just sneaks up on you. My nose was bleeding like a *faucet* back at Elk Pass—"

Sandi ignored him. "Need a tissue?"

Darby shook her head sharply, squeezing her nostrils. Blood poured down her throat in clogged mouthfuls. Droplets speckled her lap.

Oh Jesus, don't cry.

Sandi crossed the room, her big purse swinging. She grabbed a lump of brown napkins from the coffee counter and laid them in Darby's lap. She touched her shoulder. "Are you sure? It's . . . it's really bleeding."

Darby felt her face tighten up, like her skin was being stretched taut around her skull. Fiery heat on her cheeks. Her vision blurred with tears, her breaths hissing through her teeth, while Ashley calmly watched her from across the table with his hands tucked neatly in his lap.

Don't cry, Darby, or he will kill everyone here.

"I'm fine," she choked. "It's just the elevation—"

"I had my first beer at eight thousand feet," Ashley chimed

in again. "Sliced my hand on a fluorescent light, and I bled pure red water for two straight days—"

"Oh, *shut up*," Darby snarled.

He froze, startled by her sudden ferocity. This should have been another win for Darby, another small moment of prey catching predator off guard, but she already knew it was a huge mistake.

Because Sandi had noticed.

"I . . ." The lady hesitated, palms up. She glanced between them, her yellow parka crinkling as she moved. "Wait. What's really happening here?"

Silence.

Ashley chewed his lip thoughtfully, and then nodded to Lars.

No, no, no—

Lars reached into his coat pocket for his pistol. But the front door banged open beside him, hitting the wall, startling him—

"Finally found the coffee." Ed came in, boots squeaking, spattered with snowflakes, and slammed two clipped baggies of ground French roast on the table between them. "The recipe is two tablespoons for every eight ounces of boiling—oh, holy shit, that's *blood*."

"The altitude," Darby choked.

Sandi said nothing.

"Damn." Ed looked Darby up and down. "You really got it. Keep pressure on your nose, and lean forward, not backward."

She tilted her head forward.

"Good. Forward makes it clot. Backward, and it all pours down your throat and you get a stomach full of blood." He brushed snow from his shoulders. "And use those napkins. They're free."

"Thanks."

As Ed moved past, Darby glanced over to Sandi, bridging a moment of shaky eye contact. Sandi was suspicious now, eyes wide, glancing between the two brothers. The outline of Lars's concealed pistol was plainly shadowed in the overhead light.

Darby raised an index finger to her lips: *Shhh.*

Sandi nodded once.

At the same time, Ashley must have been making a hand signal to Lars. Darby turned back and only caught the end of it, but it looked like a frenzied hand-to-throat gesture: *Stop, stop, stop.* That was it; the room had just been a split second from exploding into violence. Ed had no clue that he might have just saved everyone's lives by bumbling back inside when he did with a bag of instant coffee.

Now, he reached through the security shutter and dispensed hot water. "It's not quite boiling, but it's hot enough for tea. Should be okay for some shitty coffee."

"Manna from heaven," said Ashley. "Sweet, sweet caffeine."

"Yep, that's the idea."

"You're my hero, Ed."

He nodded, his patience for Ashley's chitchat clearly wearing thin. "Good to hear."

Sandi backed up and sat on the corner bench, where she could monitor the entire room. Darby watched her lift her paperback but hold it in her lap. Her other hand tucked carefully inside her purse, behind the embroidered letters of Psalm 100:5. Gripping a canister of pepper spray, perhaps.

Please, Sandi, don't say anything.

The Wanashono rest area was a powder keg. All it would

take was a single spark—and this room was full of friction. Carefully, out of view, Darby opened the IF YOU TELL THEM, I KILL THEM BOTH note in her lap, beneath the tabletop, and wrote another message against her thigh. She capped her pen and folded the napkin tightly again, leaving a bloody thumbprint.

"Who else wants coffee?" Ed asked.

"Me," said Lars.

Sandi nodded, but didn't speak.

"Me too," Darby said as she stood up, gripping her sore nose and handing the note to Ashley, then turning to face Ed. "No sugar, no cream. And make it strong, please. Tonight is going to be one *hell* of a long night."

Behind her, she heard Ashley greedily unfold the napkin.

He was reading her message now.

1:02 A.M.

YOU WIN, THE NOTE READ. I WON'T SAY A WORD.

Ashley smirked—she had no idea how right she was.

This CU-Boulder girl was an unexpected complication, but he'd already figured her out. He'd seen her type before, although never in the flesh. See, Darby was a bona fide hero. She was one of those bystanders on a Shell station CCTV tape who goes for the robber's gun, or renders aid to a bleeding clerk. She was the type who'd throw herself under the meat-grinder wheels of a train to save a total stranger. Protecting others, doing *the right thing*, was an instinct for her, whether she knew it or not.

Contrary to popular belief, Ashley knew, that's not a strength.

It's a weakness, because it makes you predictable. Controllable. And sure enough—with just a thirty-minute conversation, a half round of circle time, and an aborted card game—Ashley already owned her.

Smashing her nose? That was just a fun little victory lap.

And he'd been surprised by how much he enjoyed watching Darby fight tears in front of Ed and Sandi, her nose a spurting red faucet. There was something great about it, something he couldn't quite put his finger on. She was humiliated, suffering in public, reminding him of some of his favorite porn. He loved the ones where the girl was secretly wearing vibrating panties in a street or restaurant, trying not to show it. Trying to hold back.

It helped that Darby was undeniably pretty, too, in a feral way. She had a ferocity to her, a vicious streak to go with her auburn hair. She didn't know how tough she could be, if pushed to the edge. He'd love to take her there. He'd love to take her to Rathdrum, to drive her out to the gravel pit and teach her how to fire his uncle's SKS. Brace the wooden Soviet stock up to her little shoulder, guide her painted fingernail around the trigger, whiff her nervous sweat as she aligned the notched iron sights.

Such a bummer, then, that he'd have to kill her tonight.

He didn't want to.

Ashley Garver had never technically killed anyone before, so tonight would be a definite first. The closest instance he could think of was still more manslaughter than murder. And not via direct action—but inaction.

He'd been a kid when it happened.

This was a year or two before he nearly lost his thumb at Chink's Drop. So he'd been five, maybe six. Back then, his parents used to offload him and Lars (just a preschooler) in the summer months with Uncle Kenny, who lived in the dry prairies of Idaho. He called himself Fat Kenny (*Hey, hey,*

hey!), which Ashley only now understood was a riff on Fat Albert. He was a jolly man who huffed when he climbed stairs, smoked clove cigarettes, and always had a joke on hand.

What do you tell a woman with a black eye?

"Shoulda listened."

What do you tell a woman with two black eyes?

Nothin'. She's already been told twice.

Each year, Ashley had returned to grade school armed with an arsenal of killer jokes. Every September he'd been the most popular kid on the playground, letting them go viral. By October or so, the school district had always held an emergency assembly about tolerance.

But there was a lot more to Uncle Kenny than his riproaring funnies. He also owned an onsite diesel station on a single-lane highway east of Spokane, popular with truckers and nobody else. Ashley used to climb the apple trees with Lars and watch the eighteen-wheelers roll in and out. Sometimes they parked on Kenny's land, chewing muddy divots in the yellow grass, arriving late at night and leaving early in the morning. They rarely entered Uncle Kenny's house, though—instead they went to his storm cellar.

It was like a fallout bunker, a single hatch door protruding from the weeds twenty yards from the laundry room. This submarine door was always, *always* padlocked. Until one morning when, under a gauze of damp fog, he'd found it wasn't.

So he'd gone inside.

Ashley remembered few details about the dark room at the bottom of the long, rotten staircase. Mostly just the odors—a musty, sweet staleness that was simultaneously putrid and oddly alluring. He'd never smelled anything like it since.

Cold cement under his feet. Electrical cords on the floor; big lights set up on tripods. Indistinct shapes, lurking in the dark.

He'd just been leaving, climbing back up the stairs, when a woman's voice called out to him: *Hey.*

He'd turned, nearly tripping. He waited for a long moment, half on the stairs, half off, gooseflesh prickling on his arms, wondering if he'd only imagined it, until finally the female voice spoke again.

Hey, there. Little boy.

This had been a shock—he hadn't known how the woman in the cellar could possibly see him. It was pitch black down there. Only as an adult did Ashley understand that her pupils had been adjusted to the darkness, while his hadn't. Like Darby's crafty little close-one-eye trick.

You're a nice boy, aren't you?

He'd cowered there on the steps, covering his ears.

No. Don't be afraid. You're not like them. The ghostly voice lowered, like she was divulging a secret: *Can you . . . Hey, can you please help me with something?*

He'd been afraid to answer.

Can you bring me a glass of water?

He wasn't sure.

Please?

Finally he gave in and raced back up the rotten steps, ran back to his uncle's rancher, and filled a blue glass in the kitchen sink. The tap water tasted like iron out here. When he came back outside, Uncle Kenny was standing by the open cellar door, his hands braced on his flabby hips.

Little Ashley froze, spilling some water.

But Uncle Kenny wasn't angry. No, he was never angry.

He'd been all jolly smiles, showing yellow horse teeth, plucking the glass from Ashley's petrified little fingers: *Thanks, kiddo. It's all right, I'll take this down to her. Hey, why don't you go walk your baby brother down to the gas station and grab yourselves two chicken flautas, on the house?*

The flautas had been dry as sandpaper, withered by the heat lamp. Lars didn't mind, but Ashley couldn't finish his.

That same year, a month or two later, Ashley had returned to Uncle Kenny's a second time for Veterans Day weekend, and he remembered finding that same cellar door propped wide open, with a rattling fan blowing air out. When he descended the steps this time he found the lights on, revealing a bare, gutted bunker, the concrete walls damp with condensation. Scrub marks on the floor. The acrid odor of bleach. The woman was gone.

Long gone.

Even at that age, Ashley had known he should confront his uncle about this, or better yet, tell his parents and let them call the police. And he'd come very close, sitting on that knowledge all weekend like it was a loaded gun. But that Saturday night, Fat Kenny made macaroni and cheese with jalapeños and whole slices of bacon in it, and told a joke so epically funny it made Ashley spray a half-chewed mouthful.

Hey, Ashley. How can you tell a nigger has been on your computer? How?

Your computer's missing.

In the end, he'd simply liked Fat Kenny too much. He was too much fun. And he was genuinely decent to four-year-old Lars, too—letting him carry tools in the workshop, teaching him how to shoot crows with a BB gun. So, bottom line, whatever those truckers were doing with the woman in the bunker ultimately didn't matter to Ashley. He'd just filed it away in a dark corner of his brain.

That was seventeen years ago.

And now, at the Wanashono rest area in Colorado, on the frigid night of December 23, the roles had been shuffled, like a classic TV show returning with a cast of new actors. Ashley himself was the new Fat Kenny, scrambling to protect a damaging secret. And Darby was the accidental witness.

History doesn't quite repeat itself, but damn, it sure can rhyme.

Ed reached behind the rattling security grate, testing the hot water dispenser, and then separated two bags of coffee grounds. "I've got a dark French roast, and a light."

"Either's fine," said Sandi.

"Dark roast, please," Ashley said. "As dark as it gets."

He didn't actually have a preference; he just liked how *dark roast* sounded. His taste buds were more or less dead, so all coffee tasted the same to him. But hell, if there was ever a night for jet-black coffee, this would be it. He stuffed Darby's brown napkin into his jeans pocket, noticing it was smeared with a crescent thumbprint of her blood.

He realized he'd lost sight of her.

Quickly, he scanned the room. Ed was there by the locked coffee stand, Sandi was seated like a fat yellow bumblebee, Lars was guarding the front door—but yes, Darby was gone. She'd vanished. She'd taken advantage of his inattention and made a move.

But it was fine. No worries. Ashley Garver would just make a move, too.

Restroom?

Restroom.

He nodded to his brother.

DARBY KNEW SHE HAD ONLY A FEW SECONDS.

She closed the men's restroom door behind her without breaking stride, passing the stained sinks, her doppelganger following her in the mirrors. Scar visible, like a white sickle. Haunted eyes in the glass.

Yes, the Wanashono rest area was a pressure cooker. She'd almost gotten Ed and Sandi killed. She needed to *get out*. She needed to reframe this battle, to relocate it somewhere else. Somewhere without the risk of collateral damage.

I'll run, she decided. *I'll run up the highway. As fast, and as hard, as I possibly can. I won't stop until I find a signal and call 911. Or I've frozen to death.*

She checked her cracked iPhone again. The battery was now at 4 percent.

She looked up at the empty window—a triangular little slice of night sky and treetops. It was almost eight feet off the floor. Getting inside had been easy, thanks to the stacked picnic tables outside. Getting outside would be much harder. The urinal she'd hit was too far back to stand on, and even on her tiptoes, she couldn't reach the window frame. She'd need one hell of a flying leap to catch it with her fingertips. She'd need a running start, and every inch of it.

She backed up, past the green stalls, past PAUL TAKES IT

IN THE ASS, all the way to the door, her butt touching the wall, and the rectangular restroom stretched out before her like a twenty-foot runway. Smooth tile under her feet, slippery with moisture. She arched her back, dug into a runner's crouch, and closed her hands into fists.

She took a full breath—the bitter smell of ammonia. She let it halfway out.

Go.

She ran.

Mirrors, urinals, stall doors, all racing past her. Air whooshed in her ears. No time to overthink. No time to be afraid. She flattened her hands into blades, pumping her legs, and took a hurtling kamikaze leap at the tiny opening—

Midair, she thought: *This is going to hurt—*

It did. She crashed into the tile wall knees first, bruising her chin, punching the air from her lungs, but (*yes!*) she'd caught the window frame with two desperate fingertips. Fingernails in the soggy old wood. She braced her wet Converse against the wall. Then she re-arched her back, locked her elbows, and tugged her body upward, gasping through clenched teeth, like she was tackling the world's most hellish chin-up bar, and pulled and pulled and *pulled—*

She heard mouth-breathing. Outside.

No.

No, no, no, please don't be real—

But yes, there it was. Directly outside, on the other side of the wall. That gentle wheeze she knew all too well, that juicy little huff. Lars, Rodent Face, had circled around the building and now waited for her outside. Watching that window, pistol in hand, ready to put a bullet in her brain the instant she clambered up and exposed her face.

Now what?

She hung there on aching fingertips, her shoes dangling off the floor, desperately wishing she'd just misheard the growl of the wind outside. But she knew she hadn't. She knew Ashley had sent obedient little Lars out there to cut off her escape. Which left a far more cunning and dangerous enemy unaccounted for.

Then she heard the restroom door click shut.

He's in the room with—

A plastic bag tugged over Darby's face from behind. She screamed, but it was trapped inside her mouth.

1:09 A.M.

JAY NISSEN SAWED THROUGH THE LAST BAR ON THE DOG kennel.

She'd cut them one at a time, sawing with the toothed knife the way the red-haired lady had instructed. Like a miniature tree cutter. Her left hand throbbed with pins and needles, so it took a long time. Twice, she'd dropped the knife and had to grope for it in the darkness. Once, she'd feared it had bounced outside the kennel and been lost forever. But she had found it.

And now?

With a push, the grating fell away and clattered against the van's door.

This was the first time the cage had been open since they took her. She didn't know how many days ago that had been. Four? Five, probably. Going more than a night without her shots made her woozy, and since then she'd fallen into an irregular rhythm of sickly four-hour naps. The sun had been up and down, rising and falling from different windows. The smells of ketchup, ranch sauce, and stale sweat dewing on glass. The crumple of Jack in the Box wrappers. Their murmuring voices, Ashley's knee-slapping jokes, the hum of blacktop, the urgent tick of the van's turn signal. Was it a week already? What were her parents doing right now?

She hadn't even heard the brothers enter her house.

She remembered walking to the fridge for a cup of apple juice, and gasping when she saw them standing in the kitchen. They'd worn Halloween masks—a zombie to the left and a snarling werewolf to the right. Both rubber faces swiveled to look at her.

Outside, the daylight had dimmed. The sun slipping behind clouds.

By the sink, Jay also saw her family's housekeeper, Tanya, in a bright red tank top, clutching her mouth with both hands. Eyes watery, back arched, like she was fighting a sneeze.

No one had spoken, neither the housekeeper nor the monsters, and Jay remembered feeling an uncomfortable sensation, like she'd interrupted a grown-up conversation. Then Tanya looked across the room at her, lowering her hands, and Jay realized the woman's tank top had been white earlier today—not blood red. She was missing a front tooth when she spoke, calm but urgent:

Run.

But Jay hadn't. She couldn't. Something about this suspended scene in the kitchen, the three adults, the jolt of cranberry-colored blood, the dreamy strangeness of it all—

Please run, Jay—

And she'd wanted to, so badly. But she stood paralyzed,

like her bones were locked up with pins, as the monsters circled the counter, stomping blurs on her right and left—

Just run, they're here for you—

And then the werewolf's big hand gripped her shoulder, powerful but surprisingly gentle, and it was all over. He'd been a looming shadow of painted fangs and fur. He was the one she now knew to be Ashley.

Tanya's voice, heartbroken as they took her: *Why didn't you run, Jay?*

She still didn't know.

Here and now, Jamie Nissen—or Jay, as she'd been called since first grade—crawled out of the dog kennel on her palms, over the itchy blankets and towels her rescuer had hidden beneath a few hours ago. The metal bars bent and twanged around her; she hoped Ashley and Lars weren't nearby to hear. She reached the rear door of the van, expecting it to be locked. Lars had always been careful to lock the van's doors, every time he—

The handle clicked in her bloody fingers.

The door swung open.

Jay froze there on her hands and knees, peering out into the darkness. Thousands of swirling snowflakes. A shivery gust of night air. A parking lot of smooth, undisturbed white, glittering with crystals. It was strangely thrilling. She'd never seen this much snow before in her entire life.

Now what?

———————

"NOW WHAT, DARBS?"

She couldn't breathe or see. Plastic stretched tight over

her face, suctioning against her front teeth. Knuckled hands around her throat, twisting the bag, squeezing her airway shut. Slippery, buried-alive panic.

"Shh, shh."

She thrashed but Ashley was too strong. He had her arms twisted backward in some kind of wrestling hold. Both of her shoulder blades were wrenched together and her hands were somewhere far behind her, pinned and useless. Like she was fighting the embrace of a straitjacket. She kicked, her feet searching for the restroom wall to use as leverage, but found only empty space. Her backbone cracked.

"Don't fight," he whispered. "It's all fine."

Pressure building inside her chest. Her lungs burning, swelling against her rib cage. She felt her own last breath—a half gasp that had been inside her throat when the bag came down—trapped against her face, foggy and wet. Warm copper spreading down her chin. Her nose was bleeding again.

And again she fought, twisting, flailing. Her legs kicked out into space. Her fingers clawed and scratched; she found the loop of the lanyard in his jacket. Keys jingled. But there was no gun, no weapon to grab. She was losing energy, too. This thrash had been weaker than the first.

This is it, she realized. *I'm going to die here.*

Right here, in a dingy restroom off State Route Six. Next to the bleached toilets, the scratched mirrors, the peeling stall doors scrawled with graffiti. Right here, right now, with that Lysol taste still in her mouth.

"Shh." Ashley moved his head like he was checking over his shoulder. "It's almost over. Just let it happen—"

She screamed silently inside the Ziploc bag. The plastic

flexed a small bubble. Then her lungs reflexively inhaled—a bracing gulp—but found only negative pressure, sucking a scant few centimeters of reused air.

"I know it hurts. I know. I'm sorry." The bag twisted tighter, clockwise, and now she saw the window. Through one clamped eye, blurred by cloudy plastic and tears, she saw that little triangular window, eight feet off the floor, dusted with snowflakes. So close. So agonizingly close. Somehow, she wished it were farther away, across the room, hopeless and unreachable. But no, it was *right there*, and she could almost reach out and touch it, if only her hands weren't pinned.

She thrashed a third time, but it was uncoordinated and limp. This time Ashley barely had to hold her. She knew this was the last one, that there couldn't possibly be a fourth rally. She was a goner now. Ed and Sandi were in the same building, on the other side of a door, ten feet away, oblivious while she suffocated to death in the arms of a killer. She felt time dilate. A thick and comfortable rest settled over her, like a heavy wool blanket.

She hated how good it felt.

"Rest now." Ashley planted a wet smooch on the top of her head, crinkling the plastic. "You tried real hard, Darbs. Get some rest now."

His revolting voice was so far away. It sounded like he was in another room. Speaking to someone else. Smothering some other girl to death. The ache in her lungs was already fading. All of these awful sensations were happening to someone else, not to Darby Thorne.

Her mind wandered, disconnecting, drifting, taking stock of all the unfinished items in her life. Her capstone painting, incomplete. Her Stafford loans, unpaid. Her Gmail password, locked forever. Her bank account with $291 in it. Her dorm room. Her wall of gravestone rubbings. Her mother at Utah Valley Hospital, waking from surgery, about to learn that her daughter had been randomly murdered at a rest stop three hundred miles away from—

No.

She fought it.

No, no, no—

She held on to this, to forty-nine-year-old Maya Thorne, languishing in the ICU. Because if Darby died right here, right now, in this restroom, she'd never get to apologize for all the things she'd said to her mother on Thanksgiving. It would all become unchangeable history. Every ugly word of it.

And suddenly she wasn't afraid. Not anymore. She tasted something far more useful than fear—anger. She was livid. She was absolutely *fucking furious* at the unfairness of it all, of what Ashley was attempting to do to her and her family, raging hard against the enveloping darkness. And something else . . .

If I die here, she knew, *no one will save Jay.*

". . . Darbs?"

She arched her back, and commanded her weary lungs to do one final task—to open and inhale as hard as possible. To suck the plastic airtight against her open mouth, so it was contracted between her front teeth like bubble gum, just a thin, withdrawn centimeter—

She bit down.

Not hard enough. The plastic slipped out of her mouth.

"Pancreatic cancer?" Ashley's lips slithered against her ear, like he'd read her mind. "Your mom has . . . you said pancreatic cancer, right?"

She tried again. She sucked the bag taut with burning lungs. Bit down.

Nothing.

"Isn't it funny, then?" His dense grip, his rotten voice. "You were so certain you'd bury your mom, but it turns out you had it backward, you dumb cunt, because *she's going to bury you—*"

Darby bit down again, and the plastic ripped.

A pinprick of ice-cold air whistled inside. Racing down her throat in a pressurized rush, like it came through a straw.

Ashley paused—"Oh"—and in a half second of confusion, his grip weakened and Darby's shoes touched the floor. A half second was all she needed. She found her footing, kicked off the tile, and hurled her body backward into his.

Ashley stumbled, off balance.

She kept running backward, kept pushing him—

He gasped: "Wait, wait, *wait—*"

She rammed him, back-first, into a sink. Vertebrae against porcelain. The faucet clicked on, knocked by an elbow. He grunted and released, her arms twisting from his grip. Her hands finally free. She grabbed the wet bag and ripped it off her face, sucking in a full breath. An inverted scream, clogged with blood, snot, and tears.

She saw color again. Air on her cheeks. Oxygen in her blood. She fell away from him, her knees mushy, catching herself on the floor with an outstretched palm. Cold tiles, speckled with her blood.

Behind her, Ashley pulled something from his pocket.

He raised an arm—

———————

—AND HE SWUNG THE ROCK-IN-A-SOCK AT THE BACK OF Darby's head, arcing the stone like a whipping bola, ready for the wet-porcelain crunch of the girl's skull—but she was already scrambling forward, moving away.

It swiped her hair.

He lunged after her, off balance from his swing, the rock banging off the wall to his left, chipping the tile. He hit his knees and watched her break away and sprint down the restroom, toward that little triangular window, with the plastic bag fluttering behind her. *She won't make it*, he told himself. But in another instant, she'd vaulted up to the window frame, caught herself by her fingernails, and hurled her body through the tiny opening like a gymnast. Ankles up, then out.

Just like that.

She was gone.

Ashley Garver was suddenly alone in the restroom. He staggered upright, nearly slipping on the bloodstained Ziploc bag.

It didn't matter, he realized, slicking his hair back with a palm, catching his breath. He'd assigned Lars to cover the outside back wall, by the stacked picnic tables, for this very situation. His brother, armed with that trusty Beretta Cougar, was the backup. Darby had escaped his restroom kill zone, yes, but in doing so she'd practically dropped herself into Lars's arms, and now she was too weak to effectively fight back—

The restroom door banged open behind him. He whirled, expecting to see the befuddled face of Ed, here to investigate the racket, and he already had a story prepared—*I slipped on the wet floor, I think I hit my head*—only it wasn't Ed standing there in the doorway.

It was Lars.

Ashley kicked the plastic bag. "Oh, *come on*."

"You sounded like you, ah, needed help—"

"Yes. I needed you out there."

"Oh—"

"Out *there*." Ashley pointed furiously. "*Outside*, not inside."

Lars's eyes widened, darting from his big brother to the empty window. He realized what he'd done, what he'd allowed to happen, and his face crumpled and reddened with sloppy tears: "I'm sorry. I'm so sorry, I didn't mean to—"

Ashley kissed him on the lips.

"Focus, baby brother." He slapped his cheek. "The parking lot. That's where she's running, right now."

He hoped he could still run, too. His lower back throbbed where the redhead had slammed him into the porcelain sink. And as he collected his senses, he noticed something else. A sudden lightness in his right jeans pocket.

His lanyard was gone.

"And . . . the bitch took our keys."

DARBY TUMBLED DOWN THE STACKED PICNIC TABLES, LANDing hard. She dropped Ashley's keys in the snow but recovered them, clambering upright.

The red lanyard had become hooked around her thumb in

the scuffle. Pure luck, really. When she'd charged him into the sink and broken free, the payload of clattering keys had come with her. Now she had them. And he didn't.

They jingled in her palm. A half dozen mismatched keys, and a black thumb drive. She stuffed the whole handful into her pocket as a new plan took shape.

What's better than running for help?

Stealing the abductors' van and *driving* for help.

With Jay inside.

A desperate gamble. She was still in shock, her fingers still slick with sweat, her breaths still surging. Her mind raced with panicked thoughts. She wasn't sure if the Astro could drive any farther than Blue could in Snowmageddon, but she'd sure as hell try. She'd stomp on the gas, rock the four-wheel drive on its shocks, try everything. She had no other options. If she stayed here at Wanashono, Ashley and Lars would murder her.

She circled the building, wading through snowdrifts, and the night air stung her throat. She passed the crowd of half-buried Nightmare Children to her left. Chewed bronze forms in the darkness, pit-bull-mauling victims frozen in playtime. That bare flagpole, wobbling under another razor-sharp gust of wind.

Ahead, the parking lot. The cars. Their van.

Just another fifty feet—

The visitor center's front door squeaked open behind her. A rectangle of projected light, and she cast a staggering shadow on the snow. A pair of crunchy footsteps followed her. The door shut and her shadow vanished.

"No." Ashley's voice, firm, like he was scolding a dog: "Don't shoot her."

She slipped, slashing a knee on jagged ice. Kept running. The pursuing footsteps flanked her now, one moving right, one cutting left. Like wolves circling their prey. She recognized them by their breathing—the congested pant of Lars on the left, the controlled huffs of Ashley on the right. She kept running and focused on the Astro. Keys jangling in her hand.

"Lars! *Don't shoot her.*"

"She's trying to steal the van—"

"You want a yellow card?"

She slipped again, catching herself. Her purse bounced off her knee. She was just ten paces from the kidnappers' vehicle now. She could see the cartoon fox on the side, racing closer, still holding that orange nail gun—

"She won't get anywhere. The snow's too deep—"

"What if she does?"

"She won't."

"What if she *does*, Ashley?"

Darby skidded, reaching the driver door, her heart thudding in her throat. She palmed snow off the lock and fumbled for the keychain, but it was too dark to identify the Chevy key. At least three of them felt thick enough to be car keys. She tried the first one. It didn't fit. She tried the second one. It fit but didn't turn—

"She's unlocking the door—"

She was on the third key, jamming it into the icy lock, when she noticed something to the right. A minor detail, but wildly wrong.

The Astro's rear door.

It should have been shut—but it hung ajar, the glass reflecting a scythe of lamplight, the upper edge collecting a rim of snowflakes. Darby hadn't left it open. It couldn't possibly have been Lars or Ashley. That left . . . Jay?

Lars panted. "She's . . . she's stopping."

"I know."

"Why's she stopping?"

As both pairs of footsteps drew closer, Ashley understood. "Oh *hell*."

1:23 A.M.

FROM HER ANGLE, DARBY COULDN'T QUITE SEE IT.

But she knew what Ashley saw—Jay's dog kennel clumsily sawed apart from the inside, the Astro's rear door pushed open, and a pair of small footprints leading out into the darkness.

He stared, mouth agape with dull shock, before glancing back to Darby: "If she tries to run, shoot her."

She turned—but Lars had already circled the van and appeared behind her with that stubby handgun held waist-high, aimed at her stomach.

She caught her breath. Surrounded again.

"I don't . . . I don't believe it." Ashley paced, his fingers digging into his scalp, and Darby noticed his hairline was every bit as severe as his younger brother's. He grew his bangs out to cover the receding bits.

She couldn't help but feel a grim satisfaction. She loved it. For all of Ashley's smugness and posturing tonight, she'd still managed to hurl one hell of a wrench into their plan. Little Jaybird was loose.

Ashley kicked the Astro's side, bruising the metal. "I don't *fucking* believe it—"

Lars edged back.

But Darby couldn't resist. There was too much white-hot adrenaline in her veins. Two minutes ago, he'd been asphyxiating her with a plastic bag and she was still furious about that, still bristling with reckless energy. "Hey, Ashley. I'm no expert on kidnappings, but doesn't it only work if there's a kid in there?"

He turned to face her.

She shrugged. "Just my amateur opinion."

"You . . ." Lars raised his pistol. "You should stop—"

"And you should eat a goddamn *breath mint*." Darby looked back to Ashley, her words shivery and raw, unspooling like twine: "Are you sure about that little speech of yours? Helpless humans just letting the big, scary monsters do their thing? Because I think I just *influenced the plot*, motherfucker—"

He stomped toward her.

She flinched, regretting her momentary loss of control, and Ashley raised the rock-in-a-sock as he charged, winding up for a skull-fracturing impact, but then at the last instant he sidestepped past her and threw it.

She opened her eyes.

He'd been aiming at a streetlight. Two hundred feet away. After a few airy moments of flight, the rock hit the post squarely, bouncing off the metal with a warbling clang. It echoed twice.

Most NFL quarterbacks couldn't do that.

Lars whispered: "Magic."

I'm a magic man, Lars, my brother.

They'd been toying with her this entire night, she realized. Manipulating her. Pretending to be strangers, working the room, dropping flagrant lies and obtuse little hints and studying how she reacted. Like a rat in their maze.

Can you cut a girl in half?

I can. But you only win gold if she survives.

That roomful of anxious laughter rang again inside her brain, as tinny as microphone feedback. Her migraine had returned.

Ashley wiped saliva from his mouth and turned back to Darby, his breath curling in the mountain air. "You don't get it yet, Darbs. It's all right. You will."

Get what?

This gave her a sick chill. Her adrenaline high, her crazy-stupid fearlessness—it was all slipping away, fading like a weak buzz. Two beers, fun while they last, but gone by dessert.

Lars peered inside the van. "How long ago did she break out?"

Ashley was pacing again. Thinking.

The silence made Darby uneasy. Like any good showman, Ashley was difficult to read, telegraphing his violence only when he meant to. His younger brother still dutifully held her at gunpoint, never letting the barrel touch her back. Never letting the weapon bob within grabbing distance.

Lars asked again. "How long ago did she break out?"

Again, Ashley didn't answer. He stopped with his hands

on his hips, studying Jay's footprints in the snow. They led north. Away from the rest stop. Up the rising land, past the overpass, along the on-ramp. Toward State Route Six.

His words simmered in her mind. *You don't get it yet, Darbs. You will.*

She estimated, based on the powder that had accumulated atop the van's rear door, that Jay had broken out and escaped roughly twenty minutes ago. Before the attack in the restroom, at least. The girl's footprints were already growing faint, filling in with dusty snowflakes.

"What's that?" Lars asked.

Ashley knelt to retrieve something that looked like a wrinkled black snakeskin. But Darby recognized it—the electrical tape they'd sealed over Jay's mouth. She'd discarded it here as she fled.

Wisely, Jay had avoided the visitor center, because she'd known Ashley and Lars were inside. So she'd gone for the highway, probably in hope of flagging down a passerby and calling the police—except the poor girl didn't know where she was. She didn't know they were well beyond the outskirts of Gold Bar, well beyond the outskirts of *anything* notable, nine thousand feet above sea level. She didn't know it was six uphill miles to the summit and ten downhill to Icicle Creek; that this bleak, wind-shredded climate might as well belong to Antarctica.

Jay was an affluent city kid from San Diego—a land of yucca palms, sandals, and sixty-degree winters.

Darby raked her mind, her head now throbbing like a hangover—what had Jay been wearing inside the kennel? A thin coat. That red Poké Ball T-shirt. Light pants. No gloves. No weather protection at all.

Finally, in a flash of horror, she *got* it.

So did Lars. "She's going to freeze to death out there—"

"We'll follow her tracks," Ashley said.

"But she could be a mile down the road—"

"We'll call out to her."

"She won't come to our voices."

"You're right." Ashley nodded to Darby. "But she'll come to *hers*."

Now both brothers were looking at her.

For a moment, the wind faded and the parking lot fell silent. Only the gentle patter of snowflakes landing around them, as Darby quietly realized why Ashley hadn't already killed her.

"Well, here we go." He shrugged. "I guess that puts us on the same team, huh? Neither of us wants a black-fingered little Jay-cicle."

Jokes. Everything was a joke to him.

She said nothing.

He clicked a pocket flashlight, spotlighting the girl's footprints with a blue-white LED beam. Snowflakes ignited like sparks. Then he aimed the light into Darby's face, an eye-watering brightness. "Start calling her name."

Darby stared at her feet, tasting stomach acid in her throat. A rancid, greasy sort of heartburn, bubbling with terrible thoughts. *I shouldn't have given her that knife. What if, by intervening tonight, I made things worse?*

What if I got Jay killed?

Lars's pistol jabbed her spine, a harsh gesture that meant *walk*. If she'd been ready for it, she could've spun around, swiped for the gun, and maybe, just maybe, seized control of it. But the opportunity passed.

"Her name is Jamie," Lars said. "But call her Jay."

"Go on. Follow the tracks and start hollering." Ashley swept his LED light at the footprints, and then looked back at her with darkening eyes. "You wanted to save her life so badly? Well, Darbs, here's your chance."

THE GIRL'S FOOTPRINTS LED THEM ALONG THE ON-RAMP TO the dirty ice banks of State Route Six before veering into the woods, up a rocky slope of snowdrifts and perched fir trees. Every step of the way, Darby silently dreaded reaching the end of these tracks and finding a small crumpled body in a red Poké Ball shirt. Instead, something even worse happened— Jay's footprints simply vanished, erased by windswept snow.

Darby cupped her hands and shouted again: "Jay."

It had been thirty minutes now. Her voice was raw.

Up here, the only navigational landmark was the sulking shadow of Melanie's Peak, due east. The land grew steeper around them. Boulders broke through the snowpack, granite faces glazed with rivulets of ice. The trees here teetered on shallow roots, leaning over, branches sagging. Sticks snapped underfoot, like tiny bones breaking in the snow.

"Jay Nissen." Darby swept the flashlight, throwing jagged shadows. "If you can hear me, come to my voice."

No answer. Only the stiff creak of the trees.

"It's safe," she added. "Ashley and Lars aren't here."

She hated lying.

But coaxing Jay out of hiding was the poor girl's only chance at survival now. Possible death at the hands of the Garver brothers was still better than certain death in a subzero blizzard. Right? It made sense, but she still despised herself for lying. It was humiliating. Made her feel naked. She felt like Ashley's little pet, speaking obediently on his behalf, her nostrils still crusted with dried blood from when he'd recently slammed her face into a table.

The brothers followed her but kept their distance, lingering ten paces back on her left and right. They were cloaked in darkness while Darby carried the only source of illumination—Ashley's LED flashlight. This was all according to Ashley's plan. Jay wouldn't dare emerge if she saw her abductors stalking behind Darby, holding her at gunpoint. At least, that had been the idea.

So far, it hadn't worked.

Jamie Nissen. The missing daughter of some wealthy San Diego family with a Christmas tree towering over a pile of unopened presents. Now she was somewhere out here in the howling Rockies, her fingertips blackening with frostbite, her organs shutting down, buried by flurried snowflakes, tears icing on her cheeks and freezing her eyelids shut. They might have already stepped over her little body, five minutes back, without even noticing.

Hypothermia is a peaceful way to go, Darby recalled reading somewhere. Apparently the discomfort of coldness passes quickly, replaced by a warm stupor. You drift off into a dumb sleep, oblivious to the awful damage inflicted upon your extremities. Crunchy fingers, dark blisters of necrotic flesh. She hoped Jay hadn't suffered.

She called out again into the darkness.

Still no answer.

To her left, she heard Lars whisper, "How much longer?"

To her right, "As long as it takes."

She knew Ashley wasn't stupid—he was running the same numbers in his mind. Thirty minutes spent following these half-gone footprints, plus a twenty-minute head start (at least), meant Jay's chances of survival in these freezing woods were poor, and getting worse every second.

Half-heartedly, Darby assessed her own options at gunpoint. Fight? Get shot. Run? Get shot in the back. She considered turning and shining the flashlight into the gunmen's eyes to blind them, but their pupils were already adjusted to the light. This was problem number one. And even if she *could* blind them for a few seconds, the snowbound terrain was too rough for a quick escape—which was problem number two.

To her left, Lars fretted. "What if we got Jay killed?"

To her right: "We didn't."

"What if we did?"

"We didn't, baby brother." A pause. "*She* might have, though."

This hit Darby like a dagger twisting in her gut. How painfully right Ashley was. It made sense, in an evil way. If she hadn't intervened tonight, Jay would still be penned up in that dog kennel inside their van, captive but very much alive. Icy fingers reached around her stomach and slowly, oh so slowly, began to squeeze. *Why did I have to get involved? Why couldn't I have just called the cops in the morning?*

She tried to focus on her own survival, on solving problem number one (the light) and problem number two (the terrain), but she couldn't.

She wished she could rewind this horrible night and undo her decisions. All of them. Every choice she'd made since she first peered through that frosty window and saw Jay's hand grasping that kennel bar. She wished she'd been content to simply play detective and gather information. She could have waited quietly until the morning, held her advantage, and maybe after the snowplows arrived and the rest-stop refugees went their separate ways, she could have discreetly tailed Ashley and Lars's van in her Honda. A quarter mile back, one hand on the steering wheel, her iPhone in the other, feeding the Colorado State Patrol detailed information. She still could have saved Jay.

(And Mom still would have pancreatic cancer.)

But no. Instead, Darby Elizabeth Thorne, a college sophomore with zero law enforcement or military training, had tried to take matters into her own hands. And now here she was, walking through the woods with a .45 aimed at her back, searching for a dead child.

To her right, a morbid laugh. "Gotta say, Darbs, as far as good Samaritans go, you're batting a thousand. First you confide in one of the abductors, and then you get the abductee killed. Nice work."

Everything was a joke to Ashley Garver. Even this, somehow.

Christ, she *loathed* him.

But now she wondered—had he been telling her the truth after all? Maybe it really was a textbook ransom plot, just like he'd described to her, and postpayment, the brothers really had intended to return Jay to her family alive. She imagined them jettisoning her at some barren bus stop in flyover country. Little Jaybird blinking in the Kansas sun after two weeks of darkness, rushing to the nearest stranger on a bench, begging them to call her parents—

Until Darby had intervened, that is. And handed the girl a Swiss Army knife so she could escape into a hostile climate she was utterly unprepared for. And then another venomous thought slipped into Darby's mind—she felt guilty for even thinking it, given what had already happened—but it burrowed in like a splinter.

They're going to kill me now.

Darby was certain of this.

Now that Jay is lost, now that they don't need my voice. And now that—

———

NOW THAT THEY WERE BEYOND EARSHOT OF THE REST area, Lars had been waiting for permission to shoot Darby in the back of the head, and Ashley had finally given it to him. The phrase "batting a thousand" was the tipoff.

It meant *kill.*

It was called Spy Code. Since they'd been kids, Ashley had buried dozens of secret messages within everyday dialogue. "Lucky me" meant *stay.* "Lucky you" meant *go.* "Extra cheese" meant *run like hell.* "Ace of spades" meant *pretend we're strangers.* Failure to obey a coded message meant an instant yellow card, and Lars's fingers were pocked with the pale scars of past errors. Tonight had already seen one frighteningly close call—he'd nearly missed "ace of spades" back at the rest area.

But he'd known this one was coming.

The pistol was ice cold in his hand. His skin stuck to the metal. It was a Beretta Cougar, a stout, stubby firearm that bulged under his coat and never felt quite right in his hands. Like gripping a big jelly bean. The Cougar was usually chambered in 9 millimeter, but this particular model was the 8045, so it fired the fatter .45 ACP cartridge. More stopping power, but punchier recoil and fewer rounds stored in the clip (the *magazine*, Ashley insisted). Eight shots, single-stacked.

Lars liked it well enough. But he'd secretly wished for the Beretta 92FS instead, like the iconic pistol that the hard-boiled detective Max Payne dual-wields in his series of Xbox games. He would never admit this to Ashley, of course. The gun had been a gift. You never, ever question Ashley's gifts, or his punishments. That's just how big brothers are—one day he'd brought Lars a stray cat from the shelter. A peppy little torbie (a mix between a tortoiseshell and a tabby) with a loud, rumbly purr. Lars had named her Stripes. Then, the next day, Ashley drenched Stripes in gasoline and hurled her into a campfire.

Like any big brother, I giveth, and I taketh away.

Lars raised the Beretta Cougar now.

As they walked, he aimed at the back of Darby's head (*aim small, miss small*). The painted night sights aligned; two neon green dots traced a vertical line up her backbone. She was still a few paces ahead of them, sweeping Ashley's flashlight through the trees, her body silhouetted perfectly by her own light. She had no idea.

He started to squeeze the trigger.

To his right, Ashley plugged his ear, bracing for the gun-shot. And Darby kept trudging through the knee-deep snow, aiming the flashlight ahead, unaware that she was inhabiting the last few seconds of her life, unaware that Lars's index finger was tightening around the Beretta's trigger, applying smooth pressure, a half ounce from drilling a .45-caliber hollow-point right through her—

She clicked the flashlight off.

Blackness.

———————

DARBY HEARD THEIR STARTLED VOICES BEHIND HER: "I can't see—"

"What happened?"

"She turned off the flashlight—"

"*Shoot her*, Lars—"

She ran like hell. Staggering through deep snow. Hard gasps stinging her throat. She'd night-blinded them both. Not by flashing them with the LED beam, which their pupils had already adjusted to—but by *taking it away*. She'd been shielding her own eyes to preserve her night vision. This was her solution to problem number one. As for problem number two—

Ashley's voice came from behind her, calm but urgent: "Give me the gun."

"Can you see her?"

"Give me the gun, baby brother—"

Even downhill, it was like running in waist-deep water. Lurching over snowdrifts, dodging trees, stumbling, banging a knee against icy rock, recovering, her heartbeat thudding in her ears, no time to stop, *don't stop*—

Ashley's voice rose: "I see her."

"How can you see her?"

He kept an eye shut, she realized with rising panic. *Just like I taught him*—

He shouted after her: "Thanks for the trick, Darbs—"

He was aiming at her right now, taking a marksman's stance. She felt the pistol's sights tingling on her back like a laser. Inescapable. No chance to outrun him. Just dwindling microseconds now, as Darby executed her desperate solution to problem number two—

What's faster than running?

Falling.

She hurled herself downhill.

The world inverted. She saw a whirl of black sky and frozen branches, plunging in a half second of free fall, and then a wall of shorn granite rushed up to meet her. Thunderous impact. Stars pierced her vision. She lost the flashlight. She rolled on knees and elbows, kicking up flecks of snow in a bruising tumble—

"Where is she?"

"I see her—"

Ten somersaults down, the ground flattened again and she landed hard and dizzy with ice down her shirt. She scrambled upright. Kept going. Hurtled through prickly undergrowth with outstretched hands, branches snapping against her palms, slashing bare skin. Then the terrain dropped again, and again she fell—

Their voices growing distant: "I . . . I lost her."

"There, there —"

Sliding on her back now. Fir trunks whooshing past. Right. Left. Right. No stop this time. The slope kept going, and so did she, slip-sliding over ramped snowdrifts, accelerating to dangerous speed. She raised her arms, trying to slow herself, but hit another rock shelf. Another impact punched the air from her chest, rag-dolling her sideways. Up and down lost all meaning. Her world became a violent tumble-dryer, an endless, crashing kaleidoscope.

Then it ended.

It took her a few seconds to realize she'd even stopped rolling. She'd landed sprawled on her back, her eardrums ringing, a dozen new bruises throbbing on her body. Time seemed to blur. For a dreamy moment, she nearly blacked out.

To her left, a fir tree made a strange little shiver, dropping an armful of snow and peppering her with wood chips.

Then she heard an echo from uphill—like a whipcrack—and she understood exactly what had happened, and she staggered upright and kept running.

———————

ASHLEY BLINKED AWAY THE BERETTA'S MUZZLE FLASH AND aimed for a second shot, but he'd lost her amid the brush and studded boulders. There was too much tree cover.

He lowered the pistol. Smoke curling in the air.

"Did you get her?" Lars asked.

"I don't think so."

"She's . . . she's getting away—"

"It's fine." He started downslope, descending carefully, finding footholds on snow-crested rock. "We'll catch her at the bottom."

"What if she gets back inside and tells Ed—"

"She ran the wrong way." Ashley pointed downhill with the gun. "See? Dumb bitch is going north. Deeper into the woods."

"Oh."

"The rest stop is back that way. *South*."

"Okay."

"Come on, baby brother." He tucked the pistol into his

jacket pocket and extended both arms for balance, his boots on slick stone. He found his LED flashlight upright in the snow where she'd dropped it.

As he scooped it up, he noticed something in the distance, something incongruous—the white shadow of Melanie's Peak. The same eastern landmark as always, cloaked in low clouds, but now it loomed on his *right* horizon. Not his left.

Which meant south was actually . . .

"Oh." Suddenly he understood. "Oh, that *bitch*."

"What?"

"She . . . she must have turned us around. She's running back to the building—"

DARBY WAS WITHIN EYESHOT OF THE REST AREA NOW.

Like a campfire in the darkness, tugging her closer with every aching step. The warm amber glow of the visitor center's single window, the parked cars, the flagpole and the half-buried Nightmare Children—

In the woods behind her, Ashley howled: "Daaaarby."

No enunciation, no readable emotion—just her name, resounding in shrieking singsong from the darkness beyond. It chilled her blood.

She'd bought herself some time. Not quite ten minutes, but enough time to steal the brothers' Astro (the keys were still in the door) and attempt a getaway. Fifty-fifty chance she'd even make it out of the submerged parking lot, but hell, those were better odds than she had in her own Honda, and probably the best she'd had all night. She thought about poor little Jay as she ran, and it hit her again like a crushing wave, a swarm of terrible thoughts racing behind her, biting at her with wicked teeth—

Why did I get involved?

She couldn't think about it.

This is my fault—

Not now.

Oh Jesus, I got a kid killed tonight—

She was approaching the parking lot, passing a green signboard, when Ashley shouted at her again from the trees, closer behind her now, his voice cracking into an ugly adolescent pitch: "We're going to catch you."

The Astro was fifty feet away. The snow was shallower in the parking lot, and it renewed her energy; she launched into a faster, lighter sprint. She passed an indistinct form buried under swept snow—what she'd initially believed to be Ashley's car. From this new angle, she glimpsed green metal. Pits of vertical rust. A white stencil. Under the snowpack, it wasn't a parked car at all—it was a *Dumpster.*

I should've known. I should've looked closer—

She kept running, heaving steps, the air stinging her throat, her calves burning, her joints aching. The kidnappers' Astro van coming closer.

She wished she'd never stopped at this stupid rest stop. She wished she'd never left her hometown for college last year. *Why can't I be like my sister, Devon?* Who was perfectly happy waiting tables at the Cheesecake Factory in Provo? Who vacuumed Mom's house every Sunday morning? Who had "Strength in Chinese" tattooed on her shoulder blade?

The Astro van was now thirty feet away.

Twenty.

Ten.

"And when we catch you, you little bitch, *I'll make you beg for that Ziploc bag—*"

She hit the Astro's driver door with her palms. Snow globs slid off the bumpy glass. Ashley's lanyard was still dangling in the lock, where she'd left it. She opened the door and glanced to the Wanashono building. She could twist the keys in the ignition, right now, and attempt an escape. And maybe she'd make it. Maybe she wouldn't.

But it would be a death sentence for Ed and Sandi.

Thinking a move ahead, she knew the brothers would then have no choice but to murder them both for the keys to Sandi's truck, so they could chase Darby down and kill her on the highway.

No, I can't leave Ed and Sandi.

I can't get anyone else killed tonight.

She wavered, gripping the open door for balance. Her knees were slushy; she almost collapsed inside. The ignition was *right there,* close enough to touch. The steering wheel was sticky, duct-taped in patches. A crunchy sea of Taco Bell trash lay on the floor. Lars's plastic model airplane. The van's interior was still as warm and moist as an exhaled breath, the upholstery still reeking of clammy sweat, dog blankets, and the piss and vomit of a dead girl.

The ignition was *right there.*

No. The snow was too deep. She'd seen the highway with her own eyes. State Route Six was buried, unrecognizable, all hopeless powder. Four-wheel drive or not, the Astro would high-center in seconds, trapping her on the on-ramp, and then the brothers would run her down and shoot her through the window—

What if it doesn't?

What if this, right now, is my only chance to escape?

The keys chattered in her right hand. She closed a fist around them. She desperately wanted to slide into the killers' vehicle, to turn the engine, to shift into gear, to just try to drive it, to *just please try*—

Coming closer: "Daaaaarby—"

Make a choice.

So she did.

She slammed the door. Pocketed Ashley's keys. And, with the Brothers Garver still pursuing somewhere behind her, she circled around the vehicle on aching bones and ran for the orange glow of the visitor center. She had to warn Ed and Sandi. She had to do the right thing. They'd all escape the Wanashono rest area together. No one else would die tonight.

Ed and Sandi, I can still save you both.

She had, at best, sixty seconds before Ashley and Lars caught up to her. Sixty seconds to make a new plan. She looked back at that cartoon fox, at the nail gun in its furry hand, that stupid slogan now a ghoulish promise:

WE FINISH WHAT WE START.

2:16 A.M.

DARBY FROZE IN THE DOORWAY.

Ed was murmuring something ("No signal this far from ") and stopped midsentence when he saw her, midstep near Espresso Peak with his Android in his palm. Sandi was kneeling by the table, and she whirled to face Darby, revealing a tiny shape standing behind her.

It was . . . it was Jay.

Oh, thank God.

The girl's dark hair was speckled with snowflakes. Her cheeks were rash red. She was shrouded in Sandi's bumblebee-yellow parka, dwarfed by its saggy sleeves. This was the first time Darby had seen the girl in full light, outside of that dog kennel, and for a shivery moment, she wanted only to close the distance between them, to lift this little child she barely knew and squeeze her into a bracing hug.

You turned around.

Oh, thank God, Jay, we lost your tracks but you turned around.

Sandi stood up, a black pepper-spray canister raised in a knuckled hand, her eyes rock hard. "Not one step closer."

Jay grabbed her wrist. "No. She rescued me—"

"Sandi," Ed hissed. "For Christ's sake—"

The door banged shut behind Darby, jolting her back into the moment. She tried to figure—how far behind her were the brothers now? A hundred yards? Fifty? She caught her breath, tears in her eyes, struggling to speak: "They're coming. They're armed, and they're right behind me—"

Ed knew who *they* were. "You're sure they're armed?"

"Yeah." She locked the deadbolt.

"With what?"

"They have a gun."

"Have you seen it?"

"Trust me, *they have a gun*." Darby glanced from Ed to Sandi, now realizing the deadbolt was pointless. "And they will *not* stop until we're dead. We need to take your truck and drive. Right now."

"What if they chase us?" Sandi asked.

"They won't." Darby showed her Ashley's keys.

Ed stopped pacing behind her, considering this. He seemed to like it.

Darby realized the ex-veterinarian was holding a lug wrench in his right hand, half-concealed under his Carhartt sleeve. A blunt weapon. He stepped past her, wiping sweat from his eyebrow. "Okay. Okay, Darby, keep your Honda keys on you, too. We can't have them stealing your car and following us—"

Jay stood up. "Let's *go*, then."

Darby liked her already.

And she noticed a yellow bracelet glinting on Jay's wrist. She hadn't seen it before in the murky darkness of the kidnappers' van. It looked vaguely medical. She wondered briefly—*What is that?*

No time to ask. Everyone crowded up to the front door, and Ed unlatched the deadbolt with a hard swipe. He rallied the group, like a reluctant coach. "On three, we'll, uh . . . we're all going to run to the truck. Okay?"

Darby nodded, noticing the odor of vodka on his breath. "Sounds good."

"Are they out there?"

Sandi peered out the smudged window. "I . . . I don't see them yet."

"All right. Sandi, you'll take Jay to the front seat and start the engine. Give it gas and go drive, reverse, drive, reverse—"

"I know *how to drive in the snow,* Eddie."

"And Dara, you're at the back tires with me, so we can push."

"Deal."

He pointed at Jay, snapping his fingers: "And somebody carry her."

Sandi hoisted the girl over her shoulder, despite her protests ("No, I can run too.") and checked the window again. "They'll get here any minute—"

"Don't try to fight them. Just run like hell," Ed whispered, leaning against the door, starting the count: "One."

Run like hell.

Darby lowered into a shaky runner's crouch at the back of the group, behind Sandi, feeling her tired calves burn. No weapons—they would only slow her down. From the door, she recalled it was fifty feet to the parking lot, over a narrow footpath cut into the snow.

"Two." Ed twisted the doorknob.

She rehearsed the next minute in her mind. She estimated the four of them could run fifty feet in maybe . . . twenty seconds? Thirty? Another ten seconds to pile into the truck, for Sandi to fumble her keys into the ignition. More time for the Ford to start moving, slogging through the dense snow. And that was assuming Ed and Darby wouldn't need to push it. Or dig the tires out. Or scrape the windows.

And somehow, in the back of her mind, she knew: *It's been too long.*

Ashley and Lars were only a minute or so behind me.

They're back already—

"Three." Ed opened the door—

Darby grabbed his wrist, vise-tight, all fingernails. "Stop—"

"What're you doing?"

"Stop-stop-stop," she said, panic tightening in her chest. "They're here already. They're hiding behind the cars. They're *waiting for us out there—*"

"How do you know?"

"I just do."

———————

"I SEE LARS," SANDI WHISPERED FROM THE WINDOW, HER hands cupped against the glass. "He's . . . he's crouched out there. Behind my truck."

Clever bastards.

"I see him, too," said Ed.

Darby relocked the deadbolt. "They were going to ambush us."

It would have been bad. The brothers could've gunned them all down, catching them single-file on that narrow path with nowhere to run. Target practice. It gave Darby a sickly shot of adrenaline, as sour as tequila—they'd been one poor decision away from being murdered. Her gut feeling had just saved their lives.

Clever, clever, clever.

"How did you know?" Ed asked her again.

"It's . . . it's what I would've done." Darby shrugged. "If I were them."

Jay smiled. "I'm glad you're not."

"I think I see Ashley, too," Sandi said. "Behind the van."

Darby imagined Ashley Garver out there in the cold, crouched in the snow with his green eyes trained on the door. She hoped he was disappointed. She hoped he was realizing, right now, that his nasty little trap had failed, that his prey had outwitted him for the third or fourth time tonight. She hoped he was keeping score. She hoped the self-proclaimed *magic man* was getting pissed off.

Sandi squinted through the glass. "I can't . . . I can't tell what they're doing—"

"They're guarding the cars," Darby said.

Ashley's words echoed in her mind, like half-remembered strands of a nightmare: *We're going to catch you. And when we do, you little bitch, I'll make you beg for that Ziploc bag—*

At the window, Ed tugged Sandi's shoulder. "Stay down."

"I see them. They're moving—"

"Stay away from the *goddamn* window, Sandi. They're going to shoot you."

Darby chewed her lip, knowing Ed was right—the glass was a major structural weakness. A bullet, or even a big rock, and the two brothers could climb the snowdrift and slide inside.

She stood in the center of the room, spotlighted under fluorescent lights, running her fingertips along the table's scratched surface. She turned a wobbly 360 degrees, scanning from east, to north, to west, to south. Four walls on a cement foundation. A front door with a deadbolt. One large window. And two smaller ones, one in each restroom.

We have the building.

But they have the cars.

"It's a stalemate," she whispered.

Sandi looked at her. "Then what happens next?"

"They'll make their move," Ed said grimly. "Then we'll make ours."

Each move would be a calculated risk. If they stepped outside they'd be shot. If the brothers attacked the building, they'd be leaving the cars unguarded. If one brother attacked, he'd be vulnerable to an ambush in close quarters. The possibilities and consequences made Darby's head spin, like trying to think six moves ahead in chess.

She realized Jay had moved to her side and now held her coat sleeve, gripping the fabric in white knuckles. "Don't believe Ashley. He lies for fun. He'll say anything to get in here—"

"We won't fall for it," Darby said, glancing to Ed and Sandi for support. They offered only weary silence. Maybe *stalemate* was the wrong word, she realized in the growing tension. Maybe a better one was *siege.*

And she realized something else—everyone was now looking at her.

She hated it. She wasn't a leader. She'd never been comfortable as the center of attention—she'd practically suffered a panic attack last year when the Red Robin servers crowded her table to sing "Happy Birthday." Again, she found herself desperately wishing for someone else to be in her place. Someone smarter, tougher, braver, who everyone could turn to. But they weren't.

There's only me.

And us.

And the monsters circling outside.

"And never insult Ashley, either," Jay warned. "He . . . he acts like it's okay at first, but he remembers for later. And he gets his payback if you hurt his feelings—"

"Trust me, Jay. Tonight, we are *way* past hurt feelings." Darby emptied her pockets and purse, placing Ashley's keychain, her Honda keys, and her iPhone on the counter. Then she unfolded the brown napkin, exposing her handwritten message to Ashley, and his message to her: IF YOU TELL THEM, I KILL THEM BOTH.

Ed read it and his shoulders sagged.

Sandi gasped, covering her mouth.

"When . . . when they realize we're not running to the truck," Darby said to everyone, "they're going to change their tactics and come for us. They have no choice, because we're all witnesses now, and we have their hostage. So this building is going to be our Alamo. For the next four hours."

She pulled the final item from her pocket—she'd almost forgotten about it—and placed it on the faux-granite countertop with an emphatic click. It was Lars's .45-caliber cartridge, gleaming gold in the harsh light.

Seeing the bullet made Sandi collapse into her seat, burying her red cheeks in her hands. "Oh Jesus Christ. We are not going to last four *minutes*—"

Darby ignored her. "First, we need to block the window."

"All right." Ed pointed. "Help me flip that table."

ASHLEY WATCHED THE WINDOW DARKEN.

A broad shape moved against the glass from the inside, rotating upward, reducing the orange light to glowing cracks. He imagined the glass creaking with pressure.

"Oh, Darbs." He spat in the snow. "I love you."

Lars glanced over to him. He was crouched in a diligent firing stance by the Ford's tailgate, his elbow resting on the bumper, his Beretta aimed at the front door.

"Don't bother," Ashley said. "They're not coming out. She called the ambush."

"How?"

"She just did." He stood up and walked a few paces, cracking his sore vertebrae, stretching his legs, inhaling the alpine air. "Jesus, isn't she something? I just . . . I just *love* that little redhead."

Perched against a vertical world of firs, white spruce, and rocky summits, the Wanashono visitor center looked like a nut to be cracked. The snowfall had ended; the sky had opened up to a pristine void. The clouds were thinning, revealing a pale crescent and piercing stars, and the world had changed with it, drawn in the icepick shadows of new moonlight. A moon begging for blood.

The fun, as always, was deciding *how*. He'd been through dozens of Lars's pets—turtles, fish, two dogs, more shelter-rescue cats than he could count—and whether it was bleach, bullets, fire, or the meaty click of a knife striking bone, there was no dignity in death. Every living creature dies afraid.

For all her cunning, Darby would learn this, too.

Ashley stood silent for a long moment, sucking on his lower lip. Finally, he decided. "Change of plans," he said. "We'll do it indoors."

"All of them?"

"Yes, baby brother. All of them."

———————

"WEAPONS," DARBY SAID. "WHAT DO WE HAVE?"

"My pepper spray."

"What else?"

Sandi pointed to Espresso Peak. "I mean, there's a coffee kitchen there, but it's locked —"

"Hang on." Ed crossed the room. "Let me try my key."

"A key? Where'd you get a—"

He smashed the padlock with his lug wrench, sending pieces skittering across the floor. Then he grabbed the security shutter by the handle and rolled it up to the ceiling. "Espresso Peak is open for Christmas."

Darby vaulted the counter, landing hard on her sore ankles, and searched the front façade—coffee machines, a bagel toaster, a cash register, syrup bottles. Then she opened the drawers, starting at the bottom and working upward. Bagged coffee beans, vanilla, powdered milk, jingling spoons—

"Anything?"

"Nothing useful."

Ed checked the back. "No landline phone, either."

"There has to be one." Darby searched the next set of drawers, peeling off a yellow Post-it note: REMINDER, PLEASE MOP RESTROOMS —TODD.

"Any knives?"

"Spoons, spoons." She slammed another drawer. "Nothing but spoons."

"What kind of coffee shop doesn't have knives?"

"This one, apparently." Darby wiped sweat from her eyes, glancing back to the cash register (too heavy), to the pastry case (not a weapon), to the toaster (nope), to the coffee machines lining the countertop. "But . . . okay, these things will dispense scalding-hot water. Someone, please, fill a carafe."

"For a weapon?" Sandi asked.

"No. For fucking *coffee*."

"We already have coffee."

"I was being sarcastic."

Pattering footsteps behind her—she'd expected Sandi to come forward—but it was Jay. The little girl carried the COFEE carafe and placed it under the spout. She stood on her tiptoes to press the button. The machine grumbled.

"Thanks, Jay."

"No problem."

Sandi was still at the front of the room. On her knees, peering outside through a three-inch gap between the flipped table and the window frame. "Ashley and Lars just moved again," she said. "They're . . . they're by their van now."

"Doing what?"

"I can't tell."

"Keep your head down," Ed reminded her.

"It's fine."

Darby opened the last drawer below the cash register and found something rattling on the bottom with pens and receipt paper—a silver key. She picked it up, peeling off another Post-it note: DON'T DUPLICATE —TODD.

The closet, she remembered.

She raced to it, inserting the key, twisting the knob. "Please, please, God, let there be a phone in here—"

Darkness inside. She thumbed a light switch—revealing a small janitor's closet, five feet by five, with crooked shelving and racks heaped with saggy cardboard boxes. The stuffy odor of mildew. A mop bucket in the corner, sloshing with gray water. And a white first-aid box on the upper shelf, filmed with dust.

And, to her left, bolted to the wall . . . a beige landline telephone.

"Oh, *thank God*—"

She grabbed the plastic receiver and mashed it to her ear—no dial tone. She tried pressing buttons. Shook it. Checked the spiral cord. Nothing.

"Any luck?" Ed asked.

She noticed another Post-it note on the wall (FIBER LINE DOWN AGAIN —TODD) and slammed the phone down. "I'm really starting to hate Todd."

"Hot water's full," Jay called out.

Darby backpedaled out of the closet, nearly bumping into Ed, and grabbed the carafe off the drip tray. "Thanks, Jay. Now fill another, please."

"Okay."

Then she carried the sloshing carafe to the visitor center's front door, feeling the steam on her palm. The water was hot enough to burn skin, and to maybe temporarily blind an attacker. But it was also rapidly cooling. In a few minutes, it would just be a harmless jug of warm water.

She was halfway there when she noticed something—a brown napkin crammed under the carafe's silver carrying handle.

Her napkin.

She halted and unfolded it. On one side, her MEET ME IN THE RESTROOM and Ashley's probably false response: I HAVE A GIRLFRIEND. On the other, IF YOU TELL THEM, I KILL THEM BOTH. And finally, underneath that, in the loopy handwriting of a child, she found Jay's message to her.

DON'T TRUST THEM.

What?

She glanced up. Jay was filling the second carafe now, holding the red button, but watching her expectantly.

Darby whispered, "Don't . . . don't trust who?"

Ed and Sandi?

Jay didn't answer. She just nodded her head in short motions. Concealing the gesture from the other two adults in the room.

Darby almost asked aloud, but couldn't.

Why? Why can't we trust Ed and—

A rough hand clapped down on her collarbone, startling her. "Three entrances, so three possible routes of attack for Beavis and Butt-Head," Ed huffed, counting on his fingers. "Front door."

"Deadbolted," Darby said.

"Front window."

"Barricaded."

"Restroom windows?"

"There's two. I broke one of them, earlier tonight, to climb inside." She felt her shoulders sag. "That's what I'm worried about."

She wasn't just worried; she was now certain—that was the route Ashley and Lars would try first. The stacked picnic tables outside formed a stairway up to the broken men's restroom window. It was another structural weakness, and Ashley was acutely aware of its existence. It had saved Darby's life twice tonight.

Ed was still considering this, and again, she whiffed that odor on his breath—vodka, or gin, maybe. *Please*, she thought. *Please, don't be drunk.*

"Can they fit through it?" he asked.

"They'll try."

"We don't have much to block it with—"

"Maybe . . ." Darby considered this, eyeing the lug wrench in Ed's hand. She remembered Sandi's pepper spray, plus the carafes of scalding water. She dashed to the restrooms, her mind racing: "Maybe we'll use that to our advantage."

"How so?"

She elbowed open the door and pointed down the long room, past the green stalls, at the empty triangular window on the far wall. "Ashley and Lars will have to crawl through, one at a time, to get inside to us. They can't go feet-first. They'll have to go head-first, so they can cover the room with their gun, and then they'll have to twist around and drop down to land on their feet."

Ed looked at her, impressed. "And *you* climbed that?"

"Here's my plan. One of us will . . ." Darby halted, remembering her conversation in this very same restroom, under the same buzzing lights, with Ashley himself. Just hours ago, they'd bickered over who would be Person A (the attacker) and who would be Person B (the backup). *From now on tonight,* she decided with a held breath, *I'm Person A.*

No more excuses.

"Dara?"

"I'll squish flat against the wall," she continued, pointing at the farthest stall. "Right in that corner there, and they won't see me when they climb inside, and—"

Ed grinned. "We can pepper spray him."

"And take his gun."

And kill them both.

The brothers were armed and physically stronger, so allowing one or both of them inside would be fatal. But this window was a natural bottleneck, and it would be their only realistic route inside, unless they managed to break the deadbolt or get through the barricaded window. And, Darby knew, if Ashley entered first with the gun, she'd stand a half-decent chance of overpowering him with pepper spray or scalding water. If she managed to steal their .45, it'd be a game changer.

Ed opened the stall door. "I'll guard the window."

"No. I'm doing this."

"Dara, it should be me—"

"I said *I'm doing it*," she snapped. "I'm the only one small enough to hide here. And I'm the one who started this."

And I'll never be Person B again.

For as long as I live.

She'd expected more of an argument, but Ed only stared. She'd also almost corrected him about her name, once and for all. But she didn't, because hell, tonight, *Dara* was close enough. And she was grateful she didn't have to mention the alcohol on his breath.

Maybe . . . *Maybe that's why Jay doesn't trust you?*

He paused. "So, you were the one who found Jay?"

"Yeah. I got her out."

"And they'd been traveling with her? Parked outside, right under our noses, while I played Go Fish with the dirtbag?"

"Yeah."

"Jesus Christ. You're . . . you know you're a hero, Dara—"

"Not yet." She winced, looking at the floor, fighting a sickly chill. Hour by hour, she'd grown to loathe that word. "And not even close. Not if I get you and your cousin killed tonight—"

"You won't," Ed said. "Hey. Look at me."

Reluctantly, she did.

"Some words of wisdom for you," he said. "Do you know the first thing they tell you in the Clairmont rehab center? When you first walk through those doors, and check in your items, and sign all the intake forms, and sit down?"

She shook her head.

"Me neither." He smiled. "But I'll let you know, okay?"

She laughed.

It didn't make her feel any better. But she pretended it had, like a rushed little pep talk in a restroom had been all she needed. She smiled, letting her scar materialize on her eyebrow. "I'll hold you to it, Ed."

"You bet."

As he returned to the lobby, she felt something still lumped in her right pocket—Ashley's keychain. She pulled it out and inspected it, fanning the keys in her palm. A black USB drive. A key to a storage unit place called Sentry Storage. And, lastly, the all-important key to the kidnappers' Chevrolet Astro.

Then she closed a fist around them, and before she could reconsider, hurled them out the window. A soft thump as they landed outside.

Call it a peace offering.

A chance for Ashley and Lars to cut their losses, take their van and attempt a getaway before the sun came up. Before the snowplows arrived. Before the cops came in with their guns drawn.

Take your keys, she wanted to shout.

No one has to die tonight.

Please, just take your keys, Ashley, and we'll all go our separate ways.

It was a nice fantasy. But somehow she figured there was no chance this standoff could end without bloodshed. The Brothers Garver had too much at stake to simply walk away. She'd already sat across the table from Ashley tonight, looked him in the eyes, and seen the ruthless clarity in them. Like light refracted through a jewel. A young man who saw people as meat. Nothing more.

And the witching hour was approaching. That time of evil,

of demonic entities, of crawling things that live in the dark. Just superstition, but Darby shivered anyway as she typed another draft text.

Hey, Mom. If you find this message on my phone . . .

She hesitated.

I want you to know that I didn't stop fighting. I didn't give up. I'm not a victim. I chose to get involved. I'm sorry, but I had to. Please know that I always loved you, Mom, and no matter what, I'll always be your little girl. And I died tonight fighting to save someone else's.

Love, Darby.

2:56 A.M.

ON HER WAY BACK INTO THE LOBBY, SHE FOLDED JAY'S cryptic little DON'T TRUST THEM napkin and tucked it in her back pocket.

Why? She wondered, a sore pit growing in her stomach.

Why shouldn't I trust Ed and Sandi?

She wanted to ask the girl, but Ed was too close. "Jay, did those assholes mention where they were driving you?" he asked. "Before they got stranded up here on the pass, I mean?"

"No." Jay shook her head. "They're here on purpose."

"What?"

"They were looking for this rest stop. They were looking at maps today on the road, finding it—"

"Why?"

"I don't know," she said. "I just know they *wanted* to be here."

Tonight, Darby thought, tying her hair up into a ponytail.

Another loose puzzle piece. Another unsolved fragment. It made her stomach hurt. She couldn't imagine why Ashley and Lars would choose this particular rest stop to park with their hostage, plainly visible among a handful of travelers.

Unless they'd planned to kill everyone here all along? The homicidal brothers had been traveling with a handgun, five gallons of gasoline, and a jug of bleach. Maybe Ashley had something evil in mind. As she considered this, Ed asked Jay something else that caught her attention: "Did they take your meds? When they took you?"

Darby's ears perked. *Meds?*

Jay wrinkled her nose. "My shots?"

"Yeah. Meds, shots, pens. Whatever your parents called them."

"I don't think so."

"Okay." He sighed, pushing his thinning hair back. "Then, tell me, Jay. How . . . how long have you gone without them?"

"I keep one in my pocket for emergencies, but I used it." She counted on her fingers. "So three . . . no, four days."

Ed exhaled, like he'd been gut-punched. "Wow. All right."

"I'm sorry—"

"No. It's not your fault."

Darby grabbed his elbow. "What's this about?"

"Apparently . . . well, she has Addison's." Ed lowered his voice and pointed at Jay's yellow bracelet. "*Addison's disease.* It's an adrenal condition with the endocrine glands, where they don't produce enough cortisol for your body to operate. One in, like, forty thousand people has it. Requires a daily medication, or your blood sugar plunges and you . . ." He stopped himself.

Darby touched Jay's wrist and read the bracelet: ADDISON'S DISEASE/STEROID DEPENDENT. She turned it over, expecting more details, like dosage instructions, a doctor's phone number, or a recommended emergency treatment—but that was it. That was all. Four stamped words.

Steroid dependent.

"So, what then?" Darby asked. "Ashley didn't know how to medicate her?"

"They've been medicating her incorrectly, I think. Dumbasses probably Googled it, then broke into a drugstore and grabbed the first thing with *steroid* in the name. Just made her sicker—"

"I thought you said you were a veterinarian."

"I am." Ed forced a smile. "Dogs get Addison's, too."

She remembered the sharp odor of vomit in Lars's van. Jay's tremors, her pale skin. This explained all of it. And now Darby wondered—if you're prescribed a daily steroid shot, how bad can missing four of them be?

To Ed, she mouthed: *How serious?*

He mouthed back: *Later.*

"Ashley and Lars are still by their van," Sandi called out from the window. "They're . . . they're doing something. I just can't tell what—"

"Preparing to attack us," Darby said. No point in sugarcoating it.

She paced the room, inventorying weapons. Two carafes of hot water. Sandi's pepper spray. Ed's lug wrench.

It was a hasty battle plan, but it made sense. When the assault came, Sandi would monitor the locked front door and barricade with Jay, calling out the attackers' movements.

Darby would guard the men's room window. If the brothers attempted their entry there, as she anticipated, she'd surprise-attack Lars or Ashley from the blind corner with a splash of scalding water. And Ed, with his wrench, would be a roamer, moving to whichever side of the visitor center he was needed.

"What's . . ." Sandi wiped her breath off the glass, squinting outside. "It's been ten minutes. Why haven't they tried to get inside yet?"

"To mess with us," Darby guessed. "To make us nervous."

"It's working."

In the building silence, her ears began to ring with pressure. The ceiling rafters felt lower. The floor was bare, blotted with loose napkins and mop tracks. Somehow, moving the table had actually made the room feel smaller. The air was stuffy, all recycled carbon dioxide and sweat.

Darby kept waiting for someone to make a joke to relieve the tension.

No one did.

On the long drive from Boulder, she'd hated the quiet stretches between songs, because that's when her mind went into overdrive. Remembering things she'd said to her mother. New pains. New regrets. And now she rethought Ed's answer to her question, when she'd asked how serious Jay's four missed injections were. He hadn't mouthed *later*.

No, she realized with a sinking heart. He'd said something different.

He'd said *fatal*.

Jay would die if she remained under the care of Ashley and Lars tonight. Even if they hadn't planned to murder her, they were still clueless about how to handle her adrenal condition. And her time was running out.

But really, it made perfect sense that the Garver brothers would turn out to be tragically inept kidnappers. Ashley may have had a cruel streak a mile wide, but he clearly wasn't methodical enough to quarterback a ransom operation. He improvised too much, and he toyed with his victims. And Lars? Just a whiskered man-child, a soft and undeveloped psyche Ashley had molded into his own morbid image. These two overgrown kids were unprepared for the complexity and scale of what they were attempting. They weren't remotely qualified for it. They were something far worse.

In a dark Walmart parking lot a few years back, watching a crackhead with a buzz cut break into their Subaru from the safe lights of the Home and Garden section, she remembered her mother holding her shoulder and telling her: *Don't fear the pros, Darby. The pros know what they're doing, and do it cleanly.*

Fear the amateurs.

"They're . . ." Sandi cupped her hands against the window. "Okay. Ashley just carried something out of his van."

Ed knelt to Jay. "When they come, you're going to get behind the counter. You'll close your eyes. And whatever happens, you won't come out. Understand?"

The girl nodded. "Okay."

Over Jay's head, Darby mouthed to Ed: *How do we treat her?*

"We . . . we get her to a hospital. That's all we can do," he whispered, leaning close. "I've only dealt with it in dogs, and I've only seen it a few times. I just know she's in a shock period right now. Her body isn't creating adrenaline—it's called an Addisonian crisis—so if things get scary or intense, her body could trigger a seizure, or coma, or worse. We need to control her stress level. And keep her environment as calm and peaceful as possible—"

Sandi gasped from the window. "Ashley's got a . . . oh God, is that a *nail gun?*"

"Yeah," Darby said, turning back to Ed. "Not happening."

ASHLEY CLICKED A BATTERY INTO HIS PASLODE IMCT CORD-less nailer and waited for the little green light to blink.

Back in his father's days (the golden years of Fox Contract-ing), to get any sort of power behind a fired nail, you needed an air compressor and several yards of rubber hose. Now it was all batteries and fuel cells—stuff you could carry in your pocket.

Ashley's model was bright *Sesame Street*–orange. Sixteen pounds. The Paslode decal had worn away. Nails fed from a cylindrical magazine, which had always reminded Ashley of the drum on John Dillinger's tommy gun. The nails' lengths were measured in pennies, for some ass-backwards medieval reason, and these ones were 16-pennies, roughly three and a half inches, designed to spear into two-by-four lumber. They could penetrate human flesh from up to ten feet away, and even at distances beyond that, they were still twirling shards of vicious metal, screaming through the air at nine hundred feet per second.

Cool, right?

Ashley may have spectacularly failed at the day-to-day man-agement of Fox Contracting, but boy howdy, he sure loved the toys that came with it. Fortunately his father was now too busy forgetting his own name and shitting in a bag to see what had become of the family legacy under Ashley's leadership. Both specialists unceremoniously laid off, the web domain expired, the phone still ringing sporadically but going straight to voicemail. Sometimes driving the Fox Contracting van with that peeling cartoon character felt like piloting a big corpse, a dried-out husk of his father's dreams and hard work.

See, when Wall Street failed, the feds stepped in and bailed them out with other people's money. When your little mom-and-pop outfit fails, well, you have to take the bailout into your own hands. It's the American way.

Ashley hefted the Paslode nailer and palmed the muzzle with his left hand, defeating the nose safety with an effortless push. Then a squeeze of the trigger . . .

Thwump.

A 16-penny pierced the front tire of Darby's Honda. The black rubber deflated with a hiss.

Lars watched.

Ashley kicked the tire, feeling it soften. Then he leaned and fired another— *thwump*—into the Honda's rear tire.

"Don't be nervous, baby brother. We'll sort this out." Ashley circled the car and pierced the other tires as he spoke— *thwump, thwump.* "Just a little dirty work tonight, and then we'll go see Uncle Kenny. Okay?"

"Okay."

His voice lowered, like he was sharing a dangerous secret: "And something else I forgot to mention. Remember his Xbox One?"

"Yeah?"

"He has the newest *Gears of War*."

"Okay." Lars's smile solidified, and Ashley felt a pang of sympathy for his dear baby brother. He wasn't cut out for this, but that wasn't his fault. How could it be? He'd had no control over whether his mother chugged two vineyards a day while she'd carried him. Poor Lars had been genetically kneecapped before he even drew his first breath. The shittiest of shitty deals.

Quickly, Ashley double-checked the light on his Paslode—still green. Cold weather was notoriously hard on these batteries, and he had only two. The last thing he needed would be for his nailer to lose power when he had it pressed to Darby's temple. How embarrassing would *that* be?

In terms of raw firepower, Lars's .45-caliber Beretta Cougar was the obvious winner—you don't enter a gunfight with a cordless nailer and expect to win. And it would take quite a few three-and-a-half-inchers to reliably put a human down. Worse, the projectiles themselves rarely penetrated anything beyond ten feet. But Ashley Garver loved the nailer, he supposed, for all the things that made it a deeply impractical man-killing weapon. He loved it because it was heavy, cumbersome, inaccurate, scary, and gruesome.

All artists express themselves through their instruments, right?

This was Ashley's.

"Come on, baby brother." He pointed with his nailer. "Get your war face on."

The Paslode's cylinder magazine held thirty-five 16-penny nails, fed in little five-nail racks. He'd fired four. He still had more than enough to turn a human into a screaming porcupine. Walking beside him, Lars racked the slide on the Beretta the way he'd been taught, dutifully checking to ensure there was a chambered round. He'd already topped off the magazine.

"*Gears of War 4*, right?" he asked as they walked. "Not last year's?"

"That's what I said."

"Okay."

"And don't you dare shoot Darby," Ashley reminded him. "She's mine."

"THEY'RE COMING."

"I know."

"Now they have a nail gun—"

"I *know*, Sandi."

Jay clasped her temples like she was warding off a headache, rocking against the flipped table legs. "Please, please, don't argue—"

"Ed, they're going to *kill us*—"

He pointed his lug wrench at her. "Shut up."

Darby took the child by the shoulders and pulled her away from the barricaded window, toward the center of the Wanashono lobby. Any stress or trauma could trigger a seizure. *This is literally life and death. I have to keep her calm.*

Would that even be possible tonight? She tried to remember the exact phrasing Ed had used—*an Addisonian crisis?*— and she crouched in front of Jay. "Hey. Jay. Look at me."

She did, her eyes brimming with tears.

"Jaybird, it'll be okay."

"No, it won't—"

"They won't hurt you," Darby said. "I promise, I won't let them."

By the door, the argument intensified: "Ed, they're going to get inside—"

"Then we'll fight them."

"You're just drunk. If we try to fight them, we will die." Sandi's voice rattled. "I will *die*, you will *die*, and she will *die*—"

"She's wrong." Darby pulled Jay farther back, behind the coffee counter. She patted the packed stones with her palm— solid enough to stop a bullet. "But stay behind this counter, like Ed said, okay? Just in case."

"They won't hurt me," Jay whispered. "They'll hurt *you*."

"Don't worry about me." She recalled the girl's eerie message on the napkin and scooted closer, lowering her voice to a whisper so the others wouldn't overhear: "But tell me. Why don't you want me to trust Ed and Sandi?"

Jay looked embarrassed. "I . . . no, it's nothing."

"Why, Jay?"

"I was wrong. It's nothing—"

"Tell me."

At the front door, Ed and Sandi's argument reached a screaming fever pitch. He held the lug wrench out at his cousin, brandishing it like a weapon, his voice thundering now: "If we cooperate, they'll kill us anyway."

She swatted it away. "It's our only chance—"

"I thought . . ." Jay hesitated, pointing over the countertop at Sandi, finally answering: "I thought, at first, that I recognized that lady. Because she looks exactly like one of my school bus drivers."

All the way in San Diego.

Darby's world froze.

"But that's impossible," Jay said. "Right?"

She didn't have an answer. What were the odds of that? What were the odds of two other travelers having come from the same West Coast city as the abducted child? Of all places? Here, hundreds of miles inland, stranded at a remote highway rest stop in the Rockies? She noticed Sandi had set her keys on the counter and she picked them up, studying the Ford fob.

The oxygen seemed to drain from the room.

San Diego.

"But . . . but, that's not her," Jay added quickly, gripping her wrist. "She just looks like her. It's just a coincidence."

No, it's not, Darby wanted to say. *Not tonight.*

Tonight, there are no coincidences—

By the front door, Ed and Sandi had stopped arguing. They were both listening now, standing in petrified attention. Then Darby heard it, too—a pair of muffled footsteps, boots crunching in the packed snow outside, approaching the door. A two-man death squad.

Ed backed away from the door, red-faced. "Oh Jesus. Everyone get ready—"

"Ed," Darby said. "Where did you say you guys are from?"

"Not now—"

"Answer the question, please."

He pointed. "They're right outside the door—"

"Answer the *goddamn question*, Ed."

The brothers' footsteps halted outside. They'd heard Darby raise her voice and now they were listening, too. Ashley was less than six feet away, waiting on the other side of that thin door. She even heard Rodent Face's familiar mouth-breathing, like a hospital ventilator.

"We . . . we drove from California," Ed answered. "Why?"

"What city?"

"*What?*"

"Tell me the city you're from."

"Why does that matter?"

"Answer me." Darby's voice wobbled with adrenaline, with two strangers inside and two killers at the door outside. They were listening, too. *Everyone* was listening. Everything hinged on what this ex-veterinarian said next—

"Carlsbad," Ed said. "We're from Carlsbad."

Not San Diego.

Darby blinked. *Oh, thank God.*

He threw up his arms. "There, Dara. You happy?"

She exhaled, like emptying her lungs after surfacing from a deep dive. It was just a coincidence. Jay had been mistaken. It's easy to match faces among half-remembered strangers, and apparently Sandi had a doppelganger in San Diego with a morning school bus route. California was a massive population center, so it wouldn't be unheard of that Ed and Sandi would just so happen to hail from the same state as the abducted girl. Everything else—just nerves. Just paranoia.

Silence outside. The brothers were still listening through the door.

"I told you," Jay whispered. "See? I was wrong—"

"Carlsbad," Ed hissed to Darby, his face glistening with sweat. "Carlsbad, USA. What else do you need, for Christ's sake? State? California. Zip code? 92018. Population? A hundred thousand—"

"Sorry, Ed. I just had to make sure—"

She was vaguely aware of Sandi moving up behind her, and she was turning to face the older woman when Ed continued—"County? *San Diego County*"—and that was the last clear thought that went through Darby's mind before a pressurized spurt of icy liquid fired into her eyes.

Then pain.

White-hot pain.

WITCHING HOURS

3:33 A.M.

ED SCREAMED: "*SANDI—*"

But Darby's world went bloody red. An acid splash. She felt the cells of her corneas sizzling with violation, simultaneously scalding hot and freezing cold. Like bleach under her eyelids. It crowded out all of her thoughts.

She hit the floor on her kneecaps, eyes slammed shut, clawing at her face, rubbing away beads of chemical burn. Tiny fingers grasped her elbow, tugging her. Jay's voice in her ears: "Darby. Rub your eyes—"

"Sandi, what the *fuck* are you doing?"

"Eddie, I'm sorry. I'm so sorry—"

Jay's voice, louder: "Rub your eyes."

Darby did, furiously, gasping with pain. Mashing them until her eyeballs squished in their sockets. She forced her eyelids open, peeling them back with her fingernails, and saw a cloudy soup of red and orange, blurred with incendiary tears. The watery outlines of flooring tiles. The room spun, hurtling around her like a rotating stage. She coughed, her throat thick with burbling snot. She saw dark droplets hitting the floor. Her nose was bleeding again.

"Hold still." Jay lifted something heavy. Darby was about to wonder what it was—but then a crash of hot water came down on her face. *The carafe*, she realized, rubbing her eyes. *Smart girl.*

Enraged shadows moved above her. Stomping footsteps.

"Darby." Jay yanked her elbow, harder. Twisting it against her shoulder socket: "Darby, come on. Crawl. *Crawl.*"

She did. Palms and kneecaps on the cold tile, half-blind, dripping. Jay guiding her with pushes and pulls. Behind her, the voices intensified, booming inside the room, pressurizing the air:

"Sandi. Just explain to me what's going on—"

"I can save you."

"Don't touch that door—"

"Please, let me save you," Sandi gasped, begging. "Eddie, honey, I can save your stupid life tonight, but only if you shut your mouth and do exactly what I say—"

Darby heard a hollow, metallic click behind her. It was familiar, but she couldn't identify it. She'd heard it several times tonight, though, enough to elicit a strain of déjà vu. Then through the fog of pain, lightning struck, and her mind screamed: *Deadbolt-deadbolt-deadbolt—*

Sandi just unlocked the front door.

THE DOORKNOB TURNED FREELY IN ASHLEY'S HAND, SUR-prising him, and he pressed his fingertips against the door and gave it a gentle push, revealing the visitor center's interior in a slow wipe. He saw Sandi Schaeffer first, standing in the doorway, her cheeks flushed tomato red.

"I have them," she panted. "I have both of them, trapped in the bathroom—"

Both of them? That was a relief to Ashley. "Jaybird is here, then?"

"Why would she not be?"

"Long story."

Sandi grimaced. "Of course. Of *course*—"

"It's under control."

"Under control? *Really?* Because I just Maced someone—"

"Yeah, thanks for that."

"All you had to do tonight was nothing and you still screwed it up." Sandi coughed in the pepper-spray vapor, rubbing her nose. "I mean . . . God almighty, how'd you let this happen? How'd you let it get this bad?"

Ashley was sick of talking. He shoved his way inside, his eyes watering in the acidic air. Sandi tottered backward, suddenly alarmed, all of her harsh words momentarily stuck in her throat. She'd seen the orange Paslode nailer in his hand, up close.

Christ, he *loved* that thing.

"It's under control," he assured her. "It's fine."

Lars came inside, too, his baby-blue ski jacket flaring under a growl of wind, the Beretta Cougar in his hand.

"You're sick," the lady snarled, taking another shaky step back. "You're both sick. You weren't supposed to hurt her—"

"We improvised."

"I was right about you. About both of you—"

"Oh yeah?" Ashley tapped Lars's chest. "Listen. This'll be good."

"I knew you were both just hillbilly white trash—"

"Aw, Sandi, you're hurtin' my feels."

"It's like you're *trying* to get caught." She spat as she talked, a string of saliva swinging off her chin, still tottering backward as they advanced on her with drawn weapons. "You told me . . . you said you'd give her clean clothes every day. You said you'd watch her diet. You'd give her books. You promised me you wouldn't harm a hair on Jay's head—"

"Technically true. Her hair's fine."

"How can you think this is funny? You're going to rot in prison. You and your little fetal-alcohol-syndrome—"

Brother, she would've finished, if Ashley hadn't shoved her. He wasn't angry. *It's all under control, remember?*

But it was still a rougher push than he'd intended. Sandi skidded backward, her shoes squealing, slamming her broad ass against the coffee counter. The radio toppled, antenna clattering. Her godawful black bowl cut covered her face, and she caught herself on the counter, gasping: "You ruined *everything*—"

Lars aimed his Beretta. "HEY."

Ashley hadn't noticed Ed until now—but yep, there he was. The goateed ex-veterinarian he'd walloped in Go Fish, who hated Apple products, whose biggest fear was facing his estranged family in Aurora this Christmas, stood now by the restrooms, a cross-shaped tire tool in his raised right hand, ready to swing.

"I can't let you," Ed said. "I can't let you near them."

"Sandi," Ashley said quietly, "please tell your cousin to drop that thing."

"It's a *lug wrench*, dumbass."

"Ed, just do what he says."

But the man stood firm, his back to the restroom doors. Perspiration beaded on his forehead, the lug wrench trembling in his hand.

Ashley didn't break eye contact as he advanced, taking a little sideways step to give his brother a better shot. "Sandi," he said calmly, speaking through the corner of his mouth, "let me be clear. If Cousin Ed here does not place the lug wrench on the floor right now, he will die."

"Eddie, please, *please*, just do what Ashley says."

Ed palmed sweat from his eyes, looking back to Sandi with dawning horror. He had to have figured it out by now, but that had seemed to clinch it: "Jesus Christ, how do you . . . how do you know these people? What's going on?"

Sandi winced. "Things got complicated—"

"What were you *doing with that little girl*, Sandi?"

"Drop it," Ashley repeated, taking another step forward. "Drop it now, and I won't hurt you. I promise."

To his right, Lars took a diligent firing stance with the Beretta Cougar, just the way Ashley had once taught him. Two knuckled hands, thumbs high, index finger curling around the trigger. But Ashley knew he wouldn't fire. Not without permission. He was waiting, oh so obediently, for a cue to execute Ed, which could come in many forms—including a baseball reference.

A drop of sweat hit the floor.

"I promise we won't hurt you," Ashley restated. "You have my word."

"Eddie, please." Sandi's voice softened. "You're drunk. Just put it down, and I'll explain everything."

But to his credit, he didn't give in. He stood firm, not even acknowledging Lars's gun, staring back at Ashley, only Ashley, like he was the only person in the world. Rock-hard eyes, daring him to do it. The lug wrench rattled with adrenaline. When he finally spoke, it was a low growl: "I knew I hated you."

"Really?" Ashley said. "I liked you."

"The moment I first met you tonight, when I shook your hand, I just . . . I somehow knew." The old animal doctor smiled a strange, sad smile. "I caught a flash, I think, of exactly who you are. Behind the circle time, behind the bad jokes and the card games. You're the sum of every trait I've ever hated in a human being. You're smug, you're irritating, you talk too much, you're not half as clever as you think you are, and under it all? You're pure evil."

And you're batting a thousand, Ashley almost said.

But then Ed sighed, and something broke behind his eyes, like he was finally recognizing the futility of this little stand-off. He raised both hands and opened his right in grudging surrender. The lug wrench dropped and banged off the tile floor. The echo rang in the air, and Ashley grinned.

Lars lowered his Beretta.

"Thank you." Sandi exhaled, tears in her eyes. "Thank you, Eddie, for—"

Thwump.

Ed made an oafish face, like a man surprised by a belch. For a confused moment, he still held eye contact with Ashley, same as before. But his eyes were wide now, panicked, searching—

"You forgot," Ashley told him. "I'm a *liar*, too."

He lowered the nailer.

Ed's eyes followed it, glistening with caged horror. His lips tightened wetly, contracting flesh, like he was trying to speak, but a surreal thing happened—his jaw wasn't moving. Not even a centimeter. His voice escaped through his nostrils, a strangled moan. A sloppy red bubble—saliva thickened with blood—blistered through his front teeth and splashed down to the floor.

Ashley stepped back, so it wouldn't spatter his shoes.

Sandi screamed. It was earsplitting.

"Lars." Ashley snapped his fingers and pointed. "*Control* her, please."

Ed slapped both hands to his throat, clearly trying to scream, too, but his body wouldn't let him. His mouth was nailed shut—literally—by a steel framing nail, pierced through his lower jaw at an upward angle, harpooning his tongue to the roof of his mouth. Ashley imagined it wriggling in there like a bloody eel. And he was genuinely curious how deep the 16-penny nail had tunneled—could its needle tip be tickling the floor of Ed's brain?

Ashley pushed the man aside with his foot. Ed slumped against the regional map of Colorado and slid down the wall, sobbing silently into his hands, blood pooling in his palms and dribbling dime-sized blots on the floor.

"Have a seat. You should know, Eddie-boy, I *hate* alcoholics . . ."

Sandi was in hysterics. She cried out again, a hyena scream, another big glob of shiny snot hanging from her chin. Lars thrust the Beretta's muzzle into her face, and she promptly shut up.

"Change of plan," Ashley said, tapping Lars's shoulder, and the fluorescent lights shuddered above him. "See, you and me, baby brother, we've already carpet-bombed this little building with forensic evidence, and we don't have nearly enough bleach, or time, to scrub everything down. So we're going to have to get creative, if you *catch my drift*."

Lars nodded once. Spy Code message received.

Ashley continued, stepping over a spreading puddle of Ed's blood. "And as for Darby and—"

Wait.

He realized something.

"Wait, wait . . ." He grabbed Sandi by the elbow, snapping his fingers in her face. "Hey. Look at me. You said . . . you trapped Darby and Jaybird in the restroom, right? The men's restroom?"

She sniffled, looking up at him with bloodshot eyes, and nodded.

No.

Lars looked at him, too, not getting it. But Ashley did.

No, no, no—

He threw Sandi to the floor, stomping past her, past Ed, toward the restrooms, and he elbowed the MEN door open to see . . . an empty room. Snowflakes wafting in through the triangular window.

Lars watched.

Ashley Garver stepped back out and slammed the door violently. "I'm so sick of that *fucking window*—"

DARBY TWISTED SANDI'S KEY AND THE TRUCK'S ENGINE
revved to life. A diesel roar shattered the silence of the parking lot.

Jay crawled into the passenger seat. "What if Ashley hears?"

She cranked the shifter knob. "He just did."

She'd already scraped away a viewing hole in the windshield and dug out a few scraping armfuls around the rear
tires. Just enough to form icy ramps, to gain some momentum. Sandi had come prepared; this F-150 was a beast of a
truck with studded tires, jangling chains, and a monstrous
eighteen inches of lift. If anything parked here could make
it down the mountain, it was this rig. And if it couldn't . . .
well, Darby remembered Ashley's lame little Ford joke: *Found
on road, dead.*

Let's hope not. She rubbed the chemical sting from her eyes.
Her face was still drenched from that carafe, the water now
freezing on her skin.

"Everyone here is bad," Jay whispered.

"Not me."

"Yeah, but everyone else—"

Darby tried not to think about it. Her head was still spinning, too. First Ashley had presented himself as an ally before
betraying her. And now Sandi had revealed her involvement
in the kidnapping plot. She couldn't possibly know where Ed
Schaeffer stood in all of this chaos, but she hoped he was still
alive in there.

If he's even on our side to begin with.

She hoped he was, but with every passing second, the
Wanashono rest area seemed to become more hostile. Her

allies dwindled. Her enemies multiplied. The conspiracy was dizzying.

"What was my *bus driver* doing here?" Jay asked.

Darby gripped the steering wheel. "Moment of truth."

She pressed the gas pedal and the Ford inched forward in the sludgy snow, tires spinning, throwing sheets of hard ice. Steady pressure under her toes. Not too hard, not too soft. Grinding, skidding motion—but it was motion.

"Come on. Come on, *come on*—"

"How far away are the police?" Jay asked.

She remembered the CDOT broadcast Ed had described to her. The jackknifed semi at the bottom of the pass. "Seven, uh, maybe eight miles."

"That's not far, right?"

Darby spun the wheel into a sloppy half-turn, sliding Sandi's truck into icy divots, twisting south now. Downhill, down the off-ramp, facing oncoming traffic—if there were any. She searched for the Ford's headlights and flicked them on. Ashley and Lars had already been alerted by the lope of the motor, so stealth was out. They were coming, right now.

"You stole her truck," Jay whispered.

"She pepper-sprayed me. We're even."

The girl laughed, a fragile little sound, as a slice of orange light appeared on the glass behind her. It was the visitor center's front door swinging open. A shaft of light, and in it, a thin figure.

It was Lars.

Rodent Face. All black shadow. The silhouette raised its right arm, as casually as a man aiming a television remote, and

Darby understood instinctively, grabbing Jay by the shoulder and hurling her down against the cold leather seat—

"Get down—"

CRACK.

The passenger window exploded. Gummy shards chattered off the dash. Jay yelped, covering her face.

Darby huddled low under a hailstorm of settling glass. The gunshot echoed like a firecracker in the thin air. Her body urged her to stay down in her seat, as low as possible, beneath Rodent Face's line of fire, but her brain knew better: *He's coming toward us. Right now.*

Go, go, go—

She found the gas pedal with her toes and stomped it. The truck surged forward, engine thrumming with power, knocking them back into the seats. The world heaved. Luggage thudded noisily in the back. Then Darby righted herself against the clammy leather, peered sideways over the steering wheel—exposing just an eye, an inch—and guided Sandi's F-150 toward the highway.

Jay grabbed her wrist. "Darby—"

"Stay down."

"Darby, he's shooting at us—"

"Yes, I *noticed*—"

CRACK. A bullet pierced the truck's windshield and Darby flinched. A chilly breeze whistled to her left; her side window was shattered, too. Snowflakes blew inside, slashing her cheek.

"He's chasing us," Jay said. "Drive faster—"

Darby was trying. She increased pressure on the gas, and the truck fishtailed but accelerated. The tires sprayed ice chips through the windows, peppering the interior with cold grit. Lars fired again—*CRACK*—and the truck's side mirror exploded. Jay screamed.

Darby tugged her down with her free hand. "Keep your head down. It's fine—"

"No, it's not."

"He's not going to catch us—"

CRACK. Another hole punched through the windshield, a jagged star shape above Darby's head. But Lars's gunshots sounded different. They were getting hollow, thinning across a widening distance.

"Yes." Her heart fluttered. "Yes, yes, yes—"

"What's happening?"

They were rolling down the exit ramp now, gaining speed. Thank Christ for momentum, for gravity, for the steepening grade. Darby gave the pedal another pump of gas. Another engine roar. The world tilted downward and kernels of safety glass skittered loosely around them like gravel.

"See? I told you—"

Lars fired again—*CRACK*—but missed the truck entirely. He was too far behind them now. Vanishing. The orange glow of the Wanashono building was vanishing, too, its familiar shapes sinking into the snowy darkness, and Darby was so glad to see it all go. Like awakening from a dread-sweat nightmare, she never wanted to see it again. Ever. Good riddance to that shitty place.

Jay peered around her seat, watching the pursuing figure of Rodent Face shrink through the perforated rear window—"Stay down"—and she raised a shaking fist. Her ring finger up.

It took Darby a moment to understand. "Uh . . . wrong finger."

"Oh." Jay corrected. "Better?"

"Better."

"Thanks," said the nine-year-old girl flipping the bird through the bullet-riddled back window of a stolen pickup truck, and Darby started to laugh. It was involuntary, rattling her lungs like a cough. She couldn't stop it.

Oh my God, we actually did it.

We got away.

Just seven or eight miles to go. She dug her iPhone from her pocket and tossed it to Jay. "Hey. Watch the screen, okay? If you see a signal bar, you hand it to me immediately—"

"The battery's almost dead."

"I know."

They scraped downhill, truck tires churning fresh powder like waterwheels. She feathered the gas pedal, keeping the Ford moving. Keeping the inertia unbroken. That's all it was now—raw, desperate forward momentum. Like driving across two states with a stomach full of Red Bull and ibuprofen, fighting to hold her caffeine buzz with a cryptic text from Devon shaking in her palm (*She's okay right now*), racing Snowmageddon over the pass. Forward, forward, forward. *Don't stop.*

Don't-stop-don't-stop—

Now they came up on State Route Six, high beams cutting over frozen mounds of windswept snow. Here she planned to merge into the oncoming northbound lane and pass under the first saucer of light. Darby felt another flicker of excitement in the bottom of her stomach. This was really happening. She'd done it. They were really escaping.

Even still, she worried—what if the brothers dug their van out, got it moving in the snow, and chased them down the highway? Then another triumphant shiver as she realized: *Ashley doesn't even know where his Astro keys are.*

He never saw me throw them out the restroom window.

Yes, yes, *yes.* It all felt too good to be true.

"Hold my phone up." She pointed. "Out the window."

Jay did this, crouched on her knees to lean out the passenger window, and Darby suddenly imagined hitting a hard stop and bouncing this poor girl out like a crash-test dummy. That'd be tough to explain to her parents.

"And buckle your seat belt," she added. "Please."

"Why?"

"Because it's the law."

"What if we need to get out and run?"

"Then—Jesus. Then you'll unbuckle it."

"Yours isn't buckled—"

"*Hey.*" Darby grinned darkly, doing her best angry-dad voice. "Don't make me turn this car around."

Jay buckled her seat belt with a metallic *snick*, and pointed at the seat behind Darby's head. "He almost shot you."

She touched the headrest behind her ponytail. Sure enough, her fingers found a ragged exit wound, leaking spongy clods of yellow foam. Lars's bullet had sliced an inch high, at most, skimming her scalp before exiting through the windshield. Saved by dumb luck. She let out a hoarse laugh. "Good thing I'm five-two, huh?"

"Good thing," Jay said. "I kind of like you."

Darby guided Sandi's truck to the highway, merging into the desolate oncoming lanes. Under normal traffic conditions, this would be a suicidal maneuver. She reflexively nudged the right turn signal, before feeling stupid. Her hands were still shaking. A strange silence settled in and she cleared her throat, struggling to fill it: "So . . . Sandi's your school bus driver, huh?"

"Ms. Schaeffer, I think."

"Was she nice?"

"She had me kidnapped."

"Aside from that."

"Not really." Jay shrugged. "I hardly remember her."

But she sure remembered you, Darby thought. *She remembered you, and your sleek McMansion, and your yuppie parents' daily schedules.* A school bus driver made a logical spotter for a ransom operation, and Ashley and Lars were obviously handling the dirty work. But why would Sandi risk meeting Beavis and Butt-Head in person, all the way out here? In a remote rest stop two states away?

She watched the snowy highway unfurl, feeling the blood return to her extremities, bracing against the frigid air blowing through the windows. Only now did she start to see the gallows humor of the whole mess, in her own misfortune and poor judgment. She'd unwittingly trusted a kidnapper for the *second time* tonight. That carafe of scalding water she'd planned to use as a weapon? Jaybird had dumped it over her face, which still tingled with first-degree burns. Nothing had gone according to plan. She couldn't help it, her teeth chattering: "I swear to God, Jay, next time you think you recognize someone else here . . . like, if the first Colorado cop we see looks like your butler back in San Diego, please *tell me*, okay?"

"We're normal. We don't have a butler."

"Fine. Your *maid*, then."

"We don't have a maid."

"Really? I bet you do."

"I don't."

"Is it because she's called a housekeeper?"

Jay looked embarrassed. *Checkmate.*

"I knew it. Did your parents invent Google or something?"

"You're teasing me."

Darby grinned. "Is it too late to ransom you myself?"

"Maybe not." Jay grinned back. "You're the one driving a stolen tru—"

Brain-jarring halt.

The entire world seemed to drop anchor. The truck nose-dived into a rise of deep snow, headlights burrowing and going dark, two tons of moving parts slamming into a hard stop. An empty Gatorade bottle flew out of the console. Loose glass shards bounced. Darby banged her jaw on the steering wheel, biting her tongue, and in a microsecond, they were stuck again, trapped again, and all of the joy turned sour and tinny, like the taste of blood in her teeth.

Oh no.

No, no, no—

Jay looked at her. "Good thing you made me fasten my seat belt."

3:45 A.M.

"OH *SHIT*."

Darby cranked into reverse. Tried again. Throttled it, again and again. No luck; the tires spun until the cab stank like scorched rubber.

The truck was stuck, facing the wrong way on the right-most northbound lane of State Route Six, just beyond the blue REST AREA sign. She craned her neck to look back through the splintered rear window—all in all, she'd made it fewer than fifty feet down the highway. A quarter mile, tops, from the Wanashono building. She could still see the orange parking lot lights through a copse of jagged Douglas firs. It didn't actually matter if Ashley and Lars found their keys, because they were still within *walking distance*.

"Shit-shit-*shit*." She punched the wheel, accidentally blaring the horn.

Jay looked back, too. "Can they catch up to us?"

Yes, yes, yes, 100 percent yes—

"No," Darby said. "We drove too far. But stay inside." She opened the driver door, sprinkling loose bits of glass, and slid out into the deep snow. She felt old and tired. Her bones ached. Her eyes still stung with pepper spray.

"What are you doing?"

"Digging us out." She circled the Ford's front bumper, squinting in the half-submerged headlights. Her stomach plunged when she saw the huge mound of displaced snow, sloughed into a rolling snowball in front of the truck's grille. It must have weighed a hundred hopeless pounds, maybe more, as dense as wet cement.

She almost collapsed at the sight of it, the enormity of it.

But then her gaze fell on the little girl behind the cracked windshield, on the verge of an Addisonian crisis. An anxiety time bomb; a single bad moment away from a seizure, or a coma, or worse.

So Darby dropped to her bruised knees and started to dig.

"Can I help?" Jay asked.

"No. You can't overexert yourself. Just focus on my cell phone, please. Tell me if it gets a signal." She lifted a crumbling snow boulder and heaved it aside. Her bare fingers throbbed with cold.

Seven miles, she thought, glancing downhill.

Seven miles to that jackknifed semi. Could that really be all? She imagined a busy accident scene down there, swarming with first responders, bustling with lights and motion. The red-and-blue pulse of police light bars. Road maintenance crews in reflective jackets. Paramedics inserting tubes into throats. Dazed victims being evacuated on gurneys.

All of that, just seven miles down the dark road. It didn't seem possible.

Seven fucking miles.

State Route Six was raised here where they'd crashed, cresting the upper lip of a switchback. The coniferous trees were at their thinnest, the land rocky and vertical. In daylight, with clear weather, this might've opened up onto a stunning mountain panorama. But here and now, it was perhaps the only stretch of Backbone Pass that had even the barest chance of catching a cell signal. To hell with Ashley's Nightmare Children. In hindsight, she understood that had almost certainly been another of his lies. Just one more wicked ruse, to make her waste her battery.

Another gust of wind breathed up the mountain, creaking branches, tugging her sleeves, lifting strange swirls of powder that slithered across the roadway like dancing ghosts.

"Hey, Jay," she panted as she dug, straining for conversation to fill the eerie silence, trying to keep the mood light, pleasant, unhurried. "What . . . what do you want to be when you grow up?"

"I'm not telling."

"Why?"

"You'll tease me again."

Darby leaned around the Ford's headlights, checking the rest stop's exit ramp for the advancing figures of Ashley and Lars. No sign of them yet. "Come on, Jay. You owe me. I took pepper spray in the face for you."

"It wasn't *for* me. It was aimed at you."

"You know what I mean—"

"A paleontologist," the girl answered.

"A what?"

"A paleontologist."

"Like . . . like a dinosaur fossil hunter?"

"Yeah," Jay said. "That's what a paleontologist does."

But Darby wasn't listening. She'd noticed the truck's tire looked strangely flabby, and now her blood froze. She brushed away another armful of snow and saw a steel circle protruding from the tire's sidewall. A nail head. She heard it now—the gentle, reptilian hiss. Leaking air.

She crawled to the other tire. Two more nails pierced into the treads.

Oh God, this was Ashley's backup plan all along.

She punched snow. "Shit."

He disabled all of the cars, just in case we managed to escape in one of them—

But it didn't make sense—why would Ashley nail-gun the tires of Sandi's truck, too, if she was an integral part of the kidnapping plot? After they'd taken all that care to meet up here in the frozen Rockies?

Jay peered over the door. "What is it?"

"Nothing." Darby scrambled back to the front of Sandi's truck and resumed digging, double-time. Her heart was racing, thudding against her ribs, as she tried to appear calm. "Jaybird, tell me. What's . . . what's your favorite dinosaur?"

"I like them all."

"Yeah, but you have to have a favorite. T. Rex? Raptor? Triceratops?"

"Eustreptospondylus."

"I . . . I have no idea what that is."

"That's why I like it."

"Describe it, please." Darby just needed to keep the conversation going, scooping armfuls of snow, her frantic thoughts churning: *He's coming for us. Right now, he's catching up to us, and he's carrying that nail gun—*

"It's a carnivore," the girl said. "Walks on two hind legs. Jurassic period. Three fingers on each hand, kind of like a raptor—"

"You could have just said 'raptor,' then."

"No. It's Eustreptospondylus."

"Sounds like a shitty dinosaur."

"You couldn't spell it," Jay said, pausing. "Oh. Your phone found a signal—"

Darby jolted upright and ran to the passenger door, reaching through the shattered window, snatching her iPhone from Jay's fingers. She didn't believe it until she saw it—a lone signal bar. Blinking urgently. "Your turn to dig," she said.

"The battery's one percent—"

"I know."

The door croaked, sprinkling more glass, and Jay jumped out. Darby held the phone with red fingers, mashing 911 with her thumb—but the phone vibrated in her hand, startling her. A NEW MESSAGE bubble blocked her touchscreen. She was about to swipe past it, until she saw the sender's number.

It was 911.

An answer to her text message, the one she'd tried to send hours ago tonight, which must have only now successfully auto-sent: Child abduction gray van license plate VBH9045 state route 6 Wanasho rest stop send police.

The answer?

Find a safe place. Officer coming ETA 30.

Darby almost dropped her phone. *ETA*, as in *estimated time of arrival*. *30* must be minutes, right? It couldn't be hours, or days—

Thirty minutes.

"Is it working?" Jay asked, panting as she dug.

Darby couldn't believe it. It felt like a hallucination. She blinked, afraid it would all disperse like a dream, but the letters were all still there, trembling in her numb hands. Her text had successfully sent at 3:56 A.M. She'd received the 911 dispatcher's response at 3:58 A.M. Just minutes ago.

Oh, thank God, the cops will be here in thirty minutes—

Her chest swelled with gulped breaths. Nervous electricity fizzed in her bones. She had questions. Tons of them. For starters, she didn't know how this reconciled with CDOT's snowplow situation—were the plows due in thirty minutes, too? Were they due first? Were they all charging up Backbone Pass at once—cops and road crews—in one big convoy? She didn't know, and truthfully, she didn't care, as long as the cops got here and shot Ashley Garver in his smirking face.

"Oh, Jay," she whispered. "I could kiss you—"

The girl's voice rose: "Darby, *stop*."

"What?"

Jay faced her now, standing in the curved glare of the Ford's headlights. Staring with snowflakes collecting on her shoulders, alarmingly still.

Darby tried to keep her voice calm. "Jay, I don't understand—"

"Don't move."

"What *is it?*"

She whispered: "He's behind you."

———————

ASHLEY WAS JUST TUGGING THE PASLODE'S TRIGGER, PRE-paring to spear a 16-penny into the back of her skull, when Darby turned to face him.

Her auburn bangs feathered off her cheekbone as she spun, her eyes coming around and up to find him. Catching a slash of moonlight, her skin was marshmallow soft. That white scar still invisible—unless she squinted or smiled. Like an actress hitting her mark, a gentle flourish framed by a cinematographer's eye, the way Eva Green greets Daniel Craig in *Casino Royale.*

Just a turn.

But Christ, *what a turn.*

Under Darby's coat and jeans, he could locate the luxurious shapes of her body. Her shoulders. Her hips. Her breasts. He wished he could print this moment, this snapshot of heartbreaking beauty, and hold on to it forever. As with all true art, you're never quite sure how it makes you feel at first, until you untangle your reactions later. And he'd have plenty to untangle. He wished it could just be something simple, like lust, because lust could be satiated with Pornhub—but ever since he'd kissed her in that grungy restroom, his feelings for Darby had become knottier and more complex.

"Hi, Darbs." He forced a smile. "Long night, huh?"

She said nothing.

No fear in those eyes. Not even a tremor.

She just looked him up and down, assessing him, like the

CU–Boulder redhead had somehow already anticipated this encounter, hours ago, and had a contingency plan prepared, which was of course impossible. Tonight had been a swirling, sweaty shitstorm of blind chance and left-field surprises. Not even a *magic man* like Ashley himself could stay on top of everything all the time.

But still, he thought, *I wish you hadn't turned around.*

It makes this harder.

He raised the cordless nailer again. He depressed the Paslode's muzzle with his left palm, tricking the safety, squeezing the two-stage trigger, drawing careful aim on her left eye—

Darby didn't flinch. "That'd be a mistake."

"What?"

"You don't want to kill me."

"Yeah? Why's that?"

"I hid your keychain," she said. "I know where your Astro keys are, and if you kill me now, you'll *never find them.* Now that Sandi's truck is stuck here, and you shot up my Honda, you've trapped yourself here. That van is the only way you and your brother will ever escape this rest stop tonight."

Silence.

She raised her hands, like a mic drop.

And from the front of Sandi's truck, Ashley heard a strange, scraping chitter. A sound he'd never heard before.

It was Jay. Laughing.

4:05 A.M.

THIRTY MINUTES.

Thirty minutes.

Survive the next thirty minutes, until the cops get here.

This repeated in her mind on the cold trek back to the rest area. Ashley had ordered her to walk in front, with Jay at her side, while he held the nail gun to their backs. He also carried her iPhone.

He'd snatched it from Darby's hand before she could delete 911's text message. He swiped through it now, the screen illuminating the snow a spectral blue as they walked, and she quietly braced for Ashley Garver's apocalyptic reaction when he learned the truth—that the cops were incoming at this very second.

But nothing happened. They walked in silence. She heard him lick his lips, adjusting his grip on the nail gun as he scrolled through her phone, and she realized—*He's not reading my texts.*

The possibility of Darby texting the police hadn't occurred to him. He was only scanning her call records, searching for successful voice calls to 911. Which, of course, she'd already tried, dozens of times, back at 9:00 and 10:00 P.M. He was scrolling through them, inspecting the time stamps.

"Call failed," he read. "Call failed. Call failed. Call failed—"

You have no idea. She wanted to laugh, but couldn't.

You're holding it in your hand.

"Good, good." He sounded like he was relaxing.

She squeezed Jay's unhurt hand, lowering her voice. "Don't be afraid. He can't kill me, because I know where his keys are—"

"That's true, Darbs," Ashley interjected. "But I can *hurt* you."

Yeah? she wanted to say. *You have half an hour, asshole.*

She desperately hoped thirty minutes was a realistic estimate for when the police would arrive, and not just a dispatcher's wild guess. Between the jackknifed semi and the blizzard, there were a lot of possible complications that might not be visible from an alert desk inside a warm sheriff's station somewhere. What if it wasn't thirty minutes, but forty? An hour? Two hours?

Ashley groped her as she walked. The nail gun prodding her backbone, his fingers exploring her pockets, front and back. Her legs. The sleeves of her coat. "Just making sure," he breathed down her neck.

He'd been searching for his keys.

The only thing keeping me alive right now is that stupid keychain. She imagined those keys now, resting in the snow outside the restroom window where they'd landed. Slowly vanishing, one snowflake at a time.

"You should just tell me now what you did with them," he whispered. "It'll be so much easier for both of us."

For a while as they walked, Darby didn't quite grasp what he meant by that. Then the realization came to her slowly, like a great shape emerging from the depths, taking monstrous form.

When they got back inside the visitor center, Ashley was going to torture her. This was a certainty. He would give her a yellow card, or a red card, or worse, until she confessed the keychain's location. And the second she did, he'd kill her. She felt her heartbeat kick up in her chest like a trapped animal. She considered running, but he'd just nail-gun her in the back. And he was far too strong for her to fight.

As they neared it, the rest area took form in the moonlight. It looked falsely serene, like a model inside a snow globe. She saw the cars—their Astro, her Honda, the buried Dumpster she'd once mistaken for Ashley's car. The icy flagpole, standing like a needle. The bronze crowd of Nightmare Children. And emerging from the darkness, half-buried in windswept snow, with its dead lamp and barricaded window, the Wanashono visitor center itself.

Big Devil, the name meant.

Then Ashley pivoted her—"Turn, turn"—and they followed the footpath from the parking lot to the front door. The final fifty feet.

I've saved Jay already, she reminded herself. *I've gotten the police involved. They have guns. They'll take care of Ashley and Lars.*

All I have to do is survive.

This long walk back had taken ten, maybe fifteen minutes, she guessed. So she was already halfway there.

Just fifteen more.

As they moved closer to the building, Darby realized something—she wasn't even afraid anymore. She was exhilarated, actually, drunk with a strange sort of excitement. She'd already been shot at, pepper-sprayed, and nearly asphyxiated with a Ziploc bag, and like a goddamn cockroach, she'd survived everything Ashley and Lars—and even Sandi—had thrown at her. Against all odds, Darby was still in this fight. It was too personal, this eight-hour psychological duel with Ashley, all of the night's tricks and turns and wins and losses. And now she had to witness her grisly checkmate. She wanted to be there the second it happened, to see the shock on Ashley's face when the first approaching police car flashed red and blue. It thrilled her, in a dark way she couldn't describe.

You'll hurt me, Ashley. You'll hurt me bad. For these last fifteen minutes or so, I'm all yours. But after that?

You're mine.

And you have no idea—

"Oh, hey." Ashley stopped. "You . . . got a text message back at the highway."

The blue glow returned. He was reading her phone again.

Darby panicked. 911 must have sent a second text message. Of *course*. The well-intentioned emergency dispatcher had no way of knowing that Darby herself was under duress, that her phone was now in the killer's hand.

"From . . ." Ashley squinted. "From someone named . . . Devon."

Then he held the cracked iPhone out to her, and when her eyes pulled into focus, whatever remained of Darby's world disintegrated.

It happened. Mom died.

"Ooh," Ashley said. "Awkward."

Then he broke her iPhone in half. "Keep walking."

THE FRONT DOOR SHUT LIKE A GUNSHOT.

Jay screamed when she saw Ed. Ashley grinned, all white teeth, grabbing her by the collar and forcing her to look. "Cool, huh?"

Ed Schaeffer was slumped in a sitting position under the Colorado map, the front of his Carhartt shiny with dark blood. He tilted his head up at them as they entered the room, and his lips weakly quivered, like he was trying to speak.

"Don't move, Eddie." Sandi knelt beside him, trying to wrap the right length of medical gauze around his ruined jaw. The white first-aid box was open on the floor, its contents scattered. "Don't move, I'm trying to help you—"

Over her trembling hands, Ed's gaze darted up to Darby—a flash of recognition—and he tried again to speak, but only managed a moaned gurgle. A mouthful of blood, ropy with snakelike clots, squirted through his locked teeth and splashed down into his lap.

Jay cried, struggling to look away, but Ashley wouldn't let her. "See?" he said into her ear. "That's a red card."

Across the room Lars watched all of this like a scarecrow, holding the .45 in one hand and a white jug of bleach in the other, as Ed's strangled scream reached a fever pitch in the confined air.

All of this horror barely registered with Darby.

She wasn't there. Not really. She was somewhere else, and this world had gone slippery, tinged with oil. Lights smeared into shafts. Her body was a cold suit, her heartbeat and breaths falling into a slow, mechanical rhythm. She imagined a tiny creature, her truest self perhaps, pulling levers and viewing camera feeds inside her own skull. She'd seen that in a movie—*Men in Black*. She recalled watching the DVD years ago, sitting with her mother on the basement sofa, sharing a Snoopy blanket. *I like Will Smith*, her mother had told her, sipping a drink that smelled like peaches. *He can rescue me anytime he'd like.*

She was gone now, Darby realized.

The body of Maya Thorne would remain in some hospital in Provo, Utah, but the tiny being that lived inside her head was lost forever.

Now Ashley squeezed her right hand, interlocking his icy fingers with hers as if they were teenagers on a date, and he guided her through the room. Past Ed and Sandi, past the stone counter, past the coffee machines. She didn't know where he was taking her, nor did she care. She numbly noticed her right foot was leaving red footprints—she'd sleep-walked through Ed's pooled blood. Like a nightmare, she just wanted it all to be over.

For it to *please* be over.

She twisted her neck, glancing back at the old *Garfield* clock on the wall. It read 5:19 A.M. For winter daylight savings, she subtracted an hour.

That made it 4:19 A.M.

She'd received 911's text message at 3:58 A.M. The walk

back had taken twenty-one minutes. Subtracted from thirty, that made nine minutes left until the police arrived here. Nine short minutes.

Survive nine more minutes.

That's all.

Ashley halted her abruptly—here, at the janitor's closet door. Still half-open, from when she'd unlocked it. He gently twirled her now, like a slow, dizzy tango, and pushed her against the wall.

"Sit here," he said.

She didn't.

"Sit, please."

She shook her head and tears tapped the floor. Her sinuses ached.

"You're not going to sit?"

She shook her head again.

"You're not tired?"

Oh, she was exhausted. Her nerves were shredded, her muscles were sagging meat. Her thoughts were blurry. But somehow, she knew that if she sat down now, it would all be over. She'd lose her will. She'd never stand up again.

For a moment, she considered just blurting it out, saying what couldn't be unsaid: *Ashley, I threw your keys out the men's restroom window. They landed just ten, maybe twenty feet away in the snow.*

You can kill me. I'm done.

Across the room, Jay wept. Rodent Face knelt by her, trying to calm her. "Don't look at Ed. Don't look at him, okay? He's fine—"

Ed took a tortured breath through his nose as Sandi wrapped another bandage around his jaw, and then he made a strange sound, like a wet burp. The clean white gauze blotted red.

"He's *fine*, Jaybird. Wanna, ah, play circle time?"

"We're all . . ." Sandi sighed, wiping Ed's blood on her pants. "We're all going to prison for the rest of our lives. You know that, right?"

Ashley ignored her. He was a black shadow, towering over Darby, studying her. Still gripping her wrist, trapping her against the half-open closet door. His eyes moved up and down her body.

Darby stared at the floor, at her size-eight Converse, clumped with snow and browned with dirt and blood. Ten days ago, they'd been new in a box.

"Were . . ." Ashley cleared his throat. "Were you close to your mom?"

She shook her head.

"No?"

"Not really."

He leaned closer. "Why not?"

She said nothing. She fought his grip on her wrist, and he gently retaliated with his other hand, pressing his nail gun against her belly. His finger on the trigger. Something about the thing's color—a sickening Crayola orange—made it look like an oversize child's toy.

He repeated himself, his hot breath lapping at her neck: "Why not, Darbs?"

"I was . . . I was kind of an awful daughter." Her voice trembled but she steadied herself. Then, like a levee breaking, it all came out: "I took advantage of her. I manipulated her. I

called her horrible things. I stole her car once, with a shoelace.
I'd leave, for days at a time, without telling her where I'd gone
or who I was out with. I must have given her ulcers. When
I . . . when I left for college, we didn't even say goodbye. I just
got in my Honda and drove to Boulder. I stole a bottle of her
gin from the cabinet on my way out."

She remembered drinking it alone in her dorm room. The
sour burn in her throat, under a bleak wallpaper of strangers'
graves, of names and birthdates drawn in charcoal shadows of
crayon and wax.

Ashley nodded, sniffing her hair. "I'm sorry."

"You're not."

"I am."

"You're lying—"

"I mean it," he said. "I'm genuinely sorry for your loss."

"I wouldn't be," Darby said through her teeth. "If it was
your mom."

She felt more tears coming, stinging her irritated eyes, but
she fought them. She couldn't start now. That would come
later. Later, later, later. After the cops kicked down the door
and raked Ashley and Lars with bullets, after Sandi was hand-
cuffed, when she and Jay were safe in an ambulance with
wool blankets draped over their shoulders. Then, and only
then, could she properly grieve.

Ashley furrowed his brow. "How'd you steal a car with a
shoelace?"

She didn't answer. It was an unremarkable story. Her
mom's Subaru had been broken into once before, and the ignition had been mangled. So it took two keys—one for the
door and one for the ignition. Darby had acquired one, but

not the other. Nothing amazing to it—she'd just followed the instructions of an eleven-minute YouTube video.

You rotten little bitch, her mom had said from the porch, watching her own Subaru pull into the driveway at 3:00 A.M.

You rotten little bitch.

"And . . ." Ashley put it together. "That's how you broke into our van, huh?"

She nodded, and another tear hit the floor.

"Wow. It's like tonight was meant to be." He grinned again. "I've always believed things happen for a reason, if that's any consolation."

It wasn't.

Death is supposed to transform you from a person into an idea. But to Darby, her mother had always been an idea. Somehow, after eighteen years of living in the same tiny two-bedroom house in Provo, eating the same food, watching the same television, sitting on the same sofa, she'd never truly known who Maya Thorne was. Not as a human being. Certainly not as the person she would have been had Darby never existed. Had she really just been the flu.

Oh God, Mom, I'm sorry.

She almost broke. But she couldn't—not in front of him. So it stuck thickly in her chest like a wet, knotted towel, a dull ache in her soul.

I'm so sorry for everything—

Ashley inspected her for another long moment, another thoughtful breath. She could smell the dense odor of his sweat. She heard his tongue move behind his lips, like he was wrestling with words he couldn't quite say. When he finally did speak again, his voice was different, overcome by some emotion she couldn't identify: "I wish you were my girlfriend, Darby."

She said nothing.

"I wish, so badly, that you and I . . . that we'd met under different circumstances. This, all this, isn't me. Okay? I'm not evil. I don't have a criminal record. I've never hurt anyone before tonight. I don't even drink or smoke. I'm just a business owner who got involved in a little thing that went south, and now I have to clean up this mess in order to protect my brother. Understand? And you're getting in the way of that. So I'm asking again, before it gets ugly—where are my keys?"

She stared back at him, rock hard, giving nothing.

Over Ashley's shoulder, she could see the clock. The characters on it. Orange Garfield still offering those roses to pink Arlene. Her blurry eyes focused on the minute hand—almost vertical now. 4:22 A.M.

Five minutes until the cops arrived.

"Did you hear me, Ashley?" Sandi stood up, drawing his attention. "Are you having a psychotic episode? Keys or no keys, it's over. We're all going to prison."

"No. We're not."

"How do you figure?"

Ashley didn't answer. Instead, his dark silhouette turned back to Darby, and his grip on her wrist changed. His fingers walked over her skin like clammy octopus tentacles, rearranging themselves around her, tightening. And he lifted her hand up, up, sliding against the wall . . .

Sandi raised her voice. "What are you *doing* to her?"

Darby craned her neck to see—he was holding her right hand against the supply closet door. Right up against the door's hinge. Pressing her fingertips flush against the golden jaws, where the brass was spotted with old lubricant and brown cavities of rust. She saw her pinkie fingernail, painted crackle-blue, her vulnerable flesh seated in there like a tiny head in a guillotine.

Five minutes.

She looked back at Ashley, her gut twisting with panic.

He had the nail gun tucked in his armpit now, leaning to grasp the doorknob with his free hand. "You might not remember this, Darbs, but earlier tonight, you made fun of me for my phobia of door hinges. Remember that? Remember what you called me?"

She closed her eyes, squeezing acidic tears, wishing it would all go away—

"Yeah, *oops*, huh?"

—But it was real. It was all really happening, right now, and it could never be undone, and her artist's fingers were about to be crushed by unsympathetic metal.

Sandi gasped. "*Jesus Christ*, Ashley—"

"Don't do it," Jay begged, fighting Lars. "Please, don't—"

But the tall shadow of Ashley Garver wasn't listening. It leaned in close to Darby, licking its lips, and she smelled something sweetly bacterial, fetid, like decaying meat. "You're giving me no choice. If you tell me, I promise I won't hurt you, okay? You have my word. Where. Are. My. Keys?"

Fiveminutes—fiveminutes—fiveminutes—

She forced herself to open her eyes, to blink away the tears, to steady her breathing, to look the monster in its green eyes. She couldn't take the bait. She couldn't submit and play this game, because the instant he knew where his keychain was, he'd kill her. There was no other option. Ashley Garver was many, *many* things, but above all else, he was a pathological liar.

"Please, Darbs, just tell me, so I don't have to hurt you. Because if you don't, you're forcing me to slam this door."

He knelt down close so she could see the pained glimmer in his eyes. She knew this was all staged. Another head of the hydra. This negotiation was just like any other act she'd witnessed tonight, just another version of Ashley to be worn for a while and then discarded, the way a python crawls out of its wrinkly gray skin.

The entire room fell silent, awaiting her answer.

Inhale. Count to five. Exhale.

"If I tell you," she whispered back, "you'll just slam the door anyway."

His eyes darkened. "Smart girl."

Then he did.

4:26 A.M.

EN ROUTE, HIGHWAY PATROLMAN CORPORAL RON HILL asked Dispatch twice to clarify the 207 call, but there was no further info available. No name. No background. Just a vehicle (gray van), a license plate (VBH9045), and a rough location, sent to 911 via text message. No further contact. No calls. All follow-ups had failed, likely due to spotty cell service and tonight's record-breaking winter storm.

It sounded like a prank.

The nastiest calls always sound like pranks at first.

His cruiser churned uphill, cylinders firing, sand and gravel clattering noisily against the undercarriage. In theory, CDOT has a particular order to its road maintenance at this altitude—plow, then deice, then sand and salt—but apparently their A-team had taken Christmas Eve off. The whole effort seemed like an exercise in herding cats, while paying them overtime. Snooping in on their CB frequencies, he was reminded of his old CO's phrase for when marines move out of formation, risking exposure to enemy fire: a *gagglefuck*.

Ron was thirty-six, baby-faced, with a wife who'd studied graphic design but settled for being a wife, and a five-year-old son who wanted to be a cop when he grew up. She hated him for that. He'd been reprimanded twice for sleeping on speed traps, and once for what the after-action report called "unnecessary verbal force," which Ron still believed to be an oxymoron.

Before tonight's 7:00 P.M. shift, he'd found his wife's suitcase in the closet.

Upright, and half-packed.

Thinking about this, he almost missed the blue sign that came up on his right, crested with snow, glaring in his high beams:

REST AREA ONE MILE.

"HEY." FINGERS SNAPPED IN DARBY'S FACE. "LOST YOU FOR a sec."

Her right hand felt like it'd been submerged in boiling water.

At first, it hadn't hurt at all—just the whoosh of displaced air and the cannon blast of the door slamming beside her right eardrum—and then the pain arrived. Deafening, shattering. At once sledgehammer blunt and needle sharp. It hurled her out of her body, out of this world. For a black instant she was nowhere, and in another, she was back in her tiny childhood house in Provo, six years old again, racing up the creaking staircase, hurtling into the warm blankets of her mother's bed, taking refuge from a witching-hour nightmare. *I've got you,* her mother whispered, flicking on the nightstand lamp.

It was just a dream, baby.

You imagined it all.

I've got you—

And then the bedroom bled away like wet paint and Darby was back in this shitty Colorado rest stop with fluorescent lights and stale coffee, this hellish place she could never escape. She'd slumped into a crouch when she lost consciousness, her back to the door, a sour taste in her throat. She was afraid to look up at her right hand. She knew what had happened. She knew the door was shut, that at least two of her fingers were crushed inside it, pulverized between merciless brass teeth—

I've got you, Darby—

"Earth to Darbs." Ashley snapped his fingers. "I need you lucid."

"Ashley," Sandi hissed. "You're *insane.* You've lost your mind—"

Darby found the courage to look at her hand, blinking away tears. Her ring and pinkie fingers were gone above the hinge, inside the door's scissor-jaws. It gave her a nauseating, shivery jolt. Her body just *ended* there. It couldn't possibly be her hand, but it was. She couldn't imagine what her fingers looked like inside the door—skin burst, tissue shredded, bones splintered. Tendons crushed and tangled into red spaghetti noodles. There was somehow less blood than she'd expected; just a long, shiny bead trickling down the doorframe.

She watched it inch down the chapped wood.

"Ashley," Sandi barked. "Are you even listening?"

Darby reached for the doorknob with her unhurt left hand,

swiping, missing it twice, finally closing her numb fingers around it, to open the closet door and free her mangled hand, to reveal the hideous, heartbreaking damage—but the door-knob didn't turn. He'd *locked* it, the bastard.

Ashley strode across the room, pocketing the key, leaving her pinned there. "All right, Sandi. It's time I leveled with you."

"Oh, *now* it's time? After all this?"

"Sandi, let me explain—"

"Oh, sure." She hurled the plastic first-aid box at him, which he swatted away, so that it clattered off the stone counter. "You gave me your word, Ashley. *No one was supposed to get hurt* through this whole thing—"

He edged closer. "I have a confession to make."

"Yeah? What's that?"

He spoke slowly, precisely, like a surgeon delivering bad news. "Our meeting here wasn't about finding a discreet public place for you to hand off your storage key to me. I mean, yes, that was *your* plan, and maybe I'll put those steroid shots to use to keep Jaybird alive for as long as they last . . ."

Sandi's eyes widened with icy terror.

"But, see, *I* had a plan, too." He kept approaching. "And, it turns out, *your* plan was only a part of *my* plan."

Sandi took another step back, paralyzed by his wide shoulders, his sheer presence, as the fluorescent lights flickered overhead.

Silence.

"You know . . ." Ashley shrugged. "I really thought you'd try to run by now."

She tried.

He was too quick.

He grabbed her elbow with that muscular grip Darby knew all too well, and with an aikido spin hurled Sandi into the floor. A shoe flew off. Her other foot kicked the vending machine as she went down, turning the glass opaque with cracks. Ashley was already on top of her, forcing her to lie facedown, his knee on her back.

Ed struggled forward, but Lars aimed his .45. "Ah, nope, nope."

Now Ashley grabbed the woman by the scalp, both fists clenched in her black bowl-shaped haircut, and yanked her head backward, against his braced knee. "You called . . . Sandi, now, you may not remember this, but earlier tonight, you said some very nasty things about Lars, about his condition. Because of choices our mother made decades ago, when he was just an embryo. How fair is that? Come on, Sandi. You know *I love my baby brother*—"

She screamed against his grip.

"Take it back, Sandi." He twisted her neck harder. "Take back what you said."

She cried out, all vowels.

"Try again. I can't hear you—"

She gasped: "I . . . I take it back—"

"Okay, well, that's a nice gesture." Ashley glanced to Lars. "So, baby brother? Do you accept Sandi's apology?"

Lars grinned, savoring the power, and shook his head twice.

"Please. *Please, I*—"

Ashley adjusted his hold on Sandi's scalp, planted his boot higher between her shoulder blades (for leverage, Darby realized), and tugged hard.

The woman's neck broke, eventually. It wasn't quick, or painless. Sandi screamed until she was out of air, her face going a rotten purple, her eyes bulging before going flat, her fingers clawing, kicking. Ashley paused once, adjusting his grip before yanking her head harder, harder, *harder*, ninety degrees backward now, until her vertebrae finally dislocated in an audible, wet string of clacks. Like popping knuckles. If she had still been conscious, she might've experienced the paraplegic horror of her body going numb. It was a straining, clumsy, grunting process, and it took a full thirty seconds before Sandi was visibly dead.

Then Ashley let go, letting Sandi's forehead thud against tile, her neck loose with separated bones. He stood up, red-faced.

Lars was clapping his scarred hands now, giggling with excitement, like he'd just seen the card trick to end them all.

I just witnessed a murder, Darby thought dully. Just now. In plain view. Sandi Schaeffer—San Diego school bus driver, coconspirator to this tangled mess of a ransom plot—was gone. A human life, a soul, extinguished. Whether it was door hinges or Lars's fetal alcohol syndrome—utter a phrase that displeases Ashley Garver, even in passing, and he doesn't forget it. He makes a note. And later, he takes his pound of flesh.

"Hey, baby brother." He caught his breath, pointing down at the woman's warm body. "Wanna hear something funny? Not that it matters now, but did this Jesus freak tell you what she was planning to spend her share on?"

"What?"

"Women's shelters. Six figures donated to battered women's shelters all over California, like a real-life Mother Teresa. Can you *believe that*?"

Lars laughed thickly.

Darby glanced up at the *Garfield* clock, but her vision smeared with Vaseline tears. Maybe three minutes until the cops arrived? Two minutes? She couldn't tell. Her mind was a swirl of razor blades. She closed her eyes, wishing desperately to be six years old again. She wished this were just another witching-hour nightmare she'd awoken from, before high school, before Smirnoff Ice and curfew and marijuana cookies and Depo-Provera, before everything got complicated, wrapped up in her mother's arms, blinking away tears, breathlessly describing the ghostly lady with the double-jointed dog legs who'd strode through her bedroom—

No, it was just a dream.

I've got you, baby. It was just a dream

Just inhale, count to five, and —

Ashley rattled the closet door. Like sandpaper on exposed nerves, a jangling, complex pain writhed up her wrist. She screamed in a choked voice she'd never heard before.

"Sorry, Darbs. You were dozing off again." He wiped sweat from his forehead. "Trust me, this was supposed to be an easy little one-off. We'd pick up Jaybird from her mansion, drive twelve hours to a storage unit in Moose Head, where Sandi had a stash of money, cabin keys, and Jay's stupid adrenaline shots, all under a fake name and a five-digit combination lock—one-nine-eight-seven-two. We'd grab that, disappear up to Sandi's family cabin, and spend a week or two negotiating a sweet ransom payoff. Right?"

He rattled the door again—another violin-screech of pain.

"*Wrong.* After we surprise-adopted Jaybird, when we were halfway across the Mojave, we learned there was a break-in at

Sandi's stupid Sentry Storage place, and all of the combination locks had been compromised. Figures, right? So they were back to using default keys, which only Sandi had, all the way back in California. And problem two—Mr. Nissen called the cops, despite our explicit instructions *not* to, and now Sandi was under all kinds of scrutiny since she's the goddamn *school bus driver* who took Jay home that day. She couldn't FedEx the key to us without risking a stakeout. Meanwhile we're out here in the Rockies with no place to stay and a sick kiddo in the van, puking up a storm. What were we to do? Huh?"

He reached forward, as if to rattle the doorknob again—Darby winced—but he showed a flash of compassion and didn't.

"So, Sandi cooked up a last-minute family Christmas trip to Denver as a cover story for the police, and on the drive she'd covertly stash the key for us in a public place, like a rest stop, so we could then access Jay's meds and our supplies. Which brings me to problem three." Ashley pointed outside. "This goddamn winter wonderland."

The pieces clicked together in Darby's mind: *Snowmageddon trapped them all here at the handoff point. With poor Ed as Sandi's unwitting prop.*

And then I showed up.

The sheer scale of it dwarfed her and made her head swim. This viper's nest she'd wandered into at 6:00 P.M., strung out on Red Bull and exhausted. She watched the long, beady drip of her own blood. It almost touched the floor now.

"I'm not stupid," Ashley said. "I've seen enough movies to know everything leaves a digital fingerprint. Since the police are involved now, collecting Jaybird's ransom from Mommy and Daddy is pretty much impossible. And the cops are all over Sandi, too. She stole Jay's cortisol shots from the school nurse's office a few months back, so they'll pin that on her pretty quick. And then she'd probably roll over on us, which makes her a liability. So we came up here to kill her after she gave us the key. Make it look like a robbery-gone-wrong, gunshot-to-the-face deal. But I wasn't expecting the blizzard, or for her to bring Cousin Ed. And I wasn't expecting *you*, obviously."

It all interlocked and made a macabre sort of sense. Except for one last unknown, burning in the back of Darby's mind with unresolved tension. "Then . . . if there's no ransom money, what're you going to do with Jay?"

"Hey." Ashley snapped his fingers in her face again. "Answer mine first, okay? Where are my keys?"

"What are you going to do with her?"

He smiled guiltily. "It'll just make you uncooperative."

"Yeah? What the hell have I been all night?"

"Trust me, Darbs. Just trust me on this one." He stood up, hefting the orange nail gun, and paced across the room. "Because, hallelujah, I've *figured you out*. I could slam that door on each of your fingers until the sun comes up, until you have nothing but bloody hamburger hands, and you still won't tell me what I need to know, because you're just not that kind of person. You're a hero, a bleeding-heart. Your whole night went to hell because you broke into a van to save a stranger. So guess what? Here's your chance to save another one."

He crouched beside Ed and pressed the nail gun to his forehead. The older man's eyelids slid groggily half-open.

"Now, Darbs," Ashley said, "I'm going to count down

from five. You're going to tell me where you hid my key-chain, or I'll kill Ed."

She shook her head, thrashing left to right, in helpless denial. Up on the wall, the *Garfield* clock now read 5:30 (4:30) A.M.

It's been thirty-two minutes. The police are late—

Ashley raised his voice. "Five."

"No. I . . . I can't—"

"Four."

"Please, Ashley—"

"Three. *Come on*, Darbs." He punched the nail gun's muzzle against Ed's forehead in cruel, bruising thrusts: "Look. At. Him."

Ed now stared across the room at her through watering eyes. Poor old Edward Schaeffer, the ex-veterinarian with an estranged family waiting for him in Aurora, Colorado. A human cover story; Sandi's unwitting collateral damage. He was moving his lips again, muffled by clammy red gauze, trying to form words with a tongue impaled to the roof of his mouth. She could feel his eyes on her, begging her to tell Ashley what he wanted to know. To *just please tell him—*

"If I tell Ashley," Darby whispered to Ed, "they'll kill us both—"

This was true, but she wished she could tell him another, greater truth, to reassure him: *The police are almost here. They're a few minutes late. Any second now, they're going to kick down that door and shoot Ashley and Lars—*

"Two."

"I . . . I can't say it." She looked at Ed, realizing what this meant, and a racking sob rattled through her lips. "I'm . . . oh God, I'm *so sorry*—"

Ed nodded slowly, knowingly, dripping globs of stringy blood into his lap. Like he somehow, impossibly, understood.

She wanted to scream it to him: *Any second, now, Ed. The cops are coming to save us. Please, God, let them get here in time*—

The patience drained from Ashley's voice. "One."

"TEN-TWENTY-THREE. APPROACHING THE STRUCTURE ON foot."

Corporal Ron Hill clasped his shoulder radio and tripped on a snow bank, catching himself on a gloved palm. The ice was rock hard here, like sculpted cement. He was just a few paces from the Wanasho visitor center.

He reached the front door, stepping under the saucer-shaped lamp. Again, no further information from Dispatch beyond the initial 207 text message, which was frustrating.

He rapped the door with his Maglite. "Highway Patrol."

He waited for an answer.

Then, a little huskier: "Police. Anyone here?"

It was still technically just a public building, but his right hand moved to the heel of his Glock 17 as he gripped the doorknob and sidestepped into the crunchy snow, using the brick wall as cover.

In entry drills, doorways are called *fatal funnels* because they're the defender's natural focal point. No way around it, unless you blow down a wall—you're literally walking into the bad guy's sights. If there really were a 207 hunkered inside this rest stop, he'd be watching the door right now down the barrel of a shotgun, perhaps crouched behind his hostages for cover.

Or, just an empty, harmless room. Not that Dispatch knew.

A sharp wind tugged his Gore-Tex jacket, peppering dry snowflakes against the door, and now Corporal Hill wasn't sure what he was waiting for. For Sara to finish packing her goddamn suitcase? To hell with it.

He twisted the doorknob.

The door creaked open.

———————

"ZERO," ASHLEY SAID.

But Darby wasn't listening, because she'd just realized something. She stared past Ashley now, at the Colorado map on the wall behind Ed—and her heart sank with a heavy, cloying dread. State Route Six was a thick blue line on the map, slithering through mountain topography, and the rest areas were marked as red circles. Wanasho, Wanashono, Colchuck, Nisqual.

This one was Wanashono. *Big Devil.*

Not Wanasho.

But she'd typed her text message to 911 earlier in the night, around 6:00 P.M., before she'd learned this. Back before she'd returned inside, reexamined the map, and realized her error—that she'd transposed two similar-looking, similar-sounding local names, both concerning devils.

My text sent the cops to the wrong rest area.

To a completely *different* one, twenty miles down Backbone Pass. On the other side of that jackknifed eighteen-wheeler. The police weren't coming after all. They were still miles away, unreachable, misdirected. No one was coming to arrest Ashley and Lars. No one was coming to save them.

She wanted to scream.

She sagged against the locked door, feeling her fingers twist inside the doorframe. Another jolt of meat-grinder pain. She felt weightless, like dropping into free fall, plunging to some unknown depth. She just wanted it all to be over.

No one is coming to save us.

We're all alone.

I got us all killed—

Ashley sighed petulantly, like a frustrated child, and now he jammed the nail gun against Ed's temple and squeezed the trigger—

"Stop," Darby gasped. "Stop. I'll tell you where your keys are, if you . . . if you promise you won't kill him."

"I promise," Ashley said.

It was a lie, she knew. Of course it was a lie. Ashley Garver was a sociopath. Words and promises were meaningless to him; you might as well attempt to negotiate with a virus. But she fell apart and told him anyway, the entire room going silent, her voice a fractured whisper: "In the snow . . . outside the restroom window. That's where I threw them."

Ashley nodded. He glanced at Lars, then Jay. Then back at her, his lips curling into a boyish grin. "Thank you, Darbs. I knew you'd come through," he said, raising the nail gun to Ed's forehead anyway.

Thwump.

4:55 A.M.

"DON'T KILL HER UNTIL I'M BACK WITH THE KEYS," ASHLEY instructed his brother. "I need to be sure she's telling the truth."

Rodent Face nodded as he dumped gasoline over Ed's and Sandi's bodies, drenching them, darkening their clothes, slicking their hair, swirling ribbons into the blood on the floor. Acrid fumes curdling the air. Then he poured a glugging trail toward Darby, mouth-breathing as he approached her, raising the fuel jug high with both hands.

She closed her eyes, bracing for it.

Icy liquid crashed down on her, pounding the back of her neck, splashing off her shoulders, plastering her hair to her face. Droplets spattered off the door behind her and pooled at her knees, shockingly cold. Gasoline in her eyes, her mouth, a pungent taste. She spat on the floor.

Lars backed up into the center of the room, holding Jay's shoulder. He set down the fuel can and it sloshed, still half-full. Right beside a roll of shop towels and that familiar white Clorox jug. It all made sense now.

Bleach to break down their DNA evidence. Towels for their fingerprints. Fire for everything else.

Something white dangled from Lars's back pocket as he leaned over to wipe the countertop. She recognized it—the rock-in-a-sock Ashley had thrown into the parking lot hours ago, now obediently retrieved by Lars. The brothers were in cleanup mode, performing the grim work of erasing any forensic clues that might pin them to the massacre here.

That's why the keys are so important, Darby realized numbly. *That's why Ashley can't leave them behind.*

They're evidence.

The worst part of it all? Their sheer, dumb optimism. These brothers weren't criminal masterminds. Not even close. Even if they torched every square inch of this building to cinders, the Colorado police would find *something*. A stray hair. A skin flake. Something distinctive about the Astro's tire tracks. A thumbprint on one of Ashley's steel nails. Or even some circumstantial detail connecting Sandi to them; something they'd overlooked in their rush to eliminate her before she cracked under police scrutiny. They'd been careless. This entire ransom plot had been naïve and stupid, and it was almost certainly doomed to fail, but not before costing innocent people their lives tonight, and to Darby, that was somehow the most offensive part of it all.

She wiped an oily strand of hair from her face. Dripping with accelerant, moments from burning to death, she knew she should be terrified, screaming, hysterical, but she couldn't summon the energy. All she felt was tired.

The front door creaked—Ashley was walking outside now.

Just a few seconds left. He'd go out behind the visitor center, and find his keychain in the snow, and then Darby's life would become as worthless as Ed's and Sandi's. A nail or bullet to the skull if she was lucky, and a flicked match if she wasn't. Either way, she'd die right here, with her right hand smashed in a door, and then her bones would blacken in this fiery grave while Ashley and Lars escaped with Jay. The burning visitor center would be a useful distraction until the authorities discovered the three skeletons inside the wreckage. By then the Brothers Garver would be hours ahead. Plenty of time to vanish into an indifferent world.

But this left one unknown.

One final, itching question.

What are they going to do with Jay?

Ashley had been planning to meet Sandi here, to murder her and sever ties. But what about Jay? If it's not for a ransom . . . then what?

Jay approached her now.

"No. Don't come any closer." She spat again. "I have gasoline on me."

But she came anyway, her little footsteps rippling the dark puddle, and sat quietly on Darby's knee. Then she buried her face in the shoulder of Darby's coat. Darby wrapped her unhurt arm around this stranger's daughter, and they huddled there together, in a shivery little embrace over their own reflections, as Ashley's footsteps faded outside.

"You didn't tell me your mom died," Jay whispered.

"Yeah. It just happened."

"I'm sorry."

"It's all right."

"Was she mean to you?"

"No. I was mean to her."

"But you still loved each other?"

"It's . . . complicated," Darby said. It was the best answer she had, and it broke her heart. *It's complicated.*

"Are your . . . are your fingers okay?"

"They're locked in a door. So, no."

"Does it hurt?"

"Let's talk about something else."

"Does it hurt, Darby?"

"It hurts less now," she lied, watching a second bead of her own blood inch down the doorframe, thicker than the first. The gas fumes were clouding her mind, smearing her thoughts like watercolors. "Can we . . . hey, can we just talk about your dinosaurs for a while?"

"No." Jay shook her head. "I don't want to."

"Come on."

"No, Darby—"

"Please, tell me about your favorite one, the Eustrepto-thing—"

"I don't *want to*—"

The tears came to Darby now, now of all times. Hard, choking sobs, like a seizure in her chest. She turned away. She couldn't let Jay see.

Then Jay shifted her weight, and Darby thought the girl was only settling in her lap—until she felt something touch her left palm. Small, metallic, ice cold.

Her Swiss Army knife. She'd forgotten all about it.

"Later," Jay whispered. "I'll tell you about it later."

Darby looked back at her, understanding in a silent flash.

Those glassy blue eyes now pleading into hers: *Here's your knife back.*

Please don't give up.

But it was too little, too late, because the two-inch blade was better in Jay's hands than hers. Knife or no knife, Darby was about to die in this room. She was trapped here, with her shattered hand locked in a door, and Ashley was coming back to finish her off. Any second now.

"You should keep the knife," she said to Jay, whispering so Lars wouldn't overhear. "It'll . . . it'll just be wasted with me. You're going to save yourself now. You understand?"

"I don't think I can—"

"It's all you now." Darby blinked away tears and racked her brain, trying to recall the layout of their Astro. "I . . . okay. You broke the kennel, so they'll probably tie you down in the back, under the windows. But try to loosen a panel on the wall, and if you can reach inside, rip out every wire you can find. One of them might power the brake lights. And if the brake lights go out, the cops might pull them over . . ."

Jay nodded. "Okay."

Long shots piled upon even longer shots. It was all so grimly futile. And Jay's adrenal crisis was as volatile as a hand grenade; any additional stress could trigger a fatal seizure. But Darby couldn't give in to despair, her thoughts swimming, her words racing: "If . . . if they get careless, try to stab one of them in the face. The eyes, okay? An injury that needs medical attention, so they have to go to the hospital—"

"I'll try."

"Whatever it takes. Promise me, Jay."

"I promise." The girl's eyes glimmered with tears. She stared up at Darby's smashed hand in the door again, unable to look away. "It's . . . it's my fault they're going to kill you—"

"No, it's not."

"It is. All of this is about me—"

"Jay, this is *not your fault*." Darby forced a dizzy smile. "You know what's funny? I'm not even a good person. Not usually. I was a rotten daughter and I planned to spend Christmas alone. My mom thought I was the flu when she was pregnant with me. She tried to kill me with Theraflu. Sometimes I used to wish she had. But tonight, at this rest stop, I'm something good, and I can't tell you how much that means to me. I got to be your guardian angel, Jay. I got to fight for a good reason. And I'm going away soon, and it'll be all on you, and you need to keep fighting. Okay?"

"Okay."

"Never. Stop. Fighting."

And then for a moment, the fumes dispersed, and Darby caught hold of a crystalline thought. Everything slipped into sharp focus.

She glanced up at the horror of her right hand—at her ring finger's top knuckle, smashed between the door's teeth. At her pinkie finger, crushed beyond recognition. At the squeezed beads of blood lining the hinge, the way red jelly blurts out of a donut. She knew it might appear hopeless, but no, there was one last option she could try. Maybe she was delirious from the gas vapors. Maybe it was pure fantasy. But maybe, just maybe . . .

I'm not trapped.

Only two of my fingers are.

It would be a horrible thing. It would be a desperate, nasty, wrenching act, and it would hurt more than she could imagine, but then she glanced over at the dark figure of Larson Garver in his stupid Deadpool beanie, who'd finished wiping up fingerprints and now stood in the center of the room with his .45 aimed at her and Jay, and she made a final vow through gritted teeth: *I'll hurt you even worse, Rodent Face. I'll take your gun.*

Then I'll kill Ashley with it.

This girl is going home.

Tonight.

"I have an idea," she whispered to Jay, concealing the Swiss Army knife under her unhurt palm. "One last idea. And I'm going to need your help."

———

LARS SAW THEM WHISPERING.

"Hey." He raised the Beretta. "Stop talking."

Darby murmured something else into Jaybird's ear, and the little girl nodded once. Then she stood up, stepping aside with silent purpose. Now Darby stared across the room at him, eyes rock hard.

"Stop *looking at me.*"

She didn't.

"Turn your head. Ah, look at the floor." He thrust the Beretta at her for emphasis, but she didn't flinch. The pistol had lost its menace. It had become a prop. She wasn't afraid of it anymore.

Lars aimed—but he'd been aiming it this entire time; how do you get more threatening than that? He tried to cock it with his thumb, like they do in the movies, but the hammer was already cocked. It was already in single-action, because it had already been fired tonight. At her. Six times.

Darby kept staring at him, making his guts coil. Something about her eyes. Something had changed. Slowly, slowly, she slid forward, hunched her knees together, and stood up, her mangled hand twisting behind her back. Her hair stuck to her face in dark tangles as she rose, like a scary movie he'd seen where a dripping Japanese ghost emerged from the floor.

He wavered, looking back at the door. "Ashley," he shouted outside into the night. "I . . . did you, ah, find the keys yet?"

No answer.

His older brother was too far away to hear. He considered moving to the men's restroom, maybe, and shouting through that busted window, but that would require turning his back on them.

"Ashley," he shouted again, backing up, bumping into the cracked vending machine. "Something . . . ah, something changed. She's looking at me."

He wanted to move to the front doorway, but that would also require him to turn his back on Darby. He was afraid to. She was clearly trapped there, helpless, with her fingers *locked in a door*, but somehow he couldn't dare to lose sight of her. With her unhurt hand, she was now reaching for something—a little plastic panel on the wall, which he hadn't paid any attention to all night, up until this moment—

The light switch, he realized, as the room went black.

"Ashley." A tremor in his voice now.

Perfect darkness.

Lars knelt to the floor and groped for his brother's flashlight. His fingertips found it beside the gas can—bumping it, sending it rolling. He chased it down, his heart banging in his ribs, clicked the button, and aimed the blue-white LED beam at the closet door.

To his relief, Darby was still there, and Jaybird, too, both standing in his spotlight, both squinting back at him. Of course they were. Why had he been so frightened? He was sick of this. He wanted to shoot Darby now. Right now. And torch this stupid building, and end this hellish night, and then he and Ashley could get to Uncle Kenny's and kill some grubs in *Gears of War.*

"Ashley." His voice was hoarse. "Can I kill her yet?"

No answer.

Just the rasp of wind outside.

"Ashley, can I *please*—"

Jay moved suddenly, startling him, and walked around the room's dark perimeter. Lars aimed his Beretta at her, and his flashlight, tracking her like a searchlight as she walked past Ed's and Sandi's bodies, past the barricaded window. "Jaybird, ah, what are you doing?" She ignored him and stopped at the doorway. Then she grabbed the front door.

She pushed it shut.

"Jaybird. *Stop.*" He turned back to Darby, spotlighting her with the flashlight. He was splitting his attention now between the two females in the dark room—Darby to his left, Jay to his right. He could illuminate only one of them at a time.

He didn't like this. Not at all.

He heard a click behind him and whirled back, aiming the beam—now Jay was on her tiptoes, engaging the dead-bolt. Locking the door. Then she turned around to face him, squinting in the glare, and he recognized that same frightening look as Darby had. Yes, they were both definitely in on it, some veiled joke that Lars didn't get. This was normal. He never got jokes. Most of the time, they were about him.

A sore cavity in his stomach told him this one was, too. Like the moment before Ashley had hurled Stripes into that campfire two summers ago: *Hey, baby brother. Wanna see a shooting star?*

"Jaybird," he repeated.

No reaction.

"Jaybird, you're . . . ah, you're gonna get a red card when Ashley gets back," he said, glancing back left to the closet door, pointing his flashlight back at Darby—

She wasn't there.

Just the door. A trickle of blood. And a mashed little red piece still wedged in the door, like the juicy inside of a rare hamburger, and it took a half second to register in Lars's thick mind as what it really was, what it meant, what had just happened, and what *was coming*—

———————

DARBY SLAMMED INTO RODENT FACE HARD, FROM THE SIDE, sending the flashlight tumbling wildly into the shadows. No time for fear. Screaming with pain and adrenaline, something raw, black, and feral.

She got under Lars's right arm, under the pistol, and knocked it aside, clattering against the tourist brochure rack. She had one chance now, one racing chance—and she also had her father's Swiss Army knife in her left hand (*Congratulations on Graduating College!*), its blade dulled from sawing through the bars of Jay's dog kennel, but still sharp enough—

and with it, she throat-punched Larson Garver squarely in his Adam's apple.

The knife slipped right in.

Blood spurted into her face. Into her eyes, her mouth. The taste of warm nickels. Lars's hand swiped at her, his sharp fingernails scratching her cheek, but he was going for his own neck. Trying to hold back the bleeding.

His other hand moved, too. Half-blinded by Rodent Face's blood, she caught a blinking snapshot, a moving blur—*gun.*

Jay screamed.

That black .45. In a panic-flash, she realized Lars hadn't dropped it after all—the clatter she'd heard must have been his flashlight—and he still had the weapon in his knuckled hand, twisting the muzzle toward her belly—

Gun-gun-gun—

———

ASHLEY WAS KNEELING TO GRAB THE KEYS FROM THE SNOW when he heard a single gunshot thump from inside the building. Like a trapped thunderclap, muffled by flat walls and doors, seconds after the girls' screams. He couldn't believe it.

Really?

He sighed. "Goddammit, baby brother."

Quickly, he checked the keychain in his phone's flashlight—yep, there it was. Sandi's stupid little Sentry Storage key, silver, circular, stamped with a little *A-37,* otherwise unremarkable. He'd found the keychain half-buried in the snow where it had landed, thirty feet from the restroom window.

Darby had been telling the truth, more or less.

And he was grateful for that. If she'd been lying, and Lars

had blown her brains out just now, they'd be leaving behind a forensic gold mine of perfectly preserved fingerprints. And they'd never access Jaybird's steroid shots, meaning the little girl would likely die long before they reached their destination. And then everything—this entire bloody clusterfuck, the AMBER Alert in California, the FBI's probable involvement, the murders of Sandi, Ed, and Darby—all of it would be wasted without making a single cent. All because dear, sweet Lars got jumpy and shot Darby without permission.

Thank God she had told the truth.

Ashley mashed the keychain into his pocket, lifted his cordless nailer from the snow, and raced back to the entrance.

"Larson James Garver," he howled as he ran, exhaling a furious mist: "You just earned yourself *an orange card*—"

———

DARBY FOUGHT FOR CONTROL OF THE GUN.

Rodent Face was on the defensive now, stumbling backward, hot blood pumping from his jugular to his own frenzied heartbeat. He was trying desperately to shake her off, to gain enough distance to control the Beretta.

Darby wouldn't let him. She held on to the weapon, her slippery fingers clasped tightly over his. Then she spun, changing direction, and tugged *away* from him, counterclockwise, twisting the pistol against the joints of his knuckles. Lars was taller and stronger, but Darby was smarter, and she knew how to use inertia against him—

Inside the trigger guard, she felt his index finger snap.

Like a baby carrot.

He screamed through his teeth. There was a wet whistle to

it; air leaking through the hole in his windpipe, blood surging in strangled bubbles. They were both spinning now, a whirling tango, hands locked on the firearm, crashing into the coffee counter's edge, tipping chairs, firing into the ceiling—*CRACK, CRACK, CRACK*—showering plaster grit, exploding a fluorescent light overhead, until the gun's slide locked empty and the trigger lost slack.

They slammed into the Colorado map, both still clutching the Beretta.

Lars let go—knowing it was empty.

Darby held on—knowing it was still useful—and punched Lars in the teeth with it. He staggered away from her, holding his neck, but tripped over the bodies of Ed and Sandi. Now Darby was on top of Rodent Face, hitting again, again, again. Bashing with the aluminum heel of the pistol. She landed a particularly good blow and felt his cheekbone break with a meaty crunch.

He kicked her away, and they separated.

Darby scooted backward on the slick floor, the empty Beretta clattering. She tried to stand up, but slipped. Gasoline was everywhere. Her palms splashed down. Still half-blind, blinking his blood from her eyes. The fuel jug had tipped in the scuffle; it was on its side, pouring with rhythmic glugs. And near it, she saw her Swiss Army knife, a serrated shadow twirling on tile.

She grabbed it.

Lars was crawling away from her, toward the locked door. Not fast enough. He was moaning thick words, something desperate, clotted with tears and blood: "Ashley-Ashley-kill-her-kill-her—"

Not happening.

Not tonight.

"Kill her *please*—"

Darby caught up to him and raised the blade high over the back of Larson Garver's skull, the metal glinting a streak of LED light. Her words from earlier tonight came back like an echo—*I'll cut his throat if I have to*—and across the room, she made sidelong eye contact with Jay.

The girl was watching, awestruck.

"Jay," Darby gasped. "Don't look."

———————

ASHLEY TWISTED THE DOORKNOB—LOCKED.

"Lars," he panted. "Open the door."

No answer.

He checked the front window, but it was still blocked by Ed's overturned table. No access. He peered through the gap and saw only darkness—the lights were off in there. Flustered, he moved back to the front door, stumbling over sloped mounds of snow, nearly dropping his nailer.

"Lars," he called out, saliva freezing on his chin. "Please . . . baby brother, if you're alive in there, say something."

Nothing.

"Lars."

Those concussive gunshots rattled in his mind, hollow and panicked. Why would Lars fire a string of rapid shots? That hadn't been controlled gunfire; that was the sound of desperation. *Spray and pray*, they called it. So what had happened in there?

Still no answer.

He reared back and kicked the door. The frame creaked, but the deadbolt held. He was getting very worried now: "Lars. I'm not mad. Okay? Just answer me—"

He was interrupted by a voice.

Not his baby brother's.

Darby's.

"He can't talk right now," she replied. "Because I *cut his throat.*"

Ashley's knees went weak. For a sputtering moment his mind short-circuited, and he forgot about the deadbolt and twisted the doorknob again. "You're . . . no, you're lying. I know you're lying—"

"Want to know his last words?"

"You *better* be lying—"

"He cried your name before I killed him."

"Darby, I swear to God, if you really killed my baby brother in there, I will *cut the meat off Jaybird's little bones*—"

"You'll never touch her," Darby said, her words hardening with a chilling certainty. "I have the gun now. And you're next."

Ashley punched the door.

A bolt of shattering pain exploded through his fist. A jangling echo throbbed up his forearm. That was a mistake—a huge mistake—and he clenched his knuckles, his breaths curling through gnashed teeth, his eyes welling with hot tears.

Broken. Definitely sprained, at minimum.

He screamed. Something he wouldn't remember. It started as Lars's name, maybe, but it morphed into howling nonsense.

He wanted to slug the door again, again, again, to break his other hand, to bash his forehead, to destroy himself against an immovable object. But that would solve nothing.

Later. He'd grieve *later.*

He leaned against the door, his forehead touching the iced metal, controlling his breathing. It was still okay. He was still in this fight. In his unhurt hand, he still had his cordless nailer. And plenty of steel 16-pennies, purchased secondhand and fingerprint-free, stacked up in the drum magazine. Ready for duty. The cold weather hadn't yet sapped the battery. The indicator light was still green.

All right, Darby.

You lost your mom. I lost my baby brother. There was an intoxicating symmetry to their suffering tonight. Two wounded souls, each reeling from loss, each nursing damaged hands, joined by the rawest pain—

This is our dance, you and I.

He could still taste her lips from when he'd kissed her in the restroom. He'd never forget it. The sweet sourness of Red Bull, coffee, and the bacteria on her teeth. The humility of it, the realness of a pretty girl with bad breath.

We're the cats on the clock.

I'm Garfield. You're my Arlene.

And hold on tight, because this is our whirling, dark dance.

He collected himself, scraping his thoughts together, his nerves buzzing: "Fine, Darbs. You want a fight? I'll give you a fight. I'm coming in there, one way or another, and I'll red-card you both, and *by the way*, you bitch—"

He caught his breath:

"I counted the shots. I know you have an empty gun."

---

45 AUTO FEDERAL, READ THE GOLDEN RIM. THE CARTRIDGE Darby had carried in her pocket all night, ever since Jay had first handed it to her. It was in her hand now, rolling across her trembling palm.

She thumbed it into the chamber of Lars's black handgun, one-handed, and let the slide clack forward with a burst of captive-spring power.

Jay looked at her.

The gun's action was closed. The hammer was cocked rearward. It was ready to fire now. She didn't know how she was so certain; she just was. Guns are visceral. She could *feel* it.

"Lars," Ashley howled outside the door. "Baby brother, if you're still alive in there, please, please, just kill her—"

Darby scooted across the wet floor to Jay and squeezed her into a hard hug. "It's almost done," she said. "Tonight's almost over."

One brother down, one to go.

Jay was pale, staring with terror. "Your hand—"

"I know."

"Your fingers— "

"It's okay."

She hadn't yet looked at her right hand. She'd been dreading it. She did now—for a split second—and then she ripped her eyes away, gasping—

Oh God.

She dared to look at the damage again, her vision clouding with tears. Her thumb, index, and middle fingers were all okay. But her ring finger was skinned raw. The fingernail was slivered, half-detached, jutting upright like a cornflake.

And her pinkie finger was *gone*. Everything from the first knuckle up. Gone, missing, severed, no longer a part of Darby Thorne's body. Still inside that door hinge across the room, crushed and unrecognizable—

Oh God, oh God, oh God—

Strangely, the actual act of ripping her hand out of it hadn't hurt at all. She'd freed herself in two sharp, clockwise twists. Just a fuzzy sort of discomfort, blunted by adrenaline. But she was rapidly losing blood now, spurting a ceaseless trickle that ran warmly down her wrist and blotted circles on the floor. She covered it with her other hand. She couldn't look at it anymore.

Like Ed had said, hours ago: *When you're facing a lunch date with the Reaper, what're a few little bones and tendons?*

And more half-remembered voices, warped and tinny, coming at her in a nauseating swirl: *Can you cut a girl in half?*

I'm a magic man, Lars, my brother.

My toast always lands jelly-side up, you could say—

Dizzy now, she checked the first-aid box on the floor, leaving sticky red handprints, pawing through the syringes and Band-Aid boxes. Searching for that thick gauze—but it was gone. Sandi had used it all on Ed.

"Can they . . ." Jay hesitated.

"Can they what?"

"You know . . . reattach fingers?"

"Yep. They sure can," Darby said, trying to sound calm. She wondered how much blood she'd lost already, and how much more she could afford to.

She gave up on the medical gauze, but beside the bleach she found something better—Lars's roll of electrical tape. She ripped off a stretch with her teeth and looped it around her right hand. Keeping her thumb free, she wrapped her three remaining fingers into a clenched block.

That took care of the bleeding. But she'd have to shoot the Beretta left-handed. She had never fired a gun before, and she was right-handed. She hoped she could still hit her target. She had only one bullet.

Jay kept staring at the injury with morbid awe, and Darby noticed she'd turned shockingly pale. Gray, like a body dredged up from underwater. "What if . . . what if they can't find your finger in the door? Because it's too smashed up—"

"It'll grow back," Darby said, biting off the last stretch of black tape.

"Really?"

"Yep."

"I didn't know fingers could grow back."

"They do." She touched Jay's forehead, the way her mother used to feel for a fever, and the girl's skin was cold. Clammy, like candle wax. She tried to remember—what were the symptoms Ed had described to her? Low blood sugar. Nausea. Weakness. Seizure, coma, death. His words echoed in fragments: *We have to get her to a hospital. It's all we can—*

"Daaaaarby." The front door thrashed in its frame and the deadbolt chattered. "We *finish what we start—*"

"He's . . ." Jay cringed. "He's so mad at us—"

"Good." Darby scooted against the wall and raised the pistol in her left hand, aiming at the door.

"Don't miss."

"I won't."

"Promise you won't miss?"

The gun rattled in her hand. "I promise."

One round in the chamber. Like a grim destiny, she'd carried it in her pocket all night, and now it was finally time to use it.

The door banged a violent thunderclap as Ashley kicked it again. Darby flinched, her finger tightening hungrily around the trigger. She wanted to fire right now, through the door, but she knew that would be risky. She knew where he was standing and roughly how high, but she couldn't count on the bullet piercing the door with enough power to kill him. She couldn't waste her only shot.

She'd have to wait. She'd have to wait for Ashley Garver to kick down the door and *step inside the room with them*, point-blank, whites-of-his-eyes, at a distance she couldn't possibly miss—

"You've shot a gun before, right?"

"Yep," she lied.

The doorframe splintered. A long sliver of wood hit the floor. Ashley screamed outside, banging his fists, a pummeling animal rage.

"But this kind of gun . . ." Jay fretted. "You've shot this kind before, right?"

"Yep."

"Are you a good shot?"

"Yep."

"Even without a finger?"

"Okay, Jay, that's enough questions—"

Thwump. A sharp, pneumatic sound interrupted her.

The window shattered behind the barricaded table, spilling crunchy shards across the floor. She saw something there, something moving in the three-inch gap between the table and the window frame. It was orange, blunt, like some big, dumb animal outside was sticking its beak in. It took Darby a few heartbeats to realize what it actually was.

Of-fucking-course.

She hurled Jay to the floor, covering her face. "Get down, *get down*—"

Thwump. The vending machine's glass exploded into white kernels. Skittles and Cheetos bags hit the floor.

The nail gun's muzzle twisted, repositioning. Ashley's first two nails had gone high, so he was adjusting his aim. Trial and error. It was the very same gap Sandi had peered through before, now being used against them.

"I hate him," Darby whispered, rolling onto her belly, whipping her slick hair from her face. "I hate him *so much*—"

"What's he doing?"

"Nothing."

"Is he shooting nails at us?"

"It's fine." She tugged Jay upright, by the wrist. "Come on, come on—"

They slid into Espresso Peak, taking cover behind the stone counter as—*thwump-thwump-thwump*—an onslaught of shrapnel pierced the air, pinging off the floor, the walls, the ceiling. The pastry case shattered. Styrofoam cups bounced. A carafe banged like a gong and hit the floor beside them, splashing warm water. But the counter and cabinets, a forty-five degree inlet, protected them from Ashley's direct fire.

"See?" Darby patted Jay, checking for injuries. "We're fine."

"You said he wasn't shooting nails at us—"

"Yeah, well, I lied."

Thwump-thwump. There were two pounding impacts on the wall above them, and something slashed Darby's cheek, like a bee sting, followed by a rush of warm blood. She ducked low and sheltered Jay from more ricochets, shielding her body with her own. She saw tears in the girl's eyes.

"No. No, Jay. It's fine. Don't cry—"

Thwump. A nail slapped wetly into Ed Schaeffer's shoulder, heaving his body in a tangle of floppy horror, and Jay screamed.

Darby held the girl close, ignoring the gash on her cheek, stroking Jay's dark hair, trying desperately to hold it together: *Oh Jesus, this is it. This is the last ounce of stress she can take. I'm going to watch helplessly as she locks up and dies—*

"Please, don't cry, Jay."

The girl sobbed louder, hyperventilating, fighting Darby's grip—

"Please, just trust me—"

Thwump. A nail thudded off a cabinet, peppering them with wood chips.

"Jay, listen to me. The police are coming," she said. "They got held up, but they're still coming. They'll check every rest stop on this highway, especially the one with an almost-identical name. They'll save us. Just a few more minutes, okay? Can you last a few more minutes?"

Just words. All of it, just words.

Jay kept sobbing, her eyes clenched, building to another bracing scream, as—*thwump*—the cash register tipped, crashing down beside them, keypad buttons skittering across the tile like loose teeth.

Darby held the nine-year-old close amid all the violence,

shielding her face from shrapnel, trying to soothe her panic. She was certain it was over—that Jay's nervous system couldn't possibly handle any more trauma—but then something came back to her. Surfacing from her memories; her mother's warm voice in her ear: *It's okay, Darby. You're fine. It was just a nightmare.*

All you have to do is—

"Inhale," she told the girl. "Count to five. Exhale."

Thwump. The *Garfield* clock exploded off the wall, showering them with plastic bits. Darby brushed away debris from Jay's hair, touching her cheek, keeping her voice level: "Just inhale. Count to five. Exhale. Can you do that for me?"

Jay took a breath. Held it. Let it go.

"See? It's easy."

She nodded.

"Again."

She took another. Let it go.

"Just like that." Darby smiled. "Just keep breathing, and we'll—"

"Daaaaarby." Ashley kicked the table and it honked on the floor, scraping a few inches. Broken glass teeth sprinkled from the window. He huffed as he pushed. "You could've been my girlfriend."

Darby rose to her knees, dizzy with gasoline fumes, pushing aside tipped Styrofoam cups, and aimed Lars's black handgun over the counter. Aligning the green-painted sights, her finger on the trigger.

"I'm not normally like this," Ashley howled outside. "Don't you *understand*, Darbs? I wasn't going to kill you. I don't even ... I mean, I don't even drink or smoke—"

Jay winced. "He's . . . he's going to get inside."

"Yeah." Darby closed her right eye, aiming the Beretta. "I'm counting on it."

"We could've gone to Idaho. Together." Ashley kicked the table again, scooting it forward another scraping inch, shedding splinters. His voice boomed in the pressurized air: "Don't you get it? We could've gone to Rathdrum. Rented the loft over my uncle's garage. I'd do jobs with Fox Contracting. You'd be my girl, and we'd leave our cities behind, you and me, and I'd show you the river I grew up on, and the trestle—"

"Is he telling the truth?" Jay asked.

Darby sighed. "I don't even think *he* knows."

Ashley Garver—a piteous creature that wore so many masks, he didn't even know what he looked like beneath them. Maybe his heart was breaking, even as he discovered he had one. Or maybe it was all just words.

"You could've been my girl," he wailed, "but you *fuckin' ruined it*—"

Darby aimed the Beretta as the table shifted again. But she couldn't fire yet. She would have to wait. She'd have to wait until Ashley Garver was visible, until he scraped the table aside and vaulted in through the broken window. Then, and only then, could she—

No.

She froze, the trigger half-pulled. The hammer cocked back, a heartbeat away from dropping. Something else, something terrible, had just occurred to her.

No, no, no . . .

The pungent taste of gasoline, sharp on her tongue. The tipped fuel jug had now drained itself empty, a half-inch spreading to coat the entire floor. Fumes crowded the air, sweating beads on the walls.

If I fire Lars's handgun, she realized with dawning horror, *the muzzle blast could ignite the vapor in the air.* The chain reaction would incinerate the entire room. There were five gallons spilled in here. The floor would become a sea of rolling fire, like the world's biggest Molotov cocktail. There'd be zero chance of escape. Darby's coat was drenched with gasoline, damp and clinging. So was Jay's parka. They'd both be burned alive.

Firing the weapon, in here, was suicide.

Darby lowered the pistol. "Shit."

"But instead, you killed my brother." Ashley kicked the table again. An exhaled, wolfish chuff. The table scraped another inch, bumping Sandi's limp ankle—he now had almost enough space to squeeze through.

Darby almost hurled the handgun in rage. "Shit, shit, *shit—*"

Jay touched her shoulder. "What?"

"I . . ." Darby rubbed blood from her eyes, reassessing, drawing desperate new plans. "You know what? It doesn't matter. He'll never touch you again. I swear to God, Jay, I am your guardian angel, and Ashley Garver will never hurt you again, because *I will kill him.*"

"I'll kill you." Ashley kicked again. "You fucking whore—"

Darby stood up, wiping gasoline off her hands. "Listen to me, Jay. We're not waiting for the police. We're not waiting for a rescue. I've been waiting all damn night and no one's rescued me. Almost everyone I've trusted tonight has turned on me. We *are* the rescue. Say it, Jay—*we are the rescue.*"

"We are the rescue."

"Louder."

"We are the rescue." Jay stood up on shaky legs.

"Can you run?"

"I think so. Why?"

Darby had one more idea. *Last-ditch* didn't even do it justice. She grabbed a handful of brown napkins from the counter and mashed them into the bagel toaster. Pressed the plunger. It clicked, like a gun's chamber closing, and inside it, the toaster's heating coils warmed.

Jay watched. "What're you doing?"

She knew she had ten, maybe twenty seconds, until the coils turned red hot.

We are the motherfucking rescue.

She grabbed a half-drunk cup of black cowboy coffee—Ed's, maybe, long cold—and chugged it on the run, squeezing Jay's fingers and racing for the restroom. Hand in hand. Running for that tiny window.

"Don't stop, Jay. Don't stop—"

"You're sure fingers grow back?"

"Yep."

ASHLEY BASHED HIS WAY INSIDE. HE VAULTED THE WINDOW on his unhurt hand, careful not to slash his palm on the jagged glass, and coughed on a pungent odor. Boy howdy, it was potent. The fuel can must've spilled, and mixed with the bleach and Sandi's pepper spray vapor, it created a truly noxious atmosphere.

He rubbed his stinging eyes as he clambered in, aiming the nailer, sweeping left to right. First he saw the crumpled bodies of Ed and Sandi near the Colorado map. Legs sprawled open in the immodesty of death. Blood mixing with the gas on the floor, swirling vivid ribbons.

Beside them, baby brother Lars.

Oh, Lars.

On his belly. His head twisted sideways in an ocean of red, his hair mussed, his eyes still drowsily half-open. His throat a meaty slash. His jugular cut to the bone; a human Pez dispenser.

The scrawny kid who'd worn an army surplus helmet and combat boots to junior high school, who loved ranch sauce on his Famous Star cheeseburgers, who'd rewatched *Starship Troopers* until his VHS copy strangled the VCR with black ribbons—he was gone now. Gone forever. He'd never play the new *Gears of War* on Xbox One, All because he got sucked into a school bus driver's ill-fated little ransom scheme. Because between the changed locks, the cops, and the blizzard, this entire week had careened wildly off the rails.

And it all would've been manageable, still, were it not for Darby Thorne.

Darbs. Darbo. That fiery little redhead from CU-Boulder who broke into their car with a *shoelace*, of all things, who handed Jaybird a knife and tipped an already volatile night irreversibly off course. He suspected his entire life had been building to this confrontation. Hers too. She was his destiny, and he was hers.

In a better universe, perhaps he'd marry her. But in this one, he'd have to kill her. And, unfortunately, he'd have to make it hurt.

Oh, Lars, Lars, Lars.

I'll make this right.

I promise, I'll—

He heard a *whoosh* to his right and he whirled, aiming the cordless nailer, expecting to see Darby and Jaybird cowering behind the coffee stand. But Espresso Peak was empty. Pierced with nails, dripping with gasoline, messy with tipped cups and plastic fragments, but empty. They weren't here.

He noticed the toaster was crammed with brown napkins. The noise he'd heard?

A cloud of gray smoke, curling from the toaster's glowing coils. A sizzle as the napkins ignited. Ashley ran his tongue along his upper lip, tasting gasoline vapor, and then it all made sense.

"Oh, *come on—*"

———

A FIREBALL RIPPED THROUGH THE RESTROOM'S TRIANGU-lar window, pushing a scorching wave of pressurized air. Darby leaped outside, a half second ahead of the blast, bouncing off a picnic table and landing hard, twisting her left ankle.

She felt a sickening *pop.*

Jay turned, a few paces ahead. "Darby!"

"I'm fine."

But she knew she wasn't. Her ankle throbbed with jarring pain. Her toes went instantly numb; a sharp mess of pins and needles inside her shoe, like invisible fingers pinching her nerves—

"Can you walk?"

"I'm fine," she said again, and another surge of fire roared through the broken window above her, drowning out her voice. Another wall of hot air threw her to her knees in the snow.

The visitor center erupted into towering flames behind them, tongues of fire pumping a column of filthy smoke. It climbed the sky, a furious tornado-swirl of glowing embers. The size and closeness of it was overwhelming. Raging heat on her back, the whining suction of devoured air. The charcoal odor of fresh fire. The snow lit up with orange daylight and the trees cast bony shadows.

Jay gripped her hand. "Come on. Stand up."

Darby tried again, but her ankle folded limply beneath her. Another surge of nauseating pain. She hobbled forward.

"Is he dead?" Jay asked.

"Don't count on it."

"What does that mean?"

"It means *no*." Darby pulled Lars's handgun from her jeans. She wasn't sure if Ashley had been inside the building when the fumes ignited; she just hoped her improvised firebomb had at least blown his eyebrows off. But dead? No. He wasn't dead, because she hadn't killed him yet. She could rest when she'd fired her stolen .45-caliber bullet right into his smirking face. No sooner.

"I hope you got him," Jay said as the inferno swelled behind them, turning the world foggy with low smoke. The moon was gone. The trees had become jagged ghosts in the firelit smog. Big Devil held its blackened shape as it burned, a cage of roiling fire around an epicenter of bone-cracking heat.

And now the glowing embers descended like fireflies from the darkness, peppering the snow around Darby and Jay. They sizzled on contact, hundreds of tiny meteors striking puffs of steam. Too fast to outrun.

"Jay. Take off your coat."

"Why?"

"There's gasoline on it." Darby tugged off her own coat and hurled it into the snow. Seconds later, a spark touched it and it erupted into blue-orange flames, like a campfire.

Jay saw this and tore hers off immediately.

"See? Told you."

More embers descended around them, more fireflies riding the winds, and Darby followed Jay one painful step at a time. She couldn't stop. Her hair was still soaked with fuel. One errant spark was all it would take, and she'd come too far and fought too hard tonight to be killed by a goddamn *spark*.

She peeled a wet strand from her face. "The parking lot. We'll get into Blue—"

"What's Blue?"

"My car."

"You named your car?"

"I'll run the engine to keep you warm. And . . ." Darby trailed off as they trudged through the smoky darkness, letting the next thought go unsaid: *And while you're sitting in Blue's passenger seat, I'll go find Ashley and shoot him in the face.*

And end it, once and for all.

Jay twisted her neck, watching the roiling flames over her shoulder as she ran, like she was expecting Ashley to emerge from the wreckage. "You . . . you killed his brother."

"Yeah. I did." It was still sinking in to Darby—yes, she'd killed someone today. She'd stabbed another human being in the neck, broken his finger and cheekbone, and slit his throat. As worn and chipped as it was, that Swiss Army knife had slipped right in, like she was cutting meat (and, technically, she was). Just dirty, grim business. And before tonight ended, she knew, she'd have to kill one more.

Jay fretted. "He loves his brother."

"*Loved*. Past tense."

"He's not going to be happy with you—"

"I . . ." Darby choked on a hoarse laugh. "I think that ship has sailed, Jay."

Just one more.

I've already killed Beavis. Only Butt-Head left.

Fifty yards back, the Big Devil building groaned like a monster turning over in its sleep, blackened ribs creaking and popping inside the firestorm. Melting snow slid off the roof in a billow of scalding steam.

Then . . . then I can finally rest.

They'd reached the Nightmare Children—those dozen or so half-gnawed kids frozen in apocalyptic playtime, buried to their waists in snow—when Jay stopped, pointing downhill, stabbing with her finger: "Look. Look, look!"

Darby wiped Lars's blood from her eyes and saw it, too.

Headlights.

Approaching the entrance ramp of the Wanashono rest area from the highway. Big, industrial high beams over a curved silver plate throwing an arc of backlit ice chips. The first CDOT snowplow was finally here.

Jay squinted. "Is . . . is that for us?"

"Yeah. That's for us."

Seeing this reassured Darby that there was still an outside world. It was still out there, it was real, it was populated with decent people who could help, and *holy Christ*, she'd almost clawed her way out of this fiery, blood-drenched nightmare. She'd almost rescued Jay. Almost.

Her knees gave out and she fell to a crouch. She was crying and laughing all at once, her face a tight mask, her scar as visible as a billboard. She didn't care. She was so close now. She watched the yellow lights float closer in the darkness, like twin lanterns. She heard the lope of an engine. "Thank you, God. Oh, *thank you*, God—"

She'd lost her phone but she knew the time was now almost 6:00 A.M. It'd been ten hours since she'd first found this girl in a padlocked dog kennel, reeking of urine, in an unattended van. In another hour, the sun would be up.

Road crews are ahead of schedule.

Or they received special direction from the cops, maybe, in light of a mysterious text message concerning a similarly named rest area—

"Darby." Jay grabbed her wrist, her voice rising with panic.

"What?"

"I see him. He's following us."

5:44 A.M.

"DAAAAARBY."

Yes, Ashley Garver was following them, a ragged shadow silhouetted against the roaring blaze. Nail gun carried in his left hand now. His right was injured, clenched under his left armpit. He was fifty yards behind them, a shambling figure in smoking clothes, raising his unhurt hand to wipe his mouth.

He was too far away to shoot.

Darby's marksmanship was too uncertain, and she couldn't waste her single bullet. So she concealed the pistol behind her waist, and at her back, the headlights intensified as the snowplow chugged closer.

She turned to Jay. A murderer approaching behind them, and the assistance of a stranger ahead of them—it should have been an easy choice.

Jay tugged her. "Let's go—"

And in a way, she realized . . . it still was.

"Darby, *let's go*. We have to run—"

"No."

"What?"

She nodded at her ankle. "I'll just slow you down. You run."

Alarm in Jay's eyes. "What? No—"

"Jay, listen to me. I have to stop him. I can't run anymore. I've been running from him all night, all freaking night, and I'm sick of it."

The headlights grew brighter, cutting shafts in the smoky fog, drawing harsh shadows in the glittering snow. They burned Darby's eyes. And behind her, the shadow of Ashley Garver staggered closer—thirty paces away now. But still not close enough. She tightened her grip on the Beretta.

"You have to run."

"No."

"*Run,*" Darby shouted, smoke in her throat. "Run to those headlights. And tell the driver to turn his truck around, to take you to a hospital."

She pushed her forward but Jay fought back. The girl shrieked, dug her feet in, tried to punch Darby in the shoulder, but then it all melted into a hug. A shivery, aching embrace under intensifying lights—

"I'll come back," Darby whispered into the girl's hair, rocking her. "I'll get him, and then I will come back to you."

"Promise."

"I promise, Jay—"

"You're lying again—"

"I pinkie-swear," she said, raising her duct-taped right hand. Jay winced. "That's not funny."

Something sliced through the air above them, tugging a handful of Darby's hair. Her first thought was *shrapnel,* but she knew better. It was a nail, a steel projectile twirling past her scalp. Ashley was shambling closer to them—but still not close enough to risk her only bullet.

Not yet.

She pushed the girl away, toward the headlights. "Now *run*."

Jamie Nissen took two shaky steps in the snow and looked back, her eyes brimming with fiery tears. "Don't miss."

"I won't," Darby said.

Then she turned back to face Ashley.

I won't.

ASHLEY WAS PERPLEXED TO SEE THEM SEPARATE—JAYBIRD ran for the incoming snowplow while Darby turned around to face him.

They were now twenty paces apart.

His right fist throbbed like it was full of gravel. The skin on his cheeks and forehead felt tight, tingly, like a sunburn. His lips were cracked, splitting and leaking down his chin. He reeked of burnt skin and hair, a dense and fatty odor curling off him in wisps of smoke. His North Face jacket had melted weirdly to his back, hanging off in molten strings.

But hell, he was alive. No rest for the wicked, right? And he was feeling pretty goddamn wicked tonight. He'd broken a woman's neck with his bare hands and nail-gunned an innocent man to death. It'd make for a hell of an episode of *Forensic Files*. To do all that, then to dive out the window of an exploding building while sustaining only second-degree burns takes the luck of the devil. Jelly-side up, indeed.

Now he noticed that Darby was limping toward him.

Away from the bright lights of safety. Away from any hope of escape.

Toward him.

He choked on a laugh that sounded like a bark. Maybe . . . maybe she'd gone a little crazy, too, in this wild pressure cooker of a night. He couldn't blame her. He wasn't even sure he could hate her—his brain was a potent sugar rush, a cocktail of confused feelings for this tenacious bitch. But feelings aside, he still had to red-card her for killing his baby brother, so he raised the cordless nailer at Darby, squinted through hot smoke, and fired again.

A hollow click.

What?

He pulled the trigger again—another click. To his horror, the Paslode's battery light now blinked an urgent red. Sapped by the cold weather. It had finally, finally happened.

"Oh *shit*—"

He looked back up. Darby was still approaching, still coming at him like his personal angel of death, limping but eerily, inhumanly calm. And he noticed something else. Something carried in her swinging hand, concealed from his view behind her hip, an angular shape, half-glimpsed—

Lars's Beretta.

No, his mind fluttered. *No, that's impossible—*

————

JAY SPRINTED INTO THE HEADLIGHTS, ARMS WAVING.

The snowplow stopped, big tires locking up, skidding sideways as the air brakes whined a shrill cry. The lights surrounded her, igniting the snow at her feet, brighter than daylight. She couldn't see anything else. Just those twin suns, overpowering.

She screamed—something she wouldn't remember.

The engine made a chuffing sound. The cab door opened. The driver was older than her father, bearded, potbellied, with a Red Sox hat. He jumped out and raced to her, already out of breath, shouting something.

She was winded, too, and she collapsed to her knees in the ice. He reached her, a stomping black shadow in the high beams, and the truck's engine made another chuffing sound. Like her aunt's German shepherd. Then the man grabbed her shoulders, his whiskery face in hers now, Dr Pepper on his breath, bombarding her with questions.

Are you okay?

She was too out of breath. She couldn't speak.

What happened?

Uphill, the flaming visitor center's roof caved in, a shattering wooden crash that unleashed more fireflies into the night, and he squinted up at it, then back to her, his rough hands on her cheeks. *You're safe now—*

She wanted to tell him about Ashley, about Darby, about the nail gun, about the life-or-death battle happening a short distance uphill. But she had no words. She couldn't assemble any thoughts. Her mind was jelly again. She just started crying, and he took her into his arms and hugged her, and the world fell apart.

He was whispering now, like a chant: *You're safe. You're safe. You're safe—*

Darby, she wanted to say.

Darby is not safe—

And then she saw it—a heartbeat of red and blue illuminated the trees. Behind the snowplow, halted bumper to bumper, was a police car. In the glow of the truck's taillights, she read a banner on the side door.

HIGHWAY PATROL.

ASHLEY GARVER RAN LIKE HELL.

Impossible. I counted the shots.

The Beretta is empty.

He told himself this, over and over, but still he wasn't brave enough to turn around and call Darby's bluff. Instead he raced back to his parked Astro, where he knew he'd left a second battery rattling around inside the Paslode box. He could reload his nail gun, at least, and then decide how to handle this new development.

He tripped on a snow bank, wincing for the crack of a gunshot and a bullet in the spine, but it never came.

He reached the Astro. Unlocked. Flung the driver door open. Scrambled inside, reaching under the passenger seat, knocking Lars's stupid plastic A-10 Warthog off the dashboard, and opened the Paslode's hard case. Two latches to unclasp with trembling fingertips.

He knew he'd heard Lars fire four gunshots in the scuffle. He was certain of it. One-two-three-four. Plus the five shots he'd fired at Sandi's truck. That equaled nine. The Beretta stored eight in the single-stacked magazine, plus one in the chamber. How could Darby have willed another .45-caliber cartridge into existence? The floor of the van, maybe; he recalled Lars opening the Federal box upside down and dumping fifty clattering rounds to the floor—

He finally hurled the case open. The lid banged against the glove box.

The first battery box was empty, so he grabbed another. Ripped off the tape. Dumped it into his palm. Opened the Paslode's trap door panel, dropped out the spent battery—

He froze.

He hadn't heard anything, but somehow he just knew. Something about the way the hairs on his neck lifted and prickled, like static electricity . . .

She's behind me.

Right now.

He turned around, slowly, slowly, and yes, there was Darby.

She'd caught up to him, standing outside the Astro's open driver door. Beretta Cougar aimed at him in knuckled hands. He'd bought this very pistol for Lars as a gift six months ago, and now it was pointed at his heart. Un-freaking-believable. Here she was—the girl he'd tried to suffocate with a Ziploc bag five hours ago, back with a furious vengeance. A nine-fingered, black-winged angel of death. She was here for him, drenched in his brother's blood, fire glowing on her sweaty skin.

"What were you going to do with Jay?" she asked. "Tell me now."

"What? *Really?*"

She aimed up, from his chest to his face. "Really."

"Okay." Ashley slid up into a sitting position on the driver's seat, keeping the nailer concealed behind his back. He realized he'd dropped the battery. "I just . . . you know what? Fine. You want to know? It's nothing special. We just have an uncle up in Idaho, we call him Fat Kenny, who said he'd give me ten thousand for a healthy white girl, plus ten percent. He runs a little ring out of his storm cellar for some truckers from out of state. Big guys who do long hauls, twenty-hour days, away from their wives, guys with . . . uh, you know. Appetites."

Darby didn't blink. She kept the Beretta trained on him, and that white scar coalesced on her eyebrow. Curved, like a sickle.

"Yeah, it's gross, and it's not my gig, but I needed to salvage things somehow." Ashley kept talking, buying time, while his unhurt hand quietly searched the seat for the Paslode's spare battery. Then he would load it and surprise the bitch with a 16-penny to the face. "So, yes, I lied to you, Darbs, when I promised it wasn't a sex thing. It was supposed to be a simple kidnapping, but then the cops got all over Sandi, and I had to change the plan, and now it's definitely, absolutely, one hundred *million* percent a sex thing, and I'm sorry."

Behind his back, his fingertips touched the Paslode battery, just a blind stroke—*there it is*—and closed around it.

"What's his name?" Darby asked.

"Kenny Garver."

"Where does he live?"

"Rathdrum."

"His *address*."

"912 Black Lake Road." Ashley slid the battery into the nailer, gently, so she wouldn't hear the click. He felt himself grinning, even at gunpoint. He held the nail gun behind his back, preparing to lift it and fire. "I mean, hell, you got me, Darbs. You win. I surrender. Let's play a round of circle time while we wait for the cops to—"

"Let's not," Darby said, pulling the trigger.

CRACK.

6:01 A.M.

ASHLEY FLINCHED AT THE GUNSHOT. HE HADN'T EXPECTED to be alive to hear it. You're never supposed to hear the one that gets you.

But he'd heard it.

And yes, he was alive.

What happened?

Darby hesitated, wobbling in stunned silence. She lowered Lars's Beretta and looked at him, her eyes wide with shock. Only then did he notice it, just below her left collarbone. On her black Art Walk hoodie. A spreading, slimy circle. Blood.

"I said *drop it!*"

Ashley turned to see a park ranger, or patrolman, or deputy, or *whatever*, standing behind the Astro, one hand on the taillight, catching his breath with a Smokey Bear hat and an aimed Glock.

He shouted again. "Drop it, girl."

Darby spun to face the cop, her lips moving. She was

trying to speak. Then the Beretta Cougar thumped to the snow—unfired—and her knees gave out. And just like that, resourceful, scrappy, brave Darby Thorne collapsed like a sack of trash onto a snow-covered parking lot.

Ashley's jaw hung open. *No way.*

No freaking way.

This is amazing.

"Stay down," the cop commanded, clasping his shoulder radio. "Shot fired, shot fired. Ten-fifty-two—"

Slouching in his seat, Ashley put it all together—the police had arrived, distracted by the fire, and naturally the first thing this hick cop saw was Darby, blood-soaked and wielding a handgun, chasing a helpless victim before cornering him inside a van, a half second from executing him. So bargain-bin Captain America here had no choice but to fire. He *had* to shoot her. That's just how it works, you know. And it was so perfect. So stunningly perfect.

The timing, the sheer misfortune. Yes, sir, he'd always been special. Supernatural forces were at work here. This was how a bona fide *magic man* eludes capture.

The cop moved in close now, gun up, kicking the Beretta away from Darby and twisting her hands up behind her back to cuff them. He was rough, yanking her elbows up into chicken wings, but judging by the pint of blood steaming off the snow, she was already having brunch with the Reaper. The handcuffs opened with a metallic *snick* and in the glow of the flames, Ashley could read the officer's stitched name: CPL. RON HILL.

The cop looked up. "Sir, let me see your hands—"

"Sure." Ashley raised the nailer.

Thwump-thwump.

DAWN

6:15 A.M.

ASHLEY GARVER WHISTLED BING CROSBY'S "WHITE CHRIST-mas" as he scavenged Corporal Hill's Glock 17, a bright yellow Taser, and a badass friction lock baton. He flipped through the cop's billfold as well, pocketing two twenties and a ten, while noting that the guy's wife looked like a total wildebeest.

The highway patrolman had squeezed off a reflexive string of gunshots as he went down, shattering the passenger window behind Ashley, punching a hole through the Astro's ceiling, and blasting a final few into the sky. One bullet might've grazed his face; he felt a stinging gash had opened up on his cheek. Or it could just be his scorched skin cracking in the alpine air.

Either way, what marvelous luck. Jelly-side up, *indeed*.

Ashley decided he'd kill the snowplow driver next. That tall diesel rig was like a stopper plugging the rest area's parking lot shut. Then he'd finesse the Astro around and get the hell out of Colorado before Corporal Hill's backup arrived.

Although—*hell, bring 'em on.*

Ashley could take them all.

He paced down the long parking lot as the Wanashono visitor center burned and collapsed behind him, approaching the headlights of the idling truck. The sky was turning pewter, a brightening gray as the sun readied to break over the horizon, and he checked the remaining ammo in the cop's Glock. These magazines were notched in the back with little numbers, so you could easily eyeball how many rounds you had left. He saw at least nine. Plus a second full mag he'd plucked from Corporal Hill's belt. He loaded that one, just in case.

Now he stood in the blinding wash of the truck's headlights, shielding his face. He concealed the Glock in his jacket pocket, where it fit comfortably. He couldn't see through the truck's windshield—too dark—but the orange driver door still hung half-ajar. CDOT stenciled on the side.

"Hey!" he shouted. "It's safe."

Silence.

He licked his lips. "Corporal Hill . . . he, uh, sent me down here to tell you the scene is secure, that the situation's under control. He shot the kidnapper. Now he needs you to transmit a message to the other trucks on your CB."

Another long silence.

Then, finally, the door creaked and a scruffy face peered out, standing on the foot rail. "I already called in and they said—"

Ashley aimed the Glock. *CRACK.*

The window exploded. A near miss, but the man fell out of the cab anyway, slamming down hard on his ass in the snow. His Red Sox hat fluttered off.

Ashley passed around the headlights, shielding his eyes.

The driver flopped onto his belly, glass bits crunching underneath him, scrambling upright, reaching for the ajar door to hoist himself back inside—*CRACK*—but Ashley put a bullet through his wrist. The man screamed hoarsely.

Ashley palmed the door shut. "Sir, it's fine."

"Don't kill me." The man crawled away sideways, on one elbow, clutching his forearm. Hot blood spurting through his fingers, blotting the snow, leaving a red trail. "Please, God, please *don't kill me*—"

Ashley followed him. "I'm not going to kill you."

"Please, don't, don't—"

"Stop moving. It's fine. I won't kill you," Ashley said, putting his foot on the man's fleshy back to pin him. "Stop struggling, sir. It's all A-okay. I promise." As he said this, he nuzzled the Glock 17 into the back of the man's neck. He started to squeeze the trigger . . . but stopped.

Again, he'd gotten that feeling. That odd electricity.

Someone was standing behind him.

What now?

He turned around, half expecting to see the ragged ghost of Darby Thorne, back for bloody revenge—but the figure standing behind him was shorter, smaller. It was Jay. Just harmless little Jaybird, in her red Poké Ball shirt, about to witness another murder. Honestly, he'd forgotten all about her. But yeah, even with Lars out of the picture, he could still deliver her to Fat Kenny, and fetch a tidy sum for as long as she lasted—

She had something in her hand.

At first he thought it was Sandi's pepper spray.

But then the nine-year-old raised it—reflecting a glint of firelight—and Ashley realized with a jolt of terror that it was something far worse. It was Lars's Beretta. She must have picked it up from the red snow by Darby's body when he hadn't been looking, and now here it was, in Jaybird's shaky little fingers.

Aimed at him.

Again.

He groaned. "Oh, *come on*—"

CRACK.

6:22 A.M.

ASHLEY GARVER FLINCHED AGAIN. AND AGAIN, HIS EAR-drums rang in answer to a gunshot he'd never expected to hear.

He opened his eyes. Jay was still standing there by the snowplow, her eyes wide with fear. The Beretta slide-locked in her white fingers. Dirty smoke lingered, curling in the headlights. The charcoal odor of burnt powder.

She missed.

He patted his stomach and chest, just to be certain. No blood, no pressure, no pain. His torso and limbs were all fine.

Yes, he realized. *From three feet away, Jaybird had missed.*

The girl's jaw quivered. She reaimed the semiautomatic and tried to fire again, but there was no slack to the trigger. Not even a click. The weapon was empty. Wherever Darby had managed to scrounge that miraculous extra cartridge from, it didn't matter, because it had whistled harmlessly past

Ashley's ear and plunked down somewhere in the frozen firs. It was gone, their last gasp of hope spent, and Ashley was still alive.

Am I immortal?

It'd all been so darkly hilarious.

The fireball hurling him out the window with only minor burns. The cop arriving and miraculously shooting the wrong person in the nick of time. And now this! Little Jaybird had him dead to rights, point-blank, but she still missed. His toast had landed jelly-side up once again. Against all odds!

He fought back a burst of pitch-black laughter. All his life, he'd been shielded, insulated from consequences by some generous, unknown force. The way he'd been born with the looks and predatory cunning Lars never had. The way his father had lost his shit to Alzheimer's just in time to hand him the reins to Fox Contracting. Even trapped a hopeless mile into the guts of Chink's Drop, he'd been rescued by the blindest, dumbest chance, and the bones in his thumb had knitted perfectly, against the doctor's prediction—yessir, he'd grown up to be quite a *magic man*, indeed, and there could be no doubt, he was destined for big things.

How big?

Hell, maybe he'd be president someday.

He couldn't resist; he laughed—but oddly, he didn't hear it. Only the tinnitus ring in his ears. Come to think of it, he wasn't even sure if his face was moving.

"Nice shooting, Jaybird," he tried to say.

No sound.

Jay lowered the Beretta. Now she appeared strangely calm,

still watching him, studying him with those little blue eyes. Not with terror—no, not anymore—but instead with curiosity.

What the hell?

Ashley tried to speak again, this time slower, his tongue carefully enunciating: "Nice shooting, Jaybird," and he heard it come out as a single groaned syllable, slurred by Novocain lips. It was his voice—yes, it came from his own lungs and airway—but it was spoken by a drooling retard he didn't recognize. This was the single most terrifying sensation he'd ever felt.

Then his eyes slipped out of focus.

Jay blurred, then doubled. Now there were two Jaybirds staring back at him, and both of them set down their twin copies of the pistol that had killed him.

A warm wetness slithered down his face, tickling his cheek. A strange odor touched the floor of his brain, dense and sour, like burnt feathers. He was furious now, trembling with rage, and he tried to say something else, to curse at Jay, to threaten a red card, to raise the officer's sidearm and shut her up forever, but it had already fallen from his fingers. To his profound horror, he'd forgotten what it was called. He recalled something . . . something like—*ock*. Was it Pock? Dock? Rock-in-a-sock? He wasn't certain of anything anymore, and words wilted and fell away like brown leaves, and he reached frantically for them, for any of them, and grasped hold of a simple one—

"Help—"

It came out unrecognizable, a moan.

Then the world inverted, the brightening sky going under as Ashley pitched over, hitting the snow on his back. The gun was somewhere to his right, but he was too mushy to reach for it. He wasn't even aware he'd landed, because in his fragmenting thoughts, Ashley Garver was still airborne, still helpless, still falling, falling, falling—

———————

"DARBY, IT'S OVER."

She was falling, too, when she heard the girl's voice and it caught her. Held her to the world like a thin tether. She opened her crusty eyes and saw the shadow of Jay hunched against a vast gray sky. "Darby, it's done. I picked up your gun and Ashley was about to kill someone else, so I shot him."

She forced her dry lips to move. "Good job."

"In the face."

"Excellent."

"You . . . you got shot, too, Darby."

"Yeah, I noticed."

"Are you okay?"

"Not really."

Jaybird leaned in and hugged her, her hair tickling Darby's face. She tried to breathe, but her ribs felt strangely tight. Like someone was standing on her chest, collapsing her lungs.

Inhale, her mother told her.

Okay.

Then count to five. Exhale—

"Darby." The girl shook her. "Stop."

"Yeah? I'm here."

"You were closing your eyes."

"It's fine."

"No. Promise me, promise, that you won't close your eyes—"

"All right." She lifted her duct-taped right hand. "I pinkie-swear."

"Still not funny. *Please*, Darby."

She was trying, but she still felt her eyelids drooping, an inevitable tug into darkness. "Jay, tell me. What was the name of your favorite dinosaur?"

"I told you already."

"Again, please."

"Why?"

"I just want to hear it."

She hesitated. "Eustreptospondylus."

"That's . . ." Darby laughed weakly. "That's such a stupid dinosaur, Jay."

The girl smiled through tears. "You couldn't spell it anyway."

Somehow, this patch of lumpy ice felt more comfortable than any bed she'd ever lain in. Every bruised inch of her body felt perfectly at rest here. Like settling into a well-earned sleep. And again, she felt her eyelids slipping shut. No pain in her chest anymore, just a dull, increasing pressure.

Jay whispered something.

"What'd you say?"

"I said thank you."

This gave Darby a little chill, and her stomach fluttered with emotions she couldn't articulate. She wasn't sure what to say to Jay, how to answer that—*you're welcome*? All she knew was that if she were given the choice, she'd do it all over again. Every minute of tonight. All of the pain. Every sacrifice. Because if saving a nine-year-old from child predators isn't worth dying for, what the hell is?

And now, bleeding out into the snow, watching the state-funded Wanashono visitor center burn and collapse into a black skeleton, Darby collapsed, too, into a deep and satisfying peace. She was so close now. So achingly close. She just had one last thing to do, quickly, before she lost consciousness: "Jay? One last favor. Reach into my right pocket, please. There should be a blue pen."

A pause. "Okay."

"Put it in my left hand."

"Why?"

"Just do it, please. And then I need you to go back to that snowplow. Tell the driver to turn it around and drive you to a hospital right now. Tell him it's an emergency, that you need steroids before you have a seizure—"

"Are you going to come with us?"

"No. I'm going to stay right here. I need to sleep."

"Please. Come with us—"

"I can't." Darby's tether had snapped and she was falling again, dropping through floors of darkness, sliding into the back of her own head, back in Provo now, back in her old childhood house with bad pipes and the popcorn ceiling, wrapped in her mother's arms. The nightmare dispelling. Her mother's warm voice in her ear: *See? You're fine, Darby. It was just a bad dream.*

And it's all over now—

"Please," Jay whispered, far away. "Please, come with me—"

Inhale. Count to five. Exhale.

Okay.

Just like that. Keep doing that.

In her darkening thoughts, she remembered Ashley's final words to her, and she pulled up her right sleeve, uncapped that pen, and wrote left-handed on her wrist. Scratchy, half-inked, all caps on her own bare skin:

KENNY GARVER.

RATHDRUM IDAHO.

912 BLACK LAKE ROAD.

KIDNAPPER.

Now it was all really, truly done. Now Jay was saved, and every last angle of Ashley's disgusting plan had been expunged, dragged into the daylight for judgment. She let the pen slide between her fingers, finally satisfied. When the cops discovered her body frozen here in the snow, they'd read her final message. They'd know they had one last door to kick down, all the way up in Idaho.

I've got you, Darby.

Okay.

Don't be afraid. The long-legged ghost wasn't real. Now her mother squeezed her tighter, impossibly tight, binding her in this perfect moment, and the terror was finally over. *It was just a nightmare, and it's all finished now. You're going to be okay. And . . . and Darby?*

Yeah?

I'm so proud of you.

DRAFT EMAIL (UNSENT)

12/24/17 5:31 p.m.

To: amagicman13@gmail.com

From: Fat_Kenny1964@outlook.com

Hey Ash . . . checking in. Everything go OK on your end?

All set up over here. I've got the bunker ready and two interested fellas already one from Milwaukee, one Portland coming in on the 30th. They haven't even seen a picture of her yet if you can believe it.

Also need to know: those meds your getting will make her better right, at least for awhile? Sick is OK, barfing is not OK.

Hope you did a clean job tying your loose ends up. You should be in Casper by now, so get here the day after Xmas then? Stay safe, keep Lars's nose clean and keep off the big roads.

Talk soon, I've got someone knocking at the front doo_

EPILOGUE

FEBRUARY 8
Provo, Utah

JAY DIDN'T REALIZE DARBY'S LAST NAME WAS SPELLED with a silent *e* until she saw it milled into a cement gravestone. Below it, the date of death: December 24.

One day before Christmas.

Seven days before New Year's.

Forty-six days ago.

She was here with her parents in Darby's hometown, on a cemetery hillside still scaled with thawing snow, because her father had insisted on making the trip. Originally, he'd wanted to fly here much earlier in January, but Jay's adrenal condition had flared up with two seizures that left her bedridden and under watch. Finally, she'd been deemed healthy enough for travel last week. All the while, her father had insisted: *We have to see Darby Thorne again. We owe her something that can't be written on a check.*

"That's the one?" he asked now. A few steps downhill, catching up.

"Yeah."

The hours and days after the incident on the Colorado highway were a sickly blur, but little moments snagged in Jay's memory. The ache of the IV needle. The roar of the rotor blades. The way the medics had circled and applauded when they carried her onto the helipad of Saint Joseph. The strange blur of the drugs. The way her mother and father came racing down that corridor in dreamy slow motion, their fingers interlocked, holding hands in a way she'd never seen them do before. Speaking in choked voices she'd never heard. The three-way hug atop her creaking bed. The taste of salty tears.

The cameras too. The fuzzy microphones. The investigators, clutching their notepads and tablets, trading gentle questions and sideways glances. The phone interviews with journalists whose accents she could barely understand. The news truck parked outside with an antenna that looked like a ship's mast. The reverent, almost fearful way people hushed their voices when speaking about the dead, like poor Edward Schaeffer. And Corporal Ron Hill, the highway patrolman who made a tragic, split-second error that cost him his life.

And Darby Thorne.

The one who started it all. The restless, bleary-eyed art student from a state college in Boulder, racing a beater Honda Civic across the Rockies, who'd first stumbled across a child locked in a stranger's van and taken heroic action to save her.

And, against all odds, succeeded.

Darby came to that rest stop for a reason, Jay's mother had said back at Saint Joseph. *Sometimes God puts people exactly where they need to be.*

Even when they don't know it.

A gust slipped through the cemetery, breathing among the taller gravestones, making Jay shiver, and now her mother caught up to the group, flipping up her sunglasses to read the letters as they coalesced on paper, clearer with every stroke of black crayon. "She . . . she had a pretty name."

"Yeah. She did."

Sunlight pierced the clouds and for a few seconds, Jay felt warmth on her skin. A curtain of light swept over the graves, shimmering over granite and frozen grass blades. Then it was gone, snuffed by a biting cold, and Jay's father slipped his hands into his coat pockets. For a long moment the three of them were silent, listening to the last scratchy rubs of crayon as the headstone transferred to paper.

"Take as long as you need," he said.

But the etching was finished already. The Scotch tape peeled off the stone, one corner at a time. Then the paper moved away, exposing the engraved letters: MAYA BELLEANGE THORNE.

"What did you mean?" Jay asked. "When I asked you if you loved each other, and you just said, 'It's complicated'?"

Darby rolled the rice paper into a cardboard tube and stood up from her mother's grave, squeezing Jay's shoulder.

"It's all right," she said. "I was wrong."

ACKNOWLEDGMENTS

THANK YOU, FIRST AND FOREMOST, TO MY FAMILY, WHO made this book possible.

To my better half, Jaclyn, who put up with me while I sank many months into this project: thank you for your honesty, your keen critical eye, and your enthusiasm—but most of all, your patience. And thank you to my parents, who always encouraged me to keep writing from the youngest age, back when I first commandeered a sluggish Windows 95 PC and typed away at my masterpiece: an epic tale of Mount Rainier erupting. I couldn't have written this novel (which luckily turned out better than the Mount Rainier one) without your support and faith over many, many years.

A tremendous thank-you across the Atlantic to Jasper Joffe of the dynamic London publisher Joffe Books for guiding this story to completion and presenting it to readers. Thank you to editor Jennifer Brehl for your expertise and sharp eyes, and to the entire team at Harper and Morrow for working their magic on this book's U.S. release.

Another thank-you to agent Lorella Belli for being my relentless and tenacious advocate across the world, and to agent Steve Fisher for guiding the film deal.

And, once more, because it bears repeating: Thanks to my mother, for recommending that I commit to writing this story after I'd described an alternative idea I was considering writing instead.

That's one more reason this book wouldn't exist if it weren't for you.

ABOUT THE AUTHOR

TAYLOR ADAMS GRADUATED FROM EASTERN WASHINGTON University with the prestigious Edmund G. Yarwood Award. His directorial work has screened at the Seattle True Independent Film Festival, and he is an avid fan of suspenseful fiction and film. He lives in Washington state.